David Alvarez

Austin, January 1993

Property of the
Grand Valley State
University Libraries

323 146
U CO OP USED BOOK
NO REFUND IF REMOVED

381-38C2
U CO OP USED BOOK
NO REFUND IF REMOVED
$ 6.70

Ahmed Essop

Hajji Musa
and the
Hindu Fire-Walker

Die plassroman

WITHDRAWN

readers international

Published by Readers International Inc., USA, and Readers
International, London. Editorial inquiries to London office at
8 Strathray Gardens, London NW3 4NY, England. US/Canadian
inquiries to Subscriber Service Department, P.O. Box 959,
Columbia, Louisiana 71418-0959 USA.

Copyright © Stories, Ahmed Essop 1978, 1988
Copyright © *The Visitation*, Ahmed Essop 1980, 1988

All texts published by permission of Ravan Press (Pty) Limited,
P.O. Box 31134, Braamfontein 2017, South Africa

Cover Art: *Immersion*, painting by Indian artist Arpana Caur,
courtesy of the October Gallery, London.
Cover design by Jan Brychta
Typesetting by Opus 43, Cumbria UK
Printed and bound in Great Britain by Richard Clay Ltd,
Bungay, Suffolk.

Library of Congress Catalog Card Number: 88-61401

British Library Cataloguing in Publication Data
Essop, Ahmed
Hajji Musa and the Hindu Fire-walker.
I. Title
823 [F]

ISBN 0-930523-51-2 Hardcover
ISBN 0-930523-52-0 Paperback

Contents

Foreword

Stories by Ahmed Essop began to appear in magazines and anthologies from 1969. They revealed such talent and freshness of matter and outlook that readers soon began to look forward to the publication of an unusually attractive and important collection. I believe that *Hajji Musa and the Hindu Fire-walker* fulfils these expectations completely.

The stories centre on the vivid aromatic world of Johannesburg's Indian community in Fordsburg, with its unique blend of religious, political, cultural and economic preoccupations. This is not to suggest that the interest is defined by a racial line. Characters of every South African extraction occur in Ahmed Essop's pages, and this is merely one element in a pattern of contrasts based on age, temperament, income, education and above all occupation — among others, waiters, philosophers and shopkeepers, housewives, journalists, gangsters and soldiers, tarts, servants and mystics, a government inspector and a Molvi find rôles in these stories.

Nor does Essop's intimate involvement with Fordsburg confine the stories to that one place. It would be more accurate to describe his world as comprehending everything that oriental Fordsburg impinges on and overflows into. He thus adds a new world to those already represented in South African fiction. With nothing more to commend it this book would take a notable place in our literature.

But there is a great deal more to commend it. Ahmed Essop is a natural master of the story-teller's art with a fine feeling for situation, character and atmosphere. Though never evasive where the harsh social realities of his chosen scene are concerned, his writing is gentle and balanced in spirit, with humour and compassion bringing various levels of comedy and tragedy into his scope. This emotional richness, as well as the vivacious variety of his scene, is reminiscent of V.S. Naipaul whose fiction Essop admires. But among South African writers, it is hard to think of another, aside from Bosman, who is capable of bringing off, on the one hand, stories as lightheartedly funny as 'Hajji Musa and the Hindu Fire-Walker', as sweepingly satirical as 'Film' and, on the other, ones as astringently poignant as 'Gerty's Brother', as mysteriously disturbing as 'Mr Moonreddy', as poetically sombre as 'The Hajji'.

Perhaps even more impressive than the range of emotional chords struck is the subtle combination of feelings within many of the stories. By the time we reach the end, for example, of 'Gladiators', 'Two Sisters', 'Obsession' or 'Ten Years', we experience such an interweaving of contrary sympathies that we might be contemplating our own fallible selves rather than characters in stories.

Yet nothing is technically forced or intellectually strained. On the contrary, Essop's style and approach, apart from the appropriate stiffening of a slightly formal manner, are as simple and direct as possible. His subtlety is born out of nothing more nor less than his fascination with the endlessly varied ways of the human heart. Thence the power to amuse, delight, move and challenge us. Thence an achievement of a timeless sort.

Lionel Abrahams

The Hajji

When the telephone rang several times one evening and his wife did not attend to it as she usually did, Hajji Hassen, seated on a settee in the lounge, cross-legged and sipping tea, shouted: "Salima, are you deaf?" And when he received no response from his wife and the jarring bell went on ringing, he shouted again: "Salima, what's happened to you?"

The telephone stopped ringing. Hajji Hassen frowned in a contemplative manner, wondering where his wife was now. Since his return from Mecca after the pilgrimage, he had discovered novel inadequacies in her, or perhaps saw the old ones in a more revealing light. One of her salient inadequacies was never to be around when he wanted her. She was either across the road confabulating with her sister, or gossiping with the neighbours, or away on a shopping spree. And now, when the telephone had gone on assaulting his ears, she was not in the house. He took another sip of the strongly spiced tea to stifle the irritation within him.

When he heard the kitchen door open he knew that Salima had entered. The telephone burst out again in a metallic shrill and the Hajji shouted for his wife. She hurried to the phone.

"Hullo . . . Yes . . . Hassen . . . Speak to him? . . . Who speaking? . . . Caterine? . . . Who Caterine? . . . Au-right . . . I call him."

She put the receiver down gingerly and informed her husband in Gujarati that a woman named "Caterine" wanted to speak to him. The name evoked no immediate association in his memory. He descended from the settee and squeezing his feet into a pair of crimson sandals, went to the telephone.

"Hullo . . . Who? . . . Catherine? . . . No, I don't know you . . . Yes . . . Yes . . . Oh . . . now I remember . . . Yes . . ."

He listened intently to the voice, urgent, supplicating. Then he gave his answer:

"I am afraid I can't help him. Let the Christians bury him. His last wish means nothing to me . . . Madam, it's impossible . . . No . . . Let him die . . . Brother? Pig! Pig! Bastard!" He banged the receiver onto the telephone in explosive annoyance.

"O Allah!" Salima exclaimed. "What words! What is this all about?"

He did not answer but returned to the settee, and she quietly went to the bedroom.

Salima went to bed and it was almost midnight when her husband came into the room. His earlier vexation had now given place to gloom. He told her of his brother Karim who lay dying in Hillbrow. Karim had cut himself off from his family and friends ten years ago; he had crossed the colour line (his fair complexion and grey eyes serving as passports) and gone to cohabit with a white woman. And now that he was on the verge of death he wished to return to the world he had forsaken and to be buried with Muslim funeral rites and in a Muslim cemetery.

Hajji Hassen had, of course, rejected the plea, and for a good reason. When his brother had crossed the colour line, he had severed his family ties. The Hajji at that time had felt excoriating humiliation. By going over to the white Herrenvolk, his brother had trampled on something that was a vital part of him, his dignity and self-respect. But the rejection of his brother's plea involved a straining of the heartstrings and the Hajji did not feel happy. He had recently sought God's pardon for his sins in Mecca, and now this business of his brother's final earthly wish and his own intransigence was in some way staining his spirit.

The next day Hassen rose at five to go to the mosque. When he stepped out of his house in Newtown the street lights were beginning to pale and clusters of houses to assume definition. The atmosphere was fresh and heady, and he took a few deep breaths. The first trams were beginning to pass through Bree Street and were clanging along like decrepit yet burning spectres towards the Johannesburg City Hall. Here and there a figure moved along hurriedly. The Hindu fruit and vegetable hawkers were starting up their old trucks in the yards, preparing to go out for the day to sell to suburban housewives.

When he reached the mosque the Somali muezzin in the ivory-domed minaret began to intone the call for prayers. After prayers, he remained behind to read the Koran in the company of two other men. When he had done the sun was shining brilliantly in the courtyard onto the flowers and the fountain with its goldfish.

Outside the house he saw a car. Salima opened the door and whispered, "Caterine". For a moment he felt irritated, but realising that he might as well face her he stepped boldly into the lounge.

Catherine was a small woman with firm fleshy legs. She was seated cross-legged on the settee, smoking a cigarette. Her face was almost boyish, a look that partly originated in her auburn hair which was cut very short, and partly in the smallness of her head. Her eye-brows, firmly pencilled, accentuated the grey-green glitter of her eyes. She was dressed in a dark grey costume.

He nodded his head at her to signify that he knew who she was. Over the telephone he had spoken with aggressive authority. Now, in the presence of the woman herself, he felt a weakening of his masculine fibre.

"You must, Mr Hassen, come to see your brother."

"I am afraid I am unable to help," he said in a tentative tone. He felt uncomfortable; there was something so positive and intrepid about her appearance.

"He wants to see you. It's his final wish."

"I have not seen him for ten years."

"Time can't wipe out the fact that he's your brother."

"He is a white. We live in different worlds."

"But you must see him."

There was a moment of strained silence.

"Please understand that he's not to blame for having broken with you. I am to blame. I got him to break with you. Really you must blame me, not Karim."

Hassen found himself unable to say anything. The thought that she could in some way have been responsible for his brother's rejection of him had never occurred to him. He looked at his feet in awkward silence. He could only state in a lazily recalcitrant tone: "It is not easy for me to see him."

"Please come Mr Hassen, for my sake, please. I'll never be

able to bear it if Karim dies unhappily. Can't you find it in your heart to forgive him, and to forgive me?"

He could not look at her. A sob escaped from her, and he heard her opening her handbag for a handkerchief.

"He's dying. He wants to see you for the last time."

Hassen softened. He was overcome by the argument that she had been responsible for taking Karim away. He could hardly look on her responsibility as being in any way culpable. She was a woman.

"If you remember the days of your youth, the time you spent together with Karim before I came to separate him from you, it will be easier for you to pardon him."

Hassen was silent.

"Please understand that I am not a racialist. You know the conditions in this country."

He thought for a moment and then said: "I will go with you."

He excused himself and went to his room to change. After a while they set off for Hillbrow in her car.

He sat beside her. The closeness of her presence, the perfume she exuded stirred currents of feeling within him. He glanced at her several times, watching the deft movements of her hands and legs as she controlled the car. Her powdered profile, the outline taut with a resolute quality, aroused his imagination. There was something so businesslike in her attitude and bearing, so involved in reality (at the back of his mind there was Salima, flaccid, cowlike and inadequate) that he could hardly refrain from expressing his admiration.

"You must understand that I'm only going to see my brother because you have come to me. For no one else would I have changed my mind."

"Yes, I understand. I'm very grateful."

"My friends and relatives are going to accuse me of softness, of weakness."

"Don't think of them now. You have decided to be kind to me."

The realism and the commonsense of the woman's words! He was overwhelmed by her.

The car stopped at the entrance of a building in Hill-brow. They took the lift. On the second floor three white youths entered and were surprised at seeing Hassen. There was a separate lift for non-whites. They squeezed themselves into a corner, one actually turning his head away with a grunt of disgust. The lift reached the fifth floor too soon for Hassen to give a thought to the attitude of the three white boys. Catherine led him to apartment 65.

He stepped into the lounge. Everything seemed to be carefully arranged. There was her personal touch about the furniture, the ornaments, the paintings. She went to the bedroom, then returned and asked him in.

Karim lay in bed, pale, emaciated, his eyes closed. For a moment Hassen failed to recognize him: ten years divided them. Catherine placed a chair next to the bed for him. He looked at his brother and again saw, through ravages of illness, the familiar features. She sat on the bed and rubbed Karim's hands to wake him. After a while he began to show signs of consciousness. She called him tenderly by his name. When he opened his eyes he did not recognize the man beside him, but by degrees, after she had repeated Hassen's name several times, he seemed to understand. He stretched out a hand and Hassen took it, moist and repellent. Nausea swept over him, but he could not withdraw his hand as his brother clutched it firmly.

"Brother Hassen, please take me away from here."

Hassen's agreement brought a smile to his lips.

Catherine suggested that she drive Hassen back to Newtown where he could make preparations to transfer Karim to his home.

"No, you stay here. I will take a taxi." And he left the apartment.

In the corridor he pressed the button for the lift. He watched the indicator numbers succeed each other rapidly, then stop at five. The doors opened — and there they were again, the three white youths. He hesitated. The boys looked at him tauntingly. Then suddenly they burst into deliberately brutish laughter.

"Come into the parlour," one of them said.

"Come into the Indian parlour," another said in a cloyingly mocking voice.

Hassen stood there, transfixed. They laughed at him in a raucous chorus as the lift doors shut. He remained immobile, his dignity clawed. Was there anything so vile in him that the youths found it necessary to maul the last recess of his self-respect? "They are white," he said to himself in bitter justification of their attitude.

He would take the stairs and walk down the five floors. As he descended he thought of Karim. Because of him he had come there and because of him he had been insulted. The enormity of the insult bridged the gap of ten years since Karim had spurned him, and diminished his being. Now he was diminished again.

He was hardly aware that he had gone down five floors when he reached ground level. He stood still, expecting to see the three youths again. But the foyer was empty and he could see the reassuring activity of street life through the glass panels. He quickly walked out as though he would regain in the hubbub of the street something of his assaulted dignity.

He walked on, structures of concrete and glass on either side of him, and it did not even occur to him to take a taxi. It was in Hillbrow that Karim had lived with the white woman and forgotten the existence of his brother; and now that he was dying he had sent for him. For ten years Karim had lived without him. O Karim! The thought of the youth he had loved so much during the days they had been together at the Islamic Institute, a religious seminary though it was governed like a penitentiary, brought the tears to his eyes and he stopped against a shop window and wept. A few pedestrians looked at him. When the shop-keeper came outside to see the weeping man, Hassen, ashamed of himself, wiped his eyes and walked on.

He regretted his pliability in the presence of the white woman. She had come unexpectedly and had disarmed him with her presence and subtle talk. A painful lump rose in his throat as he set his heart against forgiving Karim. If his brother had had no personal dignity in sheltering behind his white skin, trying to be what he was not, he was not going to allow his own moral worth to be depreciated in any way.

When he reached central Johannesburg he went to the station and took the train. In the coach with the blacks he felt at ease and regained his self-possession. He was among familiar faces, among people who respected him. He felt as though he had been spirited away by a perfumed, well-made wax doll, but had managed with a prodigious effort to shake her off.

When he reached home Salima asked him what had been decided and he answered curtly, "Nothing." But feeling elated after his escape from Hillbrow he added condescendingly, "Karim left of his own accord. We should have nothing to do with him."

Salima was puzzled, but she went on preparing the supper.

Catherine received no word from Hassen and she phoned him. She was stunned when he said: "I'm sorry but I am unable to offer any help."

"But . . ."

"I regret it. I made a mistake. Please make some other arrangements. Goodbye."

With an effort of will he banished Karim from his mind. Finding his composure again he enjoyed his evening meal, read the paper and then retired to bed. Next morning he went to mosque as usual, but when he returned home he found Catherine there again. Angry that she should have come, he blurted out: "Listen to me, Catherine. I can't forgive him. For ten years he didn't care about me, whether I was alive or dead. Karim means nothing to me now."

"Why have you changed your mind? Do you find it so difficult to forgive him?"

"Don't talk to me about forgiveness. What forgiveness, when he threw me aside and chose to go with you? Let his white friends see to him, let Hillbrow see to him."

"Please, please, Mr Hassen, I beg you . . ."

"No, don't come here with your begging. Please go away."

He opened the door and went out. Catherine burst into tears. Salima comforted her as best she could.

"Don't cry, Caterine. All men hard. Dey don't understand."

"What shall I do now?" Catherine said in a defeated tone. She was an alien in the world of the non-whites. "Is there no one who can help me?"

"Yes, Mr Mia help you," replied Salima.

In her eagerness to find some help, she hastily moved to the door. Salima followed her and from the porch of her home directed her to Mr Mia's. He lived in a flat on the first floor of an old building. She knocked and waited in trepidation.

Mr Mia opened the door, smiled affably and asked her in.

"Come inside, lady; sit down . . . Fatima," he called to his daughter, "bring some tea."

Mr Mia was a man in his fifties, his bronze complexion partly covered by a neatly trimmed beard. He was a well-known figure in the Indian community. Catherine told him of Karim and her abortive appeal to his brother. Mr Mia asked one or two questions, pondered for a while and then said: "Don't worry, my good woman. I'll speak to Hassen. I'll never allow a Muslim brother to be abandoned."

Catherine began to weep.

"Here, drink some tea and you'll feel better." He poured tea. Before Catherine left he promised that he would phone her that evening and told her to get in touch with him immediately should Karim's condition deteriorate.

Mr Mia, in the company of the priest of the Newtown mosque, went to Hassen's house that evening. They found several relatives of Hassen's seated in the lounge (Salima had spread the word of Karim's illness). But Hassen refused to listen to their pleas that Karim should be brought to Newtown.

"Listen to me, Hajji," Mr Mia said. "Your brother can't be allowed to die among the Christians."

"For ten years he has been among them."

"That means nothing. He's still a Muslim."

The priest now gave his opinion. Although Karim had left the community, he was still a Muslim. He had never rejected the religion and espoused Christianity, and in the absence of any evidence to the contrary it had to be accepted that he was a Muslim brother.

"But for ten years he has lived in sin in Hillbrow."

"If he has lived in sin that is not for us to judge."

"Hajji, what sort of a man are you? Have you no feeling for your brother?" Mr Mia asked.

"Don't talk to me about feeling. What feeling had he for me when he went to live among the whites, when he turned his back on me?"

"Hajji, can't you forgive him? You were recently in Mecca."

This hurt Hassen and he winced. Salima came to his rescue with refreshments for the guests.

This ritual of tea-drinking established a mood of conviviality and Karim was forgotten for a while. After tea they again tried to press Hassen into forgiving his brother, but he remained adamant. He could not now face Catherine without looking ridiculous. Besides, he felt integrated now; he would resist anything that negated him.

Mr Mia and the priest departed. They decided to raise the matter with the congregation in the mosque. But they failed to move Hassen. Actually, his resistance grew in inverse ratio as more people came to learn of the dying Karim and Hassen's refusal to forgive him. By giving in he would be displaying mental dithering of the worst kind, as though he were a man without an inner fibre, decision and firmness of will.

Mr Mia next summoned a meeting of various religious dignitaries and received their mandate to transfer Karim to Newtown without his brother's consent. Karim's relatives would be asked to care for him, but if they refused Mr Mia would take charge.

The relatives, not wanting to offend Hassen and also feeling that Karim was not their responsibility, refused.

Mr Mia phoned Catherine and informed her of what had been decided. She agreed that it was best for Karim to be amongst his people during his last days. So Karim was brought to Newtown in an ambulance hired from a private nursing home and housed in a little room in a quiet yard behind the mosque.

The arrival of Karim placed Hassen in a difficult situation and he bitterly regretted his decision not to accept him into his own home. He first heard of his brother's arrival during the morning prayers when the priest offered a special prayer for the recovery of the sick man. Hassen found himself in the curious position of being forced to pray for his brother. After prayers several people went to see the sick man; others went up to Mr Mia to offer help. Hassen felt out of place and as soon as the opportunity presented itself he slipped out of the mosque.

In a mood of intense bitterness, scorn for himself, hatred of those who had decided to become his brother's keepers, infinite hatred for Karim, Hassen went home. Salima sensed her husband's mood and did not say a word to him.

In his room he debated with himself. In what way should he conduct himself so that his dignity remained intact?

How was he to face the congregation, the people in the streets, his neighbours? Everyone would soon know of Karim and smile at him half sadly, half ironically, for having placed himself in such a ridiculous position. Should he now forgive the dying man and transfer him to his home? People would laugh at him, snigger at his cowardice, and Mr Mia perhaps even deny him the privilege: Karim was now *his* responsibility. And what would Catherine think of him? Should he go away (on the pretext of a holiday) to Cape Town, to Durban? But no, there was the stigma of being called a renegade. And besides, Karim might take months to die, he might not die at all.

"O Karim, why did you have to do this to me?" he said, moving towards the window and drumming the pane nervously. It galled him that a weak, dying man could bring such pain to him. An adversary could be faced, one could either vanquish him or be vanquished, with one's dignity unravished, but with Karim what could he do?

He paced his room. He looked at his watch; the time for afternoon prayers was approaching. Should he expose himself to the congregation? "O Karim! Karim!" he cried, holding on to the burglar-proof bar of his bedroom window. Was it for this that he had made the pilgrimage — to cleanse his soul in order to return into the penumbra of sin? If only Karim would die he would be relieved of his agony. But what if he lingered on? What if he recovered? Were not prayers being said for him? He went to the door and shouted in a raucous voice: "Salima!"

But Salima was not in the house. He shouted again and again, and his voice echoed hollowly in the rooms. He rushed into the lounge, into the kitchen, he flung the door open and looked into the yard.

He drew the curtains and lay on his bed in the dark. Then he heard the patter of feet in the house. He jumped up and shouted for his wife. She came hurriedly.

"Salima, Salima, go to Karim, he is in a room in the mosque yard. See how he is, see if he is getting better. Quickly!"

Salima went out. But instead of going to the mosque, she entered her neighbour's house. She had already spent several hours sitting beside Karim. Mr Mia had been there as well as Catherine — who had wept.

After a while she returned from her neighbour. When she opened the door her husband ran to her. "How is he? Is he very ill? Tell me quickly!"

"He is very ill. Why don't you go and see him?"

Suddenly, involuntarily, Hassen struck his wife in the face.

"Tell me, is he dead? Is he dead?" he screamed.

Salima cowered in fear. She had never seen her husband in this raging temper. What had taken possession of the man? She retired quickly to the kitchen. Hassen locked himself in the bedroom.

During the evening he heard voices. Salima came to tell him that several people, led by Mr Mia, wanted to speak to him urgently. His first impulse was to tell them to leave immediately; he was not prepared to meet them. But he had been wrestling with himself for so many hours that he welcomed a moment when he could be in the company of others. He stepped boldly into the lounge.

"Hajji Hassen," Mr Mia began, "please listen to us. Your brother has not long to live. The doctor has seen him. He may not outlive the night."

"I can do nothing about that," Hassen replied, in an

audacious, matter-of-fact tone that surprised him and shocked the group of people.

"That is in Allah's hand," said the merchant Gardee. "In our hands lie forgiveness and love. Come with us now and see him for the last time."

"I cannot see him."

"And what will it cost you?" asked the priest who wore a long black cloak that fell about his sandalled feet.

"It will cost me my dignity and my manhood."

"My dear Hajji, what dignity and what manhood? What can you lose by speaking a few kind words to him on his death-bed? He was only a young man when he left."

"I will do anything, but going to Karim is impossible."

"But Allah is pleased by forgiveness," said the merchant.

"I am sorry, but in my case the circumstances are different. I am indifferent to him and therefore there is no necessity for me to forgive him."

"Hajji," said Mr Mia, "you are only indulging in glib talk and you know it. Karim is your responsibility, whatever his crime."

"Gentlemen, please leave me alone."

And they left. Hassen locked himself in his bedroom and began to pace the narrow space between bed, cupboard and wall. Suddenly, uncontrollably, a surge of grief for his dying brother welled up within him.

"Brother! Brother!" he cried, kneeling on the carpet beside his bed and smothering his face in the quilt. His memory unfolded a time when Karim had been ill at the Islamic Institute and he had cared for him and nursed him back to health. How much he had loved the handsome youth!

At about four in the morning he heard an urgent

rapping. He left his room to open the front door.

"Brother Karim dead," said Mustapha, the Somali muezzin of the mosque, and he cupped his hands and said a prayer in Arabic. He wore a black cloak and a white skull-cap. When he had done he turned and walked away.

Hassen closed the door and went out into the street. For a moment his release into the street gave him a sinister jubilation, and he laughed hysterically as he turned the corner and stood next to Jamal's fruitshop. Then he walked on. He wanted to get away as far as he could from Mr Mia and the priest who would be calling upon him to prepare for the funeral. That was no business of his. They had brought Karim to Newtown and they should see to him.

He went up Lovers' Walk and at the entrance of Orient House he saw the night-watchman sitting beside a brazier. He hastened up to him and warmed his hands by the fire, but he did this more as a gesture of fraternization as it was not cold, and he said a few words facetiously. Then he walked on.

His morbid joy was ephemeral, for the problem of facing the congregation at the mosque began to trouble him. What opinion would they have of him when he returned? Would they not say: he hated his brother so much that he forsook his prayers, but now that his brother is no longer alive he returns. What a man! What a Muslim!

When he reached Vinod's Photographic Studio he pressed his forehead against the neon-lit glass showcase and began to weep.

A car passed by filling the air with nauseous gas. He wiped his eyes, and looked for a moment at the photographs in the showcase; the relaxed, happy, anonymous faces stared at him, faces whose momentary expressions were trapped in film. Then he walked on. He passed a few shops and then reached Broadway Cinema where he stopped to look at the lurid posters. There were heroes, lusty, intrepid, blasting it out with guns; women in various stages of undress; horrid monsters from another planet plundering a city; Dracula.

Then he was among the quiet houses and an avenue of trees rustled softly. He stopped under a tree and leaned against the trunk. He envied the slumbering people in the houses around him, their freedom from the emotions that jarred him. He would not return home until the funeral of his brother was over.

When he reached the Main Reef Road the east was brightening. The lights along the road seemed to be part of the general haze. The buildings on either side of him were beginning to thin and on his left he saw the ghostly mountains of mine sand. Dawn broke over the city and when he looked back he saw the silhouettes of tall buildings bruising the sky. Cars and trucks were now rushing past him.

He walked for several miles and then branched off onto a gravel road and continued for a mile. When he reached a clump of blue-gum trees he sat down on a rock in the shade of the trees. From where he sat he could see a constant stream of traffic flowing along the highway. He had a stick in his hand which he had picked up along the road, and with it he prodded a crevice in the rock. The action, subtly, touched a chord in his memory and he was sitting on a rock with Karim beside him. The rock was near a river that flowed a mile away from the Islamic Institute. It was a Sunday. He had a stick in his hand and he prodded at a crevice and the weather-worn rock flaked off and Karim was gathering the flakes.

"Karim! Karim!" he cried, prostrating himself on the rock, pushing his fingers into the hard roughness, unable to bear the death of that beautiful youth.

He jumped off the rock and began to run. He would return to Karim. A fervent longing to embrace his brother came over him, to touch that dear form before the soil claimed him. He ran until he was tired, then walked at a rapid pace. His whole existence precipitated itself into one motive, one desire, to embrace his brother in a final act of love.

His heart beating wildly, his hair dishevelled, he reached the highway and walked on as fast as he could. He longed to ask for a lift from a passing motorist but could not find the courage to look back and signal. Cars flashed past him, trucks roared in pain.

When he reached the outskirts of Johannesburg it was nearing ten o'clock. He hurried along, now and then breaking into a run. Once he tripped over a cable and fell. He tore his trousers in the fall and found his hands were bleeding. But he was hardly conscious of himself, wrapped up in his one purpose.

He reached Lovers' Walk, where cars growled around him angrily; he passed Broadway Cinema, rushed towards Orient House, turned the corner at Jamal's fruitshop. And stopped.

The green hearse, with the crescent moon and stars emblem, passed by; then several cars with mourners followed, bearded men, men with white skull-caps on their heads, looking rigidly ahead, like a procession of puppets, indifferent to his fate. No one saw him.

The Betrayal

When Dr Kamal closed his surgery door one Friday night, he felt that a door had closed on his past.

He was a tall slender man, mud-complexioned, with a balding cranium that gave him a distinguished scholarly appearance. He was not only a physician and a well-known politician, but a connoisseur and collector of works of art displaying the agony of the proletariat in fields and factories. His entire collection was on display in his gallery-cum-study at home. He had received his medical and political education in India; his ability at the game of cricket had also been developed in that country. He was a religious man and every Friday he would dutifully attend the mosque in Newtown to genuflect in prayer.

For days he had been enmeshed in a dilemma, which had originated when a new political group in Fordsburg proclaimed its inaugural meeting by means of notices stuck on walls and lamp-posts. The emergence of the group, mainly consisting of youth, posed a threat to the Orient Front of which Dr Kamal was the president. A successful public meeting could be the first stage in its growth into a powerful rival political body, a body that could in time eliminate the Orient Front as a representative organization. There was also a personal threat. Dr Kamal had achieved the presidency of the Orient Front after years of patient waiting and he was afraid that his position would lose some of its lustre with the appearance of another political body. He was also the political mentor of the Fordsburg youth and felt that his prestige and status would suffer a reduction if the new group drew deserters from the Youth League of which he was the founder. There was only one way to stop the threat: the new group had to be crushed at its inaugural meeting. But . . . how was he to reconcile this action with the fact that he had been a professed disciple of Gandhi during his political life?

He drove in his small German car to the offices of the Orient Front in Park Road. At ten o'clock he was to address a clandestine meeting of members of the Youth League. He reached the building, parked his car at the entrance, and walked slowly up a flight of stairs.

Salim Rashid, chairman of the Youth League, was waiting for him.

"We are ready, Doc."

"How many?"

"Forty-two."

"Have you explained to them what they have to do?"

"Yes. You have only to say a few words to them."

It had been Salim Rashid's idea that he should address the Youth League, after the doctor had discreetly suggested that the new political group should be annihilated, in accordance with the "ethics of political survival", before it hatched something dangerous. Had he rejected the idea, Dr Kamal would have given Salim Rashid the impression that he was afraid. The young man's argument had been that a few words from their mentor, on the eve of the clash, would be sufficient to convince the members of the rightness of their action. In order to keep the doctor's rôle a secret he would arrange a nocturnal meeting.

Salim Rashid opened a door. It led into a large room with many chairs and several tables. Some members of the Youth League were talking in groups, others were outside on the balcony. There were portraits, rather crudely garish, of Gandhi on the walls.

"Friends, attention. Dr Kamal is here to address you."

They settled down on the chairs. The doctor began:

"One of the most important duties of the Youth League — in fact it is part of its unwritten constitution — is to safeguard the integrity and retain the hegemony of its parent body the Orient Front, and prevent rival political organizations from trespassing on our traditional ground. You have a great responsibility towards the Indian people of this country. You cannot permit them to be divided. The despots will destroy us if we let this happen. Let me remind you that it has always been a thesis of mine that there is no essential conflict of principles between Gandhi and the Western political philosophers, that a violent revolt and a passive revolt are aspects of the dynamics of man's search for freedom."

He paused for a moment, coughed into his clenched hand, and continued:

"You should always remember that you are not only a vital part of the Orient Front, but also the vanguard that must protect it from harm. Remember always that you have been chosen by history to shape the future of this country."

Dr Kamal had done. The youths clapped their hands, then raised their fists and shouted a few belligerent slogans.

He left the premises immediately.

On his way home he decided to pass Gandhi Hall where the meeting was to be held the next day. His motive for passing by was rooted in a strange sudden notion that the new group too had decided to hold a secret nocturnal meeting. Fear inflamed the turbulence within him and he stopped his car, half-expecting to see a knot of people coming up the street to attend the meeting. But the street was deserted and the hall doors locked. A gust of wind rushed by, carrying with it a swarm of rasping papers. The irony of his rôle struck him with force. He, the professed disciple of Gandhi, had unleashed a demon that would profane the hall commemorative of the master's name.

He went home and locked himself in his study. This room had been the scene, in the early days when he had joined the Orient Front, of weekly lectures to the youth of Fordsburg under the title 'A Study of the Dynamics of Political Action and Political Truth', which had gained such popularity that the numbers swelled and he had formed the Youth League. Its members had come to look upon him as their oracle on political matters. In his study he had expounded to them the political philosophy of the 'triumvirate', Marx, Lenin and Gandhi. He had spoken with veneration of Gandhi's passive resistance campaigns against the 'racist oligarchs' and had extolled him as a 'Titan in the history of humanity' as he had been the first to bring into the realm of politics the concepts of truth and non-violence. He had also proudly told the youth of his meetings with Gandhi while he was a medical student in India and his abandonment of radical and revolutionary ideas in politics.

When Dr Kamal took his seat in the hall he saw that it was packed with people. He felt his chest contract and he hurriedly lit a cigarette.

"Hullo, Doc," said Rhada, the secretary of the Orient Front, sitting down beside him. "Is our Youth League present?"

"This should be an interesting meeting," he commented, pretending not to have heard the question.

"This should be their first and last meeting."

Dr Kamal was jolted. So the secretary knew of the intentions of the Youth League? Salim Rashid had assured him that the plans were all secret and that he would not be implicated. Now someone had told the secretary — and perhaps many others — and though he seemed to approve of the planned disruption and violence, there was no way of telling how he would react if things went wrong.

"There is Salim Rashid," Rhada said, pointing towards the front.

"Yes," Dr Kamal answered feebly.

"These upstarts can give us a lot of trouble if they are not stopped."

"The youth must settle matters among themselves," Dr Kamal said, with suppressed anger.

Several young men began adjusting the public address system on the stage and then one of them began to speak. He gave the audience a preliminary brief account of how he and several friends had been drawn to the politics of the People's Movement in Cape Town and had decided to form a branch in the city.

"Mr Chairman, I object!"

Salim Hoosein stood up.

"May I remind you that there is a political organization here, the Orient Front. You may have heard of it."

"I have heard of it. But I feel that there is a need for a

different kind of political organization. Let me explain . . ."

Several voices interjected:

"What do you mean?"

"Is the Front dead?"

"Are you issuing a challenge?"

The speaker pleaded for order and said that members of the audience would have ample time to ask questions later.

"Mr Chairman, are you trying to smear the Orient Front?" Salim Rashid shouted.

Before he could answer several voices accused the new group of trying to divide the Indian people in their liberatory struggle. Then someone boomed:

"Uncivilized Indians, don't you know anything about meeting procedure?"

Dr Kamal jumped up from his seat and turning in the direction of the voice said:

"I strongly object to the defamatory slur cast upon us by someone in the hall. For his information, I must state that we Indians are among the most civilized races of mankind, a people with a glorious culture . . ."

"Well, that is quite plain to all," a cynical voice near him said. "Why don't you keep quiet and let the meeting get on."

He sat down, his body quivering. The rebuke stung him with such ferocity that for a moment, while standing, he had felt his body reeling as if he was about to plunge down a vertiginous height. His dignity and status had suffered a humiliating reduction. What compelling force had made him jump up from his seat and expose his feelings to the audience, identifying himself, so it seemed to him, with the opponents of the new political group? He had come as an observer — a delusion he had managed to sustain until a few moments ago — but now he had become involved in their dispute. He should have stayed at home. The new group seemed to have many more sympathizers than he had calculated; people were taking them seriously. If the Youth League was defeated . . . he did not have time to complete the thought as, with the volume of the public address system amplified, the Chairman continued:

"Some of us felt that what we lacked here was a political body that would unify the oppressed. We are convinced that any organization opposed to racialism should not have a racial structure, such as that of the Orient Front, or the African Front . . ."

Salim Rashid leapt from his seat.

"Don't insult the Orient Front! Don't insult the organization founded by the great Mahatma Gandhi!"

He rushed forward and immediately members of the Youth League rose to follow their leader. Friends and sympathizers of the new group in the audience, shocked at first by the sudden threat of violence, jumped up from their seats and pressed towards the front to join the fray.

There was uproar and panic. Women screamed. The stage became a mass of seething, pushing, wrestling, punching, shouting combatants. From the rear of the hall one had the impression that players in a drama were involved in a mock battle.

Someone ran out of the hall to telephone the police.

When Salim Rashid leapt from his seat shouting his battle cry and rushing forward, Dr Kamal had experienced a sharp conflict within. There was the urge to flee from the violence he had contrived, and there was a petrifying inertia compelling him to remain and witness the battle. He stayed, trapped by indecision and the ambiguity of his political commitment, but when he saw the opposition's determination to fight the Youth League members, he rose from his seat. He took a few hurried steps, reached the foyer and stopped at the door. Policemen with truncheons and guns rushed past him into the hall.

Driven by a turbid amalgam of curiosity, fear and bewilderment, Dr Kamal re-entered the hall and watched horrified as this new dimension was added to the battle. Then he fled. The centre of his being that had been in turmoil during the past few weeks seemed to be undergoing a kind of physical rot and together with this feeling he sensed the approaching storm of reproach and stigma that would engulf him. He reached his car. As he drove homewards Salim Rashid's words — aroused, flaming furies — pursued him.

"Don't insult our organization . . ."

The Yogi

The wisest and most learned man in Fordsburg, many people said, was Yogi Khrishnasiva. His wisdom resided in an impenetrable deity-like silence; his learning was displayed by the volumes on philosophy, mysticism and Yoga that he always carried in his hands. His inscrutable silence led many people to believe that he was among the few devotees who had achieved union with Brahman.

There was a time when Yogi Khrishnasiva had been vocal. After completing his studies at the feet of a luminary in India he had returned to the country and toured its main cities where he had lectured to various groups and organizations. To that period belonged a number of mystical maxims (constituting the themes of his lectures) that enjoyed a brief vogue, maxims such as: non-being is life, being is death; man's life on earth is a phantasmagoric trek to nowhere; meat-eating is the root of all evil; if you have inner liberty, political liberty is unnecessary. He had had them printed on art paper with an elaborate border of Hindu deities and had issued the scrolls to individuals and groups. However, the Orient Front failed to be impressed and returned the scroll with a note saying that the Yogi was "undermining the political struggle" and that he was "nothing other than a stooge of the ruling class".

The Yogi lived with his widowed mother in Orient Mansions, an apartment block in Terrace Road. He was a small meticulous person. He could not have weighed more than a hundred pounds. There was something alert and agile about his dark, neatly-groomed face, despite the quietness that pervaded his general appearance. He was always fashionably dressed and never appeared in the traditional robes worn by mystics. As the Yogi had inherited a fortune, he did no work. His life was devoted to Yoga and the occult.

One day several youths were gathered in Mr Das Patel's café — eternally smelling of sweetmeats, sub-tropical fruit and spiced delicacies — on the ground floor of Orient Mansions. Nazeem mentioned that he had heard that Yogi Khrishnasiva had been appointed a marriage guidance counsellor by a social welfare society.

"They could not have made a better choice," commented the law student Soma. "From his lofty moral and intellectual position he can survey the field of human follies and offer his wisdom."

"Nonsense!" said Ebrahim — tall, curly-haired, dark — the political pundit. Sensing a verbal battle between the two everyone gathered around them.

"What does the Yogi, a bachelor, know about the problems of marriage?"

"Is it necessary for one to be married before one can say anything about marriage?"

"Tell me, Soma, what does the Yogi, an ascetic, know about sex?"

Soma did not reply.

"Or take a parallel example. Can one give an account of

life in a fascist dictatorship without actual experience?"

"Of course one can. In a democracy there will be a legal code; in a fascist dictatorship the individual will have no legal rights."

"Do you seriously believe that anyone outside this country can have adequate knowledge of conditions here?"

"He can read about them, surely."

"Certainly, but his knowledge will be academic."

Soma took off his spectacles and wiped them with a handkerchief. The argument was stoking up but it was veering away from the Yogi and Mr Das Patel brought them back to him.

"You talk of Yogi Khrishnasiva and now you talk of dictatorship . . . Talk of Yogi and I say he fraud."

Fraud! The word jolted them.

"I tell you he fraud. You boys too young to know."

"Tell us! Tell us!" they chorused.

But Mr Das Patel was as inscrutable as the Yogi.

"Don' worry boys. I say he fraud, big fraud. I not Das Patel for nutting. One day you see. At moment I say nutting furder."

"This is defamation of character," Soma asserted.

"Defamation of who character? The Yogi? He got no character, my dear man."

Everyone laughed.

"I say it is libellous to accuse a man without evidence."

"Look here, Soma, I not like you lawyers. You talk like old women in court and tell all Dick and Harry how clever you are. I know what I talking when I say the Yogi he fraud. Some day you see me right. Dat all."

"You are accusing a man who practises renunciation. Who will believe you?"

"Renun . . . my foot! He practise renun . . . ? I not born yesterday. You tell your fader he practise renun . . . not me."

"Soma, shut up! Shut up!" several voices shot in. They pacified Mr Das Patel. He relented a little.

"I say he sleep wit wite women. One day you see me right. Dat all."

After giving them this fresh jolt, Mr Das Patel refused to say anything further.

Someone who had gone out came back into the café to say that the Yogi was approaching. They hurried outside. As the Yogi passed by Mr Das Patel said loudly: "He practise Yoga in bed." Everyone burst into laughter. The Yogi, unshaken, went towards the entrance of Orient Mansions and climbed the stairs.

After several months Mr Das Patel's café was the arena of excitement. In the evening newspaper appeared the following item:

An Indian, Mr Indra Khrishnasiva (45), was arrested at 3 a.m. today outside a block of flats in President Street and charged under the Immorality Act. A white woman has also been taken into custody.

"I tell you boys, didn't I?" Mr Das Patel said. "I tell you dat Yogi he fraud. He only Yogi to cheat wite women to sleep wit him. I tell you he no like black women. He black but he don' like black. He like wite goose meat!"

And he laughed animatedly.

"I know Yogi Khrishnasiva dese many years. But he never come into my shop. He don' smoke, he don' drink, he don' eat, he only . . ." Mr Das Patel's wife entered the café and the word remained unuttered. When she left he burst into a wild guffaw.

"He marrich counsellor! He marrich counsellor! He counsel well dat I can tell you boys. Husban' not giving sateesfaction, dan do dis. Dan he give demonstration."

"Yes," said Aziz Khan, the writer on Islam, who had come in to buy the newspaper. "Under the guise of Yoga, he practised his abominations . . ."

"Practical Yoga," Nazeem suggested and the shop rang with laughter.

Soma, who was not amused by the levity regarding the Yogi's arrest, now decided to examine the legal implications.

"I think the Yogi can be got off. It is not easy to catch people in the very act, for obviously anyone indulging in the act takes all the necessary precautions against prying eyes. Then again, in his case, the state has to prove his guilt. The rule that the accused is innocent until found guilty applies. This rule of course does not apply in cases of political crimes . . ."

"Verbosity is a crime here . . ." Ebrahim interrupted.

"I think the Yogi will be set free because of his unimpeachable character. His lawyer need only bring witnesses . . ."

"He go free like hell. Dey put him away in jail to become real Yogi."

Everyone laughed.

"The Yogi belongs to a dead civilization," Ebrahim said. "In an era when politics governs everything, he turns his face towards the negatives of renunciation and asceticism . . . attitudes which are essentially irresponsible."

"Very high-falutin'," Mr Das Patel said, "but the plain fact is he fraud, total fraud."

The Yogi's case came up three days later and people flocked to the Magistrate's Court to listen to the proceedings. School pupils played truant, students at university decided not to attend lectures, Mr Das Patel left his wife to manage the café.

The seating accommodation in the court room was divided — one section for Europeans and the other for Non-Europeans. In the European section there were six people, two women and four men. The Non-European section was crowded and many people stood in the corridors outside.

The Yogi's face looked strained when he and the woman were brought into the court. The woman was frail in appearance, though her face was pretty. Her hair was light brown in colour and cut very short. She was neatly dressed in a blue costume.

The prosecutor opened the case by presenting the state's evidence against the Yogi and Miss Weston. He said that the police had received information that several white women were frequenting an apartment block in President Street. They decided to investigate. They came to know of the "Ganges Society" and the premises they occupied in the building. They kept a watch on the activities of members of the society. One night a police patrol observed a woman entering the building. It waited till three in the morning and when the woman and the Yogi emerged from the building, they were arrested.

The prosecutor then called several witnesses, and after handing in the report of the physician who had examined the couple immediately after arrest, closed the state's case. Counsels for the Yogi and Miss Weston had entered pleas of guilty on behalf of their clients, and now prepared for cross-examination in mitigation of punishment.

Miss Weston was called into the witness box. She told the court that being a novice she had placed her confidence in the Yogi and that he had seduced her. She was then questioned by her counsel.

"Miss Weston, you have stated that at the time of seduction you were naked. Does the practice of Yoga require the removal of clothing?"

"The guru suggested that I remove my clothing."

"Did he give a reason?"

"He said that all clothing contaminated the body and prevented the divine spirit from finding liberation."

"What happened after that?"

"The guru asked me to perform the posture called 'Prana'."

"Please explain."

"He told me to lie flat on my back, cross my legs below me, interlock my fingers on my navel, and meditate on the significance of sexual congress."

Cross-examined by the Yogi's counsel, Miss Weston denied that she had removed her clothing in order to sexually entice the Yogi.

The Yogi was next called to give evidence.

"Does the performance of Yoga require the removal of some clothing?"

"Yes."

"What garments did Miss Weston remove?"

"She removed her skirt, blouse and slip. She said her brassière was too tight and she removed it."

"Anything else?"

The Yogi hesitated before answering.

"She removed her intimate garment."

"Did you suggest that she remove it?"

"No."

"Do you think that the removal of the garment was a deliberate act of provocation and enticement?"

"Yes, positively."

The Yogi was then cross-examined by Miss Weston's counsel. To the assertion that he had misused Yoga and mysticism to seduce the lady, he answered:

"I repudiate that suggestion. I am an ascetic. All yogis are ascetics."

"Yogi Khrishnasiva, is the presence of a naked woman an impediment to the liberation of the divine spirit in man, or is she an incentive?"

He did not answer immediately, permitting himself a confident smile.

"A naked woman is neither an impediment nor an incentive."

"Could you explain that?"

The Yogi smiled again.

"We Yogis are indifferent to the state of the human body, whether in a state of dress or undress."

"Do you think that it is seemly to perform various sacred exercises without any clothing?"

"My previous premise answers this question."

"Why did you not ask Miss Weston to dress even if she had undressed of her own accord?"

"My previous premise answers this question as well."

The lawyer paused for a moment and then said:

"Yogi Khrishnasiva, in your evidence you stated that you were enticed. Did you mean by that that you made the first advances?"

"She made the first advances."

"And you succumbed?"

"I was enticed. I was overpowered."

"But you have also spoken of the indifference of the Yogi in the presence of a naked woman?"

The Yogi remained silent.

"So you cannot maintain you were indifferent?"

"No," he answered feebly.

"Then I suggest that you fraudulently employed the principles and practices of Yoga to seduce Miss Weston."

The Yogi did not answer.

That evening the proceedings in court were a subject of discussion in Mr Das Patel's café. There was a report of the trial in the newspaper and a photograph of Miss Weston and the Yogi, but the Yogi's face was partly covered with his hand. Mr Das Patel was in a state of wild excitement. He parodied the cross-examination of the Yogi and his café resounded with laughter.

The next day, before judgement was delivered, the Yogi asked if he could make a statement. He began: "Your worship, I wish to place on record that I object to this witch-hunt into the affairs of my private life . . ." But the Magistrate interrupted him with the rebuke that the court was not a forum for political speeches.

Dolly

"If any of you rich Indian bastards try to *joll* my wife I will put a knife into your guts. What you know is to show off, talk big, ride in your big cars . . ."

That was Dolly (Dooly) speaking in one of his violent, dangerous moods to bearded Mr Darsot, the spice and grain merchant. Mr Darsot dreaded meeting Dolly in the street. Yet when Dolly's scurrilities against Indians exploded, he could hardly move away, fearing a loss of dignity in ignominious retreat. Nor could he utter a word in defence, fearing to rouse Dolly's temper further. Trapped by his self-esteem and feebleness he would listen to Dolly's unsavoury oratory:

"You Indian dogs, there were not enough bitches in India so you came to South Africa. Now you look for our wives. You lock your wives up and want to *joll* ours. Bring your wife here. I will show you, you Indian bastard . . ."

Dolly would go on in this vein until he tired, or one of his friends pulled him away. Mr Darsot, displaying a tepid smile in moral victory, would hurry to seek refuge in his mansion, happy in the knowledge that he was physically unscathed.

Dolly was a small, very dark man, athletic and wiry in

build, and extraordinarily tough. I once saw two burly policemen vainly trying to pull him away from a railing to which he clung — and he only released his grip when one of them crushed his fingers with a brick. His black hair was always liberally oiled to combat its intractability. He was very ugly. His first wife had run away, unable to bear his inordinate jealousy and maniacal rages. His second wife Myrtle received a regular beating. There were times when he beat her so savagely that the police had to be called. At other times she was forced to go out with him and point out some lover (Myrtle felt that if her husband was jealous he might as well be justifiably jealous) somewhere in Fordsburg or Vrededorp. As they walked Dolly uttered menacing howls like some predacious animal. What ensued one would know after his return. If his revenge had been slaked he would shout coarsely: "Indian swine, busted his guts, showed him what Dolly is made of, the bastard!" If thwarted, he would scream obscenities at everyone in the street and bang his fists against several doors, terrifying the people within.

Myrtle was a blowsy woman, tall, frizzy-haired, with thrusting buttocks. She believed in the attractiveness of her body and she flaunted it: one would see her sitting on a balustrade, her legs daringly outstretched; or bending over a tap in the yard, her raised skirt revealing the ample flesh of her legs; or dancing, her thighs and mons Veneris embalmed in tight-fitting slacks. She had two voices: an original voice, coarse and ebulliently vulgar, which one heard during bouts of altercation with her husband, or when she reviled some woman who dared to look at her "as though I have taken your husband's you-know-what!" Her other voice was cloyingly euphonious, imitative of some woman's heard over the radio: "Oh, you're a darling honey. You do look super today, don't you?" She was often abusively referred to by women as "that Bushman bitch".

One day Bibi arrived to board and lodge with Mrs Safi, the next-door neighbour of the Dollys. She caused a sensation the day she arrived. She was the most beautiful woman to set foot in our suburb. Black-haired and blue-eyed (she was the offspring of an Indian father and a Dutch mother) with a complexion like the white flower of the gardenia, her sylph-like beauty was at variance with the earthiness of our suburb.

Dolly was mesmerized by Bibi. He expressed his adoration to us in these terms: "If any of you touch Bibi I will eat your livers." One day she was hanging up some washing in the yard when she turned around and saw him. He was gazing at her in open-mouthed rapture from beside a tap, his dark face frothing with soap.

Dolly's behaviour underwent a transformation. He no longer roamed the street Caliban-like (though he drank and smoked marijuana as usual), nor involved himself in turbulent feuds with his wife. The presence of Bibi seemed to work like alchemy in him — he was seized with a sense of shame.

And Myrtle who had once inspired so much jealousy in him (jealousy which to her was a testimony of his love) and had weathered the storms of his sadistic rages, found herself cauterized by jealousy. She would scream uncouthly and accuse him of deceiving her with Bibi in a vain effort to trigger his natural turbulent response, but he remained placid. Her jealousy then found vent in threats against Bibi. She would speak coarsely, in the presence of other women:

"That half-caste bitch will not get away with it. Who does she think she is? Because she has a white skin and blue eyes she thinks she is someone great. One of these days I will get even with her."

And she got "even" with her. One day she waited for Bibi to arrive from work, grabbed her as she passed by her doorstep, and began assaulting her. Bibi screamed and various people rushed to her assistance. When I reached them Myrtle was in the grip of several strong hands. Bibi was cowering next to a wall, her clothes torn and her hair disarranged.

When Dolly came home someone told him of the assault on Bibi. He went next-door. He saw her bruised cheek, her inflamed eye, her nail-scratched neck.

That day hideous screams reverberated through the streets as Dolly, in a rampant mood, took Myrtle into the house and turned on her with his fists.

The police were called, but tired of the feud between man and wife stood around looking bored. We waited in the street. At last Myrtle stopped howling.

Dolly unlocked the door and saw Bibi amongst us. He burst into wild laughter.

"Beauty! Beauty! Come inside. She will never touch you again."

He took Bibi by the hand and we followed them into the house.

Two Sisters

"When I want to baat den dey want to baat, when I want to go to lavatry den dey want to go also. Dey so shelfish in everyting dey do. My stepmader and my fader dey jus lock demselves in de room, sometimes de whole day. I don't know wat dey do in dere. Dere is no food in de house and if dere is den we must cook. And den dey jus come out dere room and eat all de food up."

"Why didn't you speak to your father?"

"He don't listen to us since he marry dat woman. He very nice man, but when he marry dat woman all niceness disappear. She spoil him and he don't care for us anymore. Den I tell my sister Habiba we go away. Dat not true, Habiba?"

"It true."

"A friend tell us dere's room in dis yard. Dat's how we come here."

Rookeya was talking to me and my friend Omar. The two sisters caused a sensation the day they arrived to live in the yard. They wore robe-like dresses with *ijars* (trousers). But there was nothing unusual in this. What was unusual was the colour of their hair. It was dyed blonde. They looked rather odd as blonde hair did not accord with Eastern features. They were both very hairy and waged a constant battle with the hair on their faces. "Their hairiness," my friend Omar said, "indicates that they are sweet-time girls." Rookeya was in her thirties and Habiba a few years younger.

Before long a change occurred in their mode of dress. Either because of some feminine quirk or the dictates of fashion the two sisters shed their Eastern garments (much to the consternation of Aziz Khan) and began to wear Western clothing.

Soon Omar and I were making love to the two sisters. I took the younger, Habiba. There was no real selection on our part: we gravitated towards them and indulged in some light-hearted love-making.

I found Habiba to be a woman who performed everything in jerks, as though her body were a wound-up mechanical toy. Her very walk was jerky and toy-like. She would look left, then right, and now and then look back as though fearing pursuit. Her arms would be bent almost at ninety-degree angles and she would tread the ground as though she were treading on a spike bed. When I kissed her I had the queer sensation that I was kissing a mobile skeleton.

After some time Omar and I tired of the company of the two sisters. Free of us they hitched themselves to other men.

In the morning one saw them emerge from their apartment, sprucely dressed, and descend the stairs, Rookeya always preceding Habiba protectively. They would go to Main Road and take the tram to their place of work. Both sisters worked as shop-assistants. They would return in the late afternoon, prepare food, eat, wash the dishes, and dress, sometimes in shimmering saris, and wait. Invariably men would come for them and they would be driven away in cars.

The attitude of the women in the yard towards the two sisters varied between frigid contempt and outright hostility. The married men in the yard, watched by their wives, were unable to approach them; but the unmarried ones fluttered around them despite Aziz Khan's prophecy that the "two sisters and their lovers would go hand in hand into hell".

On Saturday afternoons or Sunday mornings the two sisters, dressed in short pants or brief skirts, could be seen leaning on the iron balustrade of the balcony, talking to a group of young men gathered below, and laughing with them whenever anyone made a risqué remark or cracked a joke.

And then, as anyone could have predicted, the two sisters were impregnated. At first they became alarmed and made random accusations. Omar was one of those charged by Rookeya as being responsible for her pregnancy.

She sent for me.

"Please tell Omar dat I pregnant and he fader of child. I marry him anytime. I frighten to tell him because he little bit young."

"And how do you know?"

"We women we know who de fader. Is dat not so, Habiba?"

"It so."

"Habiba, who is the father of your child?"

"He Hamid Majid of Newtown. He got shop."

"And does he know?"

"I already tell him of baby, but he say he married and has six children. He say he look after baby."

"You are lucky."

"I also lucky," Rookeya said, smiling.

I left to convey to Omar the allegation of paternity.

"How does that woman know that I made her pregnant?"

"Feminine intuition perhaps."

"She thinks I am some stupid joker."

Omar refused to face Rookeya. He feared that she might have some irrefutable evidence. What would his parents say? What would all the people say? Father of a harlot's child! He would be taunted by school children; his teachers would point him out as an example of degenerate youth.

After a few days he decided to face Rookeya and "settle things" with her.

They quarrelled. There were "tears, tantrums and hysterics" (according to Omar) but nothing was settled.

Rookeya sent for me again.

"Tell Omar it my baby. I make it and no man make it. Tell Omar I love him and he not worry."

"But surely the child must have a father?"

"My child need no fader. It glad it has no fader, it tell me so. I feel it inside me, telling me so. My own fader not care for us, derefore my baby need no fader."

"And Habiba?"

"Habiba also not worry about fader of baby. Dat not true, Habiba?"

"It true."

And as the days passed the two sisters' wombs swelled. This provoked the anger and outraged the sense of morality of the people in the yard.

"Fine example they set our young girls," said Mrs Musa to my landlady. "Can't they see I have growing girls."

"Lucky I got no girls to worry about."

"I must tell my husband to do something. I cannot go on living alongside two pregnant and unmarried women. And my eldest daughter is so friendly with them."

Mrs Cassim, who was half-Chinese, said: "My mother used to tell me that in China unmarried girls never become pregnant."

"Yes, that is true," agreed Halima, the Malay woman. "Even in Cape Town the women are better behaved. They go out with men but they behave themselves."

"I wonder how they managed to get pregnant together," said Mrs Cassim.

"Perhaps one man sleep with both during the same night," suggested my landlady, and for a moment the seriousness of the discussion was forgotten in laughter.

"They practise polygamy," said Dorothy, the builder Solomon's wife, trying to raise another laugh.

"I beg your pardon, Mrs Solomon," Mrs Musa retorted, annoyed that her religion should be misunderstood. "That is not polygamy. They are not married to one man."

Hajji Fatima, who had been to Mecca the previous year, stated that in an Islamic country such as Arabia the two women would be stoned to death.

"They should cut off their pudenda," said Dorothy (she was an avid reader of cheap novels), and although no one had heard the word before they understood what she meant. But it was something too bloody to contemplate. There was something more decent and clean in stoning.

While other women talked, Aziz Khan's wife decided to act. One afternoon she glided out of her house, looked up at the apartment of the two sisters and stationed herself at the bottom of the stairs. Excitement flared through the yard and people gathered around her. When the two sisters arrived, she scrutinized their bulging bellies, spat and screamed:

"O Muslim women! O Muslim women! What have you done! What have you done! O Allah punish the women who call themselves Muslims and sin before you. O Muslims! O how you have fallen!"

And she fell down and wept. The two sisters looked at her in fear, hurried up the stairs and locked themselves in their apartment.

There was something so tragic in Mrs Khan's performance that gloom spread through the yard. Children were constantly reminded to keep quiet. People would emerge from their houses and look at the apartment of the two sisters as though something tragic was happening in there.

Aziz Khan, a whipcord lean man in over-sized clothing, with the face of an overfed baby, said to us:

"If I had the time I would write a book on the nefarious activities of the two sisters. They pre-eminently exemplify the moral degeneration into which present-day Muslims are falling. They should be locked up in prison and starved to death."

When someone suggested that they were not wholly responsible for their pregnancies, he answered:

"Are you suggesting that they were unable to guard their most sacred private places? Islam would never have attained its ineffable heights if it had allowed its daughters to run wild, to indulge in all sorts of acts of concupiscence."

After a few months the two sisters gave birth to two girls.

There was much talk in the yard about the birth of the babies. Some felt sorry for the babies and wished to adopt them; others suggested that they be given to the carnivores in the zoo; others wanted to set fire to the apartment.

Aziz Khan felt that the time had come for action and that the two sisters and their babies should be "ousted" from the yard. "For their continued residence is a threat to the moral fibre of the people living in the yard and a blot on the fair name and fame of our religion and our holy Prophet."

First he went to the gangster Gool, approaching him at his house immediately after noon prayers on Friday. But Gool, perhaps more interested in satisfying his hunger or finding moral talk odious, briskly disposed of him, shutting the door contemptuously.

His next call was on Molvi Haroon, priest at the Newtown mosque and head of the Islamic Society. Abdulla, a disciple of Aziz Khan, accompanied him and gave us the following account of the interview:

"Aziz informed the Molvi of the serious moral problem facing us, and do you know what he said? He said that the punishment of the two women rested in the hands of Allah! Aziz, incensed at this cowardly fence-sitting, called him a 'stupid dwarf '. The Molvi grabbed his staff and Aziz thrust his left fist at him. I dragged Aziz out of the house."

Aziz Khan's next call was on Mr Joosub, the landlord of the tenements in the yard. Mr Joosub was an eccentric who was clad in a *koortah* (a white cotton smock) even on cold days. His head was always shaved and his beard bushy and long. He was obsessed by religion and would pray to Allah everywhere, even at street intersections. Once during the festival of Eid he came into the yard with a monkey. The monkey had a tasselled red fez strapped to its head. "This monkey Muslim! This monkey Muslim!" he shouted to the spectators, especially directing his remarks to the servants. "But you no Muslim, you no Muslim!" Then he scattered handfuls of coins — which turned out to be cents.

Mr Joosub expressed his willingness to oust the "two bitches" from the yard. He would do so personally. He was king of several backyards in Fordsburg and would not tolerate the presence of "bitches" in his domains.

He came one Sunday afternoon in his chauffeur-driven Mercedes. He stood at the foot of the stairs leading to the apartment of the two sisters and made several threatening pugilistic gestures. Excited people gathered around him. He struggled up the stairs, breathing hard and clutching the railing. When he reached the landing he paused to rest for a few minutes. The sisters were standing near the doorway. First he approached Rookeya and smacked her resoundingly on the cheek, shouting, "Pig! Bitch! Pig!" in Gujarati. Habiba, who tried to escape past him, received a blow on the head. She fell and nearly came tumbling down the stairs. Mr Joosub then entered the apartment. The two sisters, shivering with fright, went towards the door to see what he would do next. Soon he appeared in the doorway, holding a primus stove in his hands; the brass contraption glinted in the sunlight as he flung it over the railing. It fell with a clanging sound and several parts were shattered by the impact. Next a chair came hurtling down, followed by a pot and a bath. Other household articles followed in quick succession as the mania for destruction gripped Mr Joosub: crockery, linen, clothing. The two sisters, frightened, impotent, watched through the doorway as their landlord entered the apartment and gave way like marionettes as he emerged with some article.

Then, suddenly, Rookeya and Habiba screamed as Mr Joosub appeared in the doorway, holding one of the infants. They flung themselves on him. Mr Joosub tried to fend them off with one hand, while with the other he clutched the screaming infant.

At this stage Solomon made his way through the crowd and climbed the stairs. When he reached the landing he gently pushed the sisters aside, held Mr Joosub by the neck, shook him, took the infant and gave it to its mother, then gave Mr Joosub a hard push against the door frame so that his face bumped painfully against it. Retaining a firm hold of Mr Joosub he dragged him down the stairs. When they reached the ground the crowd gave way for them and the children burst into applause. Solomon conducted Mr Joosub to his Mercedes, opened the door and without any ceremony pushed him into the car. The chauffeur, knowing his cue, reversed the car out of the yard and drove off.

We didn't see Mr Joosub again for some time. But the sisters decided it was dangerous living in premises belonging to a madman. They found another apartment in Newtown and moved away.

Father and Son

Shortly after the two sisters left, the premises they had occupied were renovated and expensively furnished. Everyone was eager to see the arrival of the new occupants. There was a rumour that Mr Joosub himself was coming to live in the yard in order to keep his tenants under surveillance, but the rumour proved false when one morning we saw a car enter the yard and from it emerge Mr Mayet the well-known jeweller and a young woman. Mr Mayet was over seventy years old. He wore an astrakhan fez and a newly-tailored suit. His beard was turning grey. He walked with a slight stoop and had to be assisted up the stairs by his chauffeur. The woman was tall and dusky in complexion. She was elegantly dressed in a white costume and her hair was elaborately coiffured. Her eyes were almond-shaped. She smiled at all those gazing at her.

Mr Mayet and the woman entered the apartment. The chauffeur carried in several portmanteaus and then left. The couple stayed in the apartment for the rest of the day and night. Before dawn on the next day, during the time of prayers at the mosque, Mr Mayet was seen leaving the yard.

The presence of the woman aroused a great deal of curiosity. Everyone wanted to see her, but she kept indoors. When she appeared on the balcony after a few days several people inquired of her who she was and where she came from. She told them that her name was Maimuna, that she came from Cape Town and that she was Mr Mayet's second wife.

There was much talk and gossip about Maimuna. There were those who were against her: her only motive for marrying an old man was to waste his money or inherit it. And there were those who were for her: the jeweller must have lured her with his money (or jewels) and tricked her family. Aziz Khan supported this view.

"There can be only one explanation for this mismatch of the century — the Malay woman's poor family must have been deceived into selling her to that doddering old idiot. There is just no depth to which the rich will not descend."

When someone pointed out to him that he should not object as Mr Mayet was practising polygamy, he replied:

"Polygamy is a sacred religious institution and is not there for the moronic lust of the idle rich."

A week later Aziz Khan issued a pamphlet entitled, "Polygamy and Lust", but he avoided any reference to the jeweller.

Maimuna was a pleasant woman and she gained many friends. She entertained the women in her apartment, at first during the day and later at night as well when her husband began staying away every alternate night. Many women envied her. She was good-looking, had two servants, wore expensive clothes and jewellery and could telephone for a car at any time.

And then Asif arrived, entering the yard in a tangerine Alfa Romeo sports car. Asif was Mr Mayet's eldest son. He had been to England and had spent several years — largely unfruitful academically — at London University. He had come to meet his "second mother". He was slender, handsome, eternally wearing sun-glasses. He was never seen without a silk scarf around his neck and a cigarette in his mouth.

Asif began visiting Maimuna rather too often for the liking of some people and Myrtle declared that Asif was "*jolling* his second mother". The gossip-mongers were very excited and every time Asif's Alfa Romeo came into the yard they came out of their homes to look at him. Sometimes Asif came with his father and always helped him up the stairs. As time passed Asif's visits to his "second mother" became more frequent and lasted many hours, so that his sports car looked like a permanent fixture in the yard.

Aziz Khan and his disciples were outraged at the "highly immoral and objectionable behaviour of the black Englishman. Father and son delighting in the same cesspool!"

Not only did Asif spend much of his time with his "second mother" in the apartment, but he began taking her out in his car, especially on the nights when his father stayed away.

"I have a good mind to phone Mr Mayet and tell him of his incestuous son of a goat fornicating with his mother," Aziz Khan said to us. Anyway, whether by Aziz Khan or someone else Mr Mayet came to know of the affair. He came one night when he was not expected and no sooner had he stepped out of his car than Asif's Alfa drove into the yard.

"You ape! You ape!" Mr Mayet shouted in Gujarati.

Father and son confronted each other. There was a terrible row. Mr Mayet disinherited his son in front of a crowd of people who had gathered to witness the spectacle. Asif answered back and dismissed his father as a "rotten old tree". People began to take sides and altercations broke out. Aziz Khan and several of his disciples attempted to attack Asif, others intervened, there was scuffling and shouting. In the mêlée several friends of Maimuna scratched Mr Mayet. Frightened at the commotion he had caused and fearing the arrival of the police, he quickly retreated to his car and was driven away by his chauffeur amid shouts of "Coward!" and "Serves you right!"

When peace returned Asif went away and Maimuna retired to her apartment.

The next day Asif arrived with two friends, but he did not come in his sports car. Maimuna telephoned her husband and told him to come to her immediately. She was sorry about the whole affair; she was innocent; he had been misinformed by jealous people. She had gone to the cinema; she had met Asif after the show and she had asked him to bring her home.

Mr Mayet came and when he knocked at the door Asif's friends opened it and one of them said:

"You are divorced."

"Divorced? Who divorced me?"

"Maimuna. We are the witnesses."

The people who had gathered below the stairs saw Mr Mayet step backwards.

"Asif, Asif," he said several times and began to weep. Then he turned and walked down the stairs, helped by his chauffeur.

Hajji Musa and the Hindu Fire-Walker

"Allah has sent me to you, Bibi Fatima."

"Allah, Hajji Musa?"

"I assure you, Allah, my good lady. Listen to me carefully. There is something wrong with you. Either you have a sickness or there is an evil spell cast over your home. Can you claim that there is nothing wrong in your home, that your family is perfectly healthy and happy?"

"Well, Hajji Musa, you know my little Amir has a nasty cough that even Dr Kamal cannot cure and Soraya seems to have lost her appetite."

"My good woman, you believe me now when I say Allah has sent me to you?"

Bibi Fatima's husband, Jogee, entered the room. Hajji Musa took no notice of him and began to recite (in Arabic) an extract from the Koran. When he had done he shook hands with Jogee.

"Listen to me, Bibi Fatima and brother Jogee. Sickness is not part of our nature, neither is it the work of our good Allah. It is the work of that great evil-doer Iblis, some people call him Satan. Well, I, by the grace of Allah," (he recited another extract from the Koran), "have been given the power to heal the sick and destroy evil. That is my work in life, even if I get no reward."

"But Hajji Musa, you must live."

"Bibi Fatima, Allah looks after me and my family. Now bring me two glasses of water and a candle."

She hurried to the kitchen and brought the articles.

"Now bring me the children."

"Jogee, please go and find Amir in the yard while I look for Soraya."

Husband and wife went out. Meanwhile Hajji Musa drew the curtains in the room, lit the candle and placed the two glasses of water on either side of the candle. He took incense out of his pocket, put it in an ashtray and lit it.

When husband and wife returned with the children they were awed. There was an atmosphere of strangeness, of mystery, in the room. Hajji Musa looked solemn. He took the candle, held it about face level and said:

"Look, there is a halo around the flame."

They looked and saw a faint halo.

He placed the candle on the table, took the glasses of water, held them above the flame and recited a verse from the Koran. When he had done he gave one glass to the boy and one to the girl.

"Drink, my children," he said. They hesitated for a moment, but Bibi Fatima commanded them to drink the water.

"They will be well," he said authoritatively. "They can now go and play."

He extinguished the candle, drew the curtains, and sat down on the settee. And he laughed, a full-throated, uproarious, felicitous laugh.

"Don't worry about the children. Allah has performed miracles and what are coughs and loss of appetites." And he laughed again.

Bibi Fatima went to the kitchen to make tea and Jogee and I kept him company. She returned shortly with tea and cake.

"Jogee," she said, "I think Hajji Musa is greater than Dr Kamal. You remember last year Dr Kamal gave me medicines and ointments for my aching back and nothing came of it?"

"Hajji Musa is no ordinary doctor."

"What are doctors of today," Hajji Musa said, biting into a large slice of cake, "but chancers and frauds? What knowledge have they of religion and the spiritual mysteries?"

"Since when have you this power to heal, Hajji Musa?"

"Who can tell the ways of Allah, Bibi Fatima. Sometimes his gifts are given when we are born and sometimes when we are much older."

"More tea?"

She filled the cup. He took another slice of cake.

"Last month I went to Durban and there was this woman, Jasuben, whom the doctors had declared insane. Even her own yogis and swamis had given her up. I took this woman in hand and today she is as sane as anyone else."

"Hajji Musa, you know my back still gives me trouble. Dr Kamal's medicine gave me no relief. I have even stopped making *roti* and Jogee is very fond of *roti*."

"You should let me examine your back some day," the healer said, finishing his tea.

"Why not now?"

"Not today," he answered protestingly. "I have some business to attend to."

"But Hajji Musa, it will only take a minute or two."

"Well that's true, that's true."

"Will you need the candle and water?"

"Yes."

She hurriedly went to refill the glass with water.

"Please, Jogee and Ahmed, go into the kitchen for a while," she said, returning.

We left the room, Jogee rather reluctantly. She shut the door. I sat down on a chair and looked at a magazine lying on the table. Jogee told me he was going to buy cigarettes and left. He was feeling nervous.

I was sitting close to the door and could hear Hajji Musa's voice and the rustle of clothing as he went on with the examination.

"I think it best if you lie down on the settee so that I can make a thorough examination . . . Yes, that is better . . . Is the pain here? Bibi Fatima, you know the pain often has its origin lower down, in the lumbar region. Could you ease your *ijar* a little? The seat of the pain is often here . . . Don't be afraid."

"I can feel it getting better already, Hajji Musa."

"That is good. You are responding very well."

There was silence for some time. When Jogee returned Hajji Musa was reciting a prayer in Arabic. Jogee puffed at his cigarette.

When Bibi Fatima opened the door she was smiling and looked flushed.

"Your wife will be well in a few days," Hajji Musa assured the anxious man. "And you will have your daily *roti* again. Now I must go."

"Hajji Musa, but we must give you something for your trouble."

"No, nothing, Bibi Fatima. I forbid you."

She was insistent. She told Jogee in pantomime (she

showed him five fingers) how much money he should give. Jogee produced the money from his pocket, though inwardly protesting his wife's willingness to pay a man who asked no fees. Bibi Fatima put the money into Hajji Musa's pocket.

In appearance Hajji Musa was a fat, pot-bellied, short, dark man, with glossy black wavy hair combed backwards with fastidious care. His face was always clean-shaven. For some reason he never shaved in the bathroom, and every morning one saw him in the yard, in vest and pyjama trousers, arranging (rather precariously) his mirror and shaving equipment on the window-sill outside the kitchen and going through the ritual of cleaning his face with the precision of a surgeon. His great passion was talking and while shaving he would be conducting conversations with various people in the yard: with the hawker packing his fruit and vegetables in the cart; with the two wives of the motor mechanic Soni; with the servants coming to work.

Hajji Musa was a well-known man. At various times he had been a commercial traveller, insurance salesman, taxi driver, companion to dignitaries from India and Pakistan, Islamic missionary, teacher at a seminary, shopkeeper, matchmaker and hawker of ladies' underwear.

His career as a go-between in marriage transactions was a brief inglorious one that almost ended his life. One night there was fierce knocking at his door. As soon as he opened it an angry voice exploded: "You liar! You come and tell me of dat good-for-nutting Dendar boy, dat he good, dat he ejucated, dat he good prospect. My foot and boot he ejucated! He sleep most time wit bitches, he drink and beat my daughter. When you go Haj? You nutting but liar. You *baster*! You *baster*!" And suddenly two shots from a gun rang out in quick succession. The whole incident took place so quickly that no one had any time to look at the man as he ran through the yard and escaped. When people reached Hajji Musa's door they found him prostrate, breathing hard and wondering why he was still alive (the bullets had passed between his legs). His wife and eight children were in a state of shock. They were revived with sugared water.

Hajji Musa's life never followed an even course: on some days one saw him riding importantly in the chauffeur-driven Mercedes of some wealthy merchant in need of his services; on others, one saw him in the yard, pacing meditatively from one end to the other, reciting verses from the Koran. Sometimes he would visit a friend, tell an amusing anecdote, laugh, and suddenly ask: "Can you give me a few rands till tomorrow?" The friend would give him the money without expecting anything of tomorrow, for it was well known that Hajji Musa, liberal with his own money, never bothered to return anyone else's.

Hajji Musa considered himself a specialist in the exorcism of evil jinn. He deprecated modern terms such as neurosis, schizophrenia, psychosis. "What do doctors know about the power of satanic jinn? Only God can save people who are no longer themselves. I have proved this time and again. You don't believe me? Then come on Sunday night to my house and you will see."

On Sunday night we were clustered around Hajji Musa in the yard. As his patient had not yet arrived, he regaled us with her history.

"She is sixteen. She is the daughter of Mia Mohammed the Market Street merchant. She married her cousin a few years ago. But things went wrong. Her mother-in-law disliked her. For months she has been carted from doctor to doctor, and from one psychiatrist to another, those fools. Tonight you will see me bring about a permanent cure."

After a while a car drove into the yard, followed by two others. Several men — two of them tall, bearded brothers — emerged from the car, approached Hajji Musa and shook hands with him. They pointed to the second car.

"She is in that car, Hajji Musa."

"Good, bring her into the house." And he went inside.

There were several women in the second car. All alighted but one, who refused to come out. She shook her face and hands and cried, "No! No! Don't take me in there, please! By Allah I am a good girl."

The two brothers and several women stood beside the opened doors of the car and coaxed the young lady to come out.

"Sister, come, we are only visiting."

"No, no, they are going to hit me."

"No one is going to hit you," one of the women said, getting into the car and sitting beside her. "They only want to see you."

"They can see me in the car. I am so pretty."

Everyone living in the yard was present to witness the spectacle, and several children had clambered onto the bonnet of the car and were shouting: "There she is! There she is! She is mad! She is mad!"

"Come now, Jamilla, come. The people are laughing at you," one of the brothers said sternly.

Hajji Musa now appeared wearing a black cloak emblazoned with sequin-studded crescent moons and stars, and inscribed with Cufic writing in white silk. His sandals were red and his trousers white. His turban was of green satin and it had a large round ruby (artificial) pinned to it above his forehead.

He proceeded towards the car, looked at Jamilla, and then said to the bearded brothers, "I will take care of her." He put his head into the interior of the car. Jamilla recoiled in terror. The lady next to her held her and said, "Don't be frightened. Hajji Musa intends no harm."

"Listen, sister, come into the house. I have been expecting you."

"No! No! I want to go home." Jamilla began to cry.

"I won't let anyone hurt you."

Hajji Musa tried to grab her hand, but she pushed herself backwards against the woman next to her, and screamed so loudly that for a moment the healer seemed to lose his nerve. He turned to the brothers.

"The evil jinn is in her. Whatever I do now, please forgive me."

He put his foot into the interior of the car, gripped one arm of the terrified Jamilla and smacked her twice with vehemence.

"Come out jinn! Come out jinn!" he shouted and dragged her towards the door of the car. The woman beside Jamilla pushed her and punched her on her back.

"Please help," Hajji Musa said, and the two brothers pulled the screaming Jamilla out of the car.

"Drive the jinn into the house!" And they punched and pushed Jamilla towards the house. She pleaded with several spectators for help and then in desperation clung to them. But they shook her off and one or two even took the liberty of punching her and pulling her hair.

Jamilla was pushed into the house and the door closed on her and several of the privileged who were permitted to witness the exorcism ceremony. As soon as she passed through a narrow passage and entered a room she quietened.

The room was brilliantly lit and a fire was burning in the grate. A red carpet stretched from wall to wall and on the window-sill incense was burning in brass bowls. In front of the grate were two brass plates containing sun-dried red chillies.

We removed our shoes and sat down on the carpet. Jamilla was made to sit in front of the grate. She was awed and looked about at the room and the people. Several women seated themselves near her. Hajji Musa then began to recite the chapter "The Jinn" from the Koran. We sat with bowed heads. When he had done he moved towards the grate. His wife came into the room with a steel tray and a pair of tongs. Hajji Musa took some burning pieces of coal and heaped them on the tray. Then he scattered the red chillies over the coals. Smoke rose from the tray and filled the room with an acrid suffocating smell. He seated himself beside Jamilla and asked the two brothers to sit near her as well. He pressed Jamilla's head over the tray and at the same time recited a verse from the Koran in a loud voice. Jamilla choked, seemed to scream mutely and tried to lift her head, but Hajji Musa held her.

As the smell of burning chillies was unbearable, some of us went outside for a breath of fresh air. Aziz Khan said to us:

"That primitive ape is prostituting our religion with his hocus-pocus. He should be arrested for assault."

We heard Jamilla screaming and returned quickly to the

room. We saw Hajji Musa and the two brothers beating her with their sandals and holding her face over the coals.

"Out Iblis! Out Jinn!" Hajji Musa shouted and belaboured her.

At last Jamilla fell into a swoon.

"Hold her, Ismail and Hafiz." Hajji Musa sprinkled her face with water and read a prayer. Then he asked the two brothers to pick her up and take her into an adjoining room. They laid her on a bed.

"When she wakes up the jinn will be gone," Hajji Musa predicted confidently.

We went outside for a while. Aziz Khan asked a few of us to go with him in his car to the police station. But on the way he surprised us by changing his mind.

"It's not our business," he said, and drove back to the yard.

When we returned Jamilla had opened her eyes and was sobbing quietly.

"Anyone can ask Jamilla if she remembers what happened to her."

Someone asked her and she shook her head.

"See," said the victorious man, "it was the evil jinn that was thrashed out of her body. He is gone!"

There had been the singing of hymns, chanting and the jingling of bells since the late afternoon, and as evening approached there was great excitement in the yard. Everyone knew of the great event that was to take place that evening: the Hindu fire-walker was going to give a demonstration.

"There is nothing wonderful about walking on fire," Hajji Musa declared in a scornful tone. "The Hindus think they are performing miracles. Bah! Miracles!" And he exploded in laughter. "What miracles can their many gods perform, I ask you? Let them extract a jinn or heal the sick and then talk of miracles."

"But can you walk on fire or only cook on fire?" Dolly asked sardonically. There was laughter and merriment.

"Both, my dear man, both. Anyone who cooks on fire can walk on fire."

"If anyone can, let him try," said the law student Soma. "In law words are not enough; evidence has to be produced."

"Funny you lawyers never get done with words. After gossiping for days you ask for a postponement."

Everyone laughed boisterously.

"Hajji Musa," Dolly tried again, "can you walk on fire?"

"Are you joking, Dolly? When I can remove a jinn, what is walking on fire? Have you seen a jinn?"

"No."

"See one and then talk. Evil jinn live in hell. What is walking on fire to holding one of hell's masters in your hands?"

"I say let him walk on fire and then talk of jinn," said Rama the dwarfish Hindu watchmaker, but he walked away fearing to confront Hajji Musa.

"That stupid Hindu thinks I waste my time in performing tricks. I am not a magician."

A fire was now lit in the yard. Wood had been scattered over an area of about twenty feet by six feet. An attendant was shovelling coal and another using the rake to spread it evenly.

Meanwhile, in a room in the yard, the voices of the chanters were rising and the bells were beginning to jingle madly. Every now and then a deeper, more resonant chime would ring out, and a voice would lead the chanters to a higher pitch. In the midst of the chanters, facing the small altar on which were placed a tiny earthenware bowl containing a burning wick, a picture of the god Shiva surrounded by votive offerings of marigold flowers, rice and coconut, sat the fire-walker in a cross-legged posture.

The yard was crowded. Chairs were provided but these were soon occupied. The balconies were packed and several agile children climbed onto rooftops and seated themselves on the creaking zinc. A few dignitaries were also present.

The chanters emerged from the doorway. In their midst was the fire-walker, his eyes focused on the ground. He was like a man eroded of his own will, captured by the band of chanters. They walked towards the fire which was now a glowing bed, with blue flames leaping here and there.

The chanters grouped themselves near the fire and went on with their singing and bell-ringing, shouting refrains energetically. Then, as though life had suddenly flowed into him, the fire-walker detached himself from the group and went towards the fire. It was a tense moment. The chanters were gripped by frenzy. The coal bed glowed. He placed his right foot on the fire gently, tentatively, as though measuring its intensity, and then walked swiftly over from end to end. He was applauded. Two boys now offered him coconuts in trays. He selected two, and then walked over the inferno again, rather slowly this time, and as he walked he banged the coconuts against his head several times until they cracked and one saw the snowy insides. His movement now became more like a dance than a walk, as though his feet gloried in their triumph over the fire. The boys offered him more coconuts and he went on breaking them against his head.

While the fire-walker was demonstrating his salamander-like powers, an argument developed between Aziz Khan and Hajji Musa.

"He is not walking over the fire," Hajji Musa said. "Our eyes are being deceived."

"Maybe your eyes are being deceived, but not mine." Aziz answered.

"If you know anything about yogis then you will know how they can pass off the unreal for the real."

"What do you mean, *if* I know anything about yogis?"

"He thinks he knows about everything under the sun," Hajji Musa said jeeringly to a friend. He turned to Aziz.

"Have you been to India to see the fakirs and yogis?"

"No, and I don't intend to."

"Well, I have been to India and know more than you do."

"I have not been to India, but what I do know is that you are a fraud."

"Fraud! Huh!"

"Charlatan! Humbug!"

"I say, Aziz!" With a swift movement Hajji Musa clutched Aziz Khan's wrist.

"You are just a big-talker and one day I shall shut your mouth for you."

"Fraud! Crook! You are a disgrace to Islam. You with your chillies and jinn!"

"Sister . . .!" This remark Hajji Musa uttered in Gujarati.

"Why don't you walk over the fire? It's an unreal fire." And Aziz laughed sardonically.

"Yes, let him walk," said the watchmaker. "Hajji Musa big-talker."

"The fire is not as hot as any of your jinn, Hajji Musa," Dolly said slyly, with an ironic chuckle.

"Dolly, anyone can walk on fire if he knows the trick."

"I suppose you know," Aziz said tauntingly.

"Of course I do."

"Then why don't you walk over the fire?"

"Jinn are hotter!" Dolly exclaimed.

"Fraud! Hypocrite! Degraded infidel, you will never walk. I dare you!"

"I will show you, you fool. I will show you what I can do."

"What can you show but your lying tongue, and beat up little girls!"

"You sister . . .! I will walk."

While the argument had been raging, many people had gathered around them and ceased to look at the Hindu fire-walker. Now, when Hajji Musa accepted the challenge, he was applauded.

Hajji Musa removed his shoes and socks and rolled up his trousers. All eyes in the yard were now focused on him. Some shouted words of encouragement and others clapped their hands. Mr Darsot, though, tried to dissuade him.

"Hajji Musa, I don't think you should attempt walking on fire."

But Dolly shouted in his raucous voice:

"Hajji Musa, show them what you are made of!"

Hajji Musa, determined and intrepid, went towards the fire. The Hindu fire-walker was now resting for a while, his body and clothes wet with sweat and juice from the broken coconuts, and the chanters' voices were low. When Hajji Musa reached the fire he faltered. His body tensed with fear. Cautiously he lifted his right foot over the glowing mass. But any thought he might have had of retreat, of giving up Aziz Khan's challenge and declaring himself defeated, was dispelled by the applause he received.

Crying out in a voice that was an invocation to God to save him, he stepped on the inferno:

"Allah is great!"

What happened to Hajji Musa was spoken of long afterwards. Badly burnt, he was dragged out of the fire, drenched with water and smothered with rags, and taken to hospital.

We went to visit him. We expected to find a man humiliated, broken. We found him sitting up in bed, swathed in bandages, but as ebullient and resilient as always, with a bevy of young nurses eagerly attending to him.

"Boys, I must say fire-walking is not for me. Showmanship . . . that's for magicians and crowd-pleasers . . . those seeking cheap publicity."

And he laughed in his usual way until the hospital corridors resounded.

The Target

Mahmood was the target of many fists. One would see him running down Terrace Road, a crowd of pursuers at his heels. They would catch him, contract their biceps and treat him as a punching-ball until the people in the yard where he lived ran to his rescue.

Mahmood was my relative and I would often visit his mother and sister. He was ruddy in complexion, fat, with a brilliantined wad of brownish hair on his small head and dark grey eyes beneath sleek eyebrows.

There was a time when Mahmood was involved in a protracted war (largely waged by the opposite party) with the Kanti family. He decided to propose marriage to Safia, a thirteen-year-old schoolgirl, but he went to her house on his own instead of sending an emissary as was the custom. On the first occasion he was chased out of the house by the girl's mother and sisters wielding broomsticks and kitchen utensils. On the second occasion Safia's father and brothers displayed their pugilistic skill. Mahmood persisted in his pursuit of the youthful Safia despite the continual beatings by her family. They would either besiege him in the street and use him as a volleyball, or allow him to enter the house and use him as a guinea-pig in a variety of experiments in

martyrdom. But Mahmood, miraculously, not only sur-
vived but won the admiration of Safia who pleaded with
her parents to end hostilities. This earned her the anger of
her family and she was banished to her uncle's home in a
distant country town. But she communicated secretly with
Mahmood from there. Her hero reached her and took her
away. The fugitives were found within an hour, at the
railway station waiting for a train. Mahmood was basted
and bundled into the train when it arrived and Safia
taken captive. When Safia's parents came to hear of the
incident they immediately sent for her. They were convinced she was deflowered — anything could have
happened to her during the hour she was with Mahmood —
and decided to go to Mahmood's house and offer her hand
in marriage. He promptly rejected the offer ("I have my
dignity," he explained later) and suffered another tempest
of blows.

Thereafter Mahmood found it hazardous to walk in Mint
Road. "The road is not theirs," he declared truculently.
Whenever he did he was sure to find a stone hurled at him,
or a woman's voice rich in curses, or Safia's brothers
sprinting at his heels as he fled.

One day a gang of whites came chasing Mahmood into the
yard. He screamed for help. Fortunately for him Solomon
and Dolly were present. They cornered the gang and made
good use of the opportunity, which did not come often, to
beat up some whites.

After a few days we were surprised to see a tribal warrior
fully accoutred, with horns on his head, guarding the door
of Mahmood's house. His wife was also present, a stout
woman lavishly bedecked with beads from head to foot.

When I asked Mahmood why he had engaged the couple he answered cryptically:

"I am practising integration."

The warrior with his shield, spear and club became the object of a great deal of curiosity. Children were always staring at him and people took photographs. He would pose for the photographers, and when they had done he would go up to them, stretch out his left hand and raise his spear with his right hand. Money would quickly be put into his palm. The only word in his English vocabulary was "Good!" which he uttered with a zestful bellow. His wife assisted Mahmood's mother with the household chores, and when she was not busy would sit beside her husband in the sun, combing her pyramid of hair and applying lipstick to her lips and cheeks while looking into a tiny piece of broken mirror.

With the warrior for protection Mahmood strutted about without fear of attack. Soon he began going out with the warrior at night.

"Where do you go with him?" I asked.

"Visiting friends," he answered. But one day I discovered that he was visiting enemies rather than friends when I saw the warrior's club stained with blood.

Mahmood's period of respite from the fists of his enemies did not last long. Somebody reported to the police that he was employing the warrior and his wife without the necessary permit. The couple were arrested, charged, fined (Mahmood paid the fines) and ordered to remove themselves to their tribal reserve. Mahmood was fined as well for "employing unregistered labour".

Shortly after the warrior left, Mahmood became one of the "directors" of the Blue Danube Social Club in Mayfair, as a consequence of which occupation he on several occasions returned home with a blackened eye, a sprained wrist or a bruised head. After one particularly bad spell of directing he told me:

"There was a whole *span* of ducktails at the Club. My father always told me not to interfere with ducktails. But they got stuck into me."

In Mahmood's thoughts his late father was an ever-present reality whose precepts he faithfully upheld, though his actions were seldom in accord with them and often antithetical.

"But why don't you resign as a director?"

"I have a stake in the Club."

"But you will never get out of trouble."

"They will get tired of beating me. They will come to know me better and they will stop. My father always said that if people know you, you will never get into trouble."

It was an unusual way of getting known. Mahmood did not seem to realize that as there were many fists in need of a target it would take an inordinately long time before everyone came to know him.

One day Mahmood introduced me to "Najma". She was a white. She was a short girl, gawky in her walk, exposing much of her fleshy legs. Her face was a fashion photographer's dream: a chubby pink face, a mop of blonde hair, cerulean eyes in a penumbra of cobalt eye shadow, cheeks rouged and lips vermilion. I did not inquire where he had met her but I inferred from her appearance that she was a frequenter of his Club.

"She is going to change her religion," Mahmood said. "She is joining us."

I looked at "Najma". She smiled approvingly.

"Aziz Khan is giving her religious lessons."

"A good idea."

Mahmood came closer to me and whispered:

"The gang is against her changing her religion."

"Gang?"

"Those who come with her to the Club."

I saw "Najma" often in Mahmood's house. Aziz Khan's religious instructions were taking effect. She was now of little interest to a photographer. She no longer used make-up, and wore a black scarf that covered her head, her forehead and her shoulders. Her pants were pantaloon-type and her dress a wide smock. She was sitting on the edge of the settee, swinging her legs.

"How do you like your new religion?" I asked her.

"I am getting used to it. My instructor says I am making good progress. It will be very easy, he tells me, because Christians were Muslims before the priests came to spoil everything."

As I was not aware of this historical fact I did not comment.

"My instructor tells me that I must be at all times 'soberly and modestly clad' and I am doing my best as you can see. Is that not so Mahmood?"

Mahmood agreed.

"Sometimes he is so amusing. He tells me that doing you know what is a blessing and compulsory."

She tittered.

"And I must not talk to foreign males. But that is a little difficult as you can see."

She tittered again.

"I shouldn't be talking to you because you may . . ."

"That's au-right," Mahmood interrupted. "He is one of us.

Come, let's have lunch."

Mahmood's mother and sister had laid the table and retired to an inner room. They were not very enthusiastic about "Najma" and pretended she was not present.

Mahmood filled "Najma's" plate with food and spoonfuls of pepper relish. "Najma" valiantly swallowed the food and relish. She drank glasses of water.

"She must get used to our food," Mahmood said, looking at her. "Inside and out she must be a Muslim." He spooned more relish for her.

"My father always said that if you convert someone you must do it properly."

When I left Mahmood and "Najma" were sitting together on the settee, holding hands.

A week later I asked Mahmood how "Najma" was getting on with her religious instructions. He answered:

"That guy is wasting her time."

From the scornful tone of his voice I gathered that Aziz Khan was not confining himself strictly to religious prescriptions.

A month later a few friends and I were in Mayfair at night and decided to visit the Blue Danube Club. The Club was on the second floor of the building, above a warehouse. The doorkeeper, a testy youth, would not let us in without payment and we asked to see Mahmood. Grudgingly he went to fetch Mahmood and when he came Mahmood persuaded the youth to let us in by explaining that we were visitors from Durban. We climbed the stairs and entered a large room lit by coloured lights. A band was playing in a corner and couples were dancing. I saw "Najma" (she was no longer "soberly and modestly clad") tightly clasped in the arms of a youth. I pointed her out to Mahmood.

"She is *jolling* again with guys," he said.

We watched the dancers as they began to jive to rousing music.

"If any of you feel for a dance, go ahead," Mahmood said to us.

We declined and said we preferred to watch.

After a while "Najma" spotted me and coming over with her partner said, "Hi! Enjoying yourself?" They left the Club. I saw Mahmood scowling at her as she went out.

The next day I heard that Mahmood had been so severely beaten that he required treatment in hospital. I went to see him. He looked like a mummy. His head was bandaged; one eye was swollen and closed; one arm was in plaster.

"What happened?" I asked.

"The gang got me."

He lifted his head with an agonized groan.

"My father always told me to keep away from white girls — and clubs."

Aziz Khan

I first met Aziz Khan — described in various Muslim journals as the "author of the renowned pamphlets 'Muslims in Decay' and the 'Decline and Fall of the Morality of Muslims' " and as the "illustrious modern Saracen" — the day he handed me a cyclostyled copy of his pamphlet "The Degeneracy of Muslim Marriages" at a wedding reception.

When I entered the hall decorated with balloons and tinsel, the tables heaped with cakes and delicacies, I saw a number of his pamphlets lying on the floor and being trampled upon by the guests. The hall had been divided into two sections, one for the gaily dressed womenfolk, one for the men.

As the bride and bridegroom had not yet arrived I decided to read Aziz Khan's pamphlet. It began: "One is amazed and aghast at the complete and utter degeneracy of our present-day Muslim marriages. The pristine purity of our hallowed ceremonies and customs has been sullied by the importation of Westernized forms dating back atavistically to the days when naked European heathens sojourned in primeval forests. It is about time that someone brought the shocking state of affairs to the notice of the public. One has only to look at the womenfolk to understand the extent to which the mania for modernism has advanced. Our women are no longer soberly and modestly clad at wedding functions, but shamelessly manifest themselves in shining gaudy frippery, displaying their bosoms and buttocks in the most outrageous manner to leering, lustful, lascivious eyes. Is there anything more odious than the sari — essentially a Hindu garment?"

I looked at the women in the hall. They were beautifully dressed. Several girls in pink dresses, glossy hair piled on their heads, eyes glamorously blackened with kohl and the palms of their hands dyed with henna, were moving from table to table arranging flowers in vases. I looked at the men grouped around tables, chatting to one another in a self-contained way. I read on:

"The most despicable of all practices frowned upon by our Holy Prophet is the mingling of the sexes in halls where wedding functions are held. During our so-called Islamic weddings all kinds of shameless fraternization between the sexes occur, spiced with lascivious talk that would shame the very sons of Iblis. Have we Muslims degenerated to such an extent that we are unable to see the morass of sin we are wallowing in and the slippery spirals leading us to the fire of Doom? Where are our Ulamas and Molvis, the learned men steeped in Islamic law and traditions? They too seem to have succumbed to the modernistic fad of the intermingling of the sexes."

There was the loud hooting of cars outside the hall. This signalled the arrival of the bride. She soon entered with her train and walked along the aisle that separated the sexes. She was dressed in the usual white. The bridesmaids were dressed in blue. They went towards the stage, climbed several steps and seated themselves.

As the bridegroom and his party had not yet arrived, I read on:

"As for the ritual which Muslims have imbibed from the dehumanized Westerners, I refer to that pagan institution the Betrothal, the less said about it the better. Totally foreign to the pristine purity of Muslim culture, one can only scoff at the despicable practice of giving an engagement ring (the man actually holds the woman's hand to fit the ring on the finger) and very often indulging in that impure act, a legacy of filthy barbarians — kissing!"

There followed a paragraph on the "endless expenses involved in these so-called civilized weddings", one on the "diabolical desire to have better and bigger weddings", and another on "the waste of food that could feed battalions of starving people for months". The final paragraph read: "And as for that practice of displaying the bride on the stage so that everyone can leer at her and imagine all sorts of lewd things, such as what is going to happen to her on her bridal couch and so forth — the practice is so heinous and satanic that I can hardly bring myself to refer to it. All decent people will be revolted at this anti-Islamic, pro-Occidental custom of exposing the bride . . ."

The bridegroom and his party entered the hall. The bridegroom went towards the stage and after shaking his bride's hand joined his friends at a table.

As I folded the pamphlet the very man who had handed it to me at the door settled down in a vacant seat opposite and smilingly said:

"Have you found my treatise interesting?"

"Very."

"I thank you," he said, extending a hand to me.

He did not consider it odd in any way to be present at a

wedding reception (I presumed he had been invited) after issuing a pamphlet of strictures. He seemed to be enjoying himself and I did not care to question his presence.

This same Aziz Khan not long after ignited one of the greatest religious issues among Muslims, that concerning the beard of man.

It was on a Friday when people went as usual to the Newtown mosque for prayers, which were conducted by Molvi Haroon. Afterwards the same dignitary delivered a lecture which consisted of a medley of aphorisms, historical anecdotes, Sufism and moral precepts on the keeping of beards. The beard, the Molvi declared, was the mark of a Muslim and the beardless ones should not scoff at those who were devout enough to cultivate beards.

The reference to the beard was not a matter for controversy — the congregation regarded the lecture as a verbal exercise and would have gone on merrily using the razor. But Aziz Khan immediately rose from the carpet and challenged the Molvi:

"Molvi Haroon, can you quote the passage in the Holy Koran which unequivocally states that the beard is compulsory on all Muslims?"

Issuing a challenge in the mosque is unusual. Everyone was jolted. Molvi Haroon smiled pityingly at his adversary and shrewdly posed the following question:

"Tell me, did the messenger of Allah, our holy Prophet, have a beard or not?"

Aziz asked his question again, and again the Molvi posed his parrying question. It was a stalemate. Infuriated, Aziz walked out of the mosque, followed by some twenty of his disciples.

After a few days Aziz Khan's pamphlet on the beard made its appearance. Part of it read:

"The men who claim to be the repositories of Islamic wisdom, the Molvis and other self-styled pundits, have again and again exposed themselves to the public as a set of fools. What could be more asinine and moronic than the statement by that doyen of priests, Molvi Haroon, that those without beards are not Muslims? What knowledge has this rebarbative microbe of the ineluctable beauty of Islam . . ."

Aziz Khan's pamphlet made the issue a public one, and the Islamic Academy hurriedly convened a Muslim Council to settle the matter. Aziz Khan's fame reached its zenith. Everyone marvelled at his audacity in challenging an army of luminaries. He went about, in the company of his disciples, addressing meetings which sometimes ended in violence between the bearded and beardless, with victory usually going to the beardless as they were in the majority.

After a week-end of deliberation the Muslim Council issued a counter-pamphlet. It began:

"Proudly they strut about our streets, with naked chins shamelessly exposed, professing themselves to be re-formers and doctors of learning. But any foolish ape can see that they are driven by their base egos to bark like mad dogs, casting aspersion on the beard of our Prophet (on whom be peace)."

The pamphlet went on to describe the historical circum-stances that led to Muslims cultivating beards: their opposition to the Mushrikeen (heathens) and Cafirs (unbelievers), and their hatred of the fire-worshipping Persians. It continued:

"The beard has been the pillar of Islam from the

beginning when Allah drove his beloved Adam from paradise to the present day when the world is infested with beardless Cafirs. Who can deny that Adam — the handsomest man in the annals of Creation — possessed a beard? We ask these hypocritical reformers this simple question: Did Adam have a razor and blades? Who but the valiant sons of Islam sporting their beards smashed that mighty of mighties, the Roman Empire? And who but the bearded warriors of Islam withstood the avalanche of pig-eating crusaders? But, alas! When the beards of the Muslims came under the razors of the infidels their glorious empires vanished along with them."

The final paragraph stated:

"We take this opportunity to issue this dire warning to the beardless mob of Islam-haters, that if you continue maligning the beard of our Prophet, the Almighty will send ambassadors to BREAK YOUR NECKS. May the curse of Allah and his Malla-ika (angels) and of the Ambiya (contemporaries of the Prophet) and the entire Ummate Muslima (Muslim world) fall upon you."

To this pamphlet Aziz Khan replied with another, concluding with these words: "If the so-called Muslim Council thinks that there are any other ambassadors of Allah than the Prophets of Islam, then on the Day of Reckoning they will be consigned to roast on the spits of Hell."

A few months later Aziz Khan, who was a commercial traveller, was forced to stop his car along a country road by another car that blocked the way. Three men emerged. Aziz recognized Gool and his associates.

"Follow that car," Gool said, opening the door of Aziz's car and getting in. The two men returned to Gool's car and started it.

"I have some business with you," Gool said in explanation, lighting a cigar.

"Where are you taking me?" Aziz asked.

"You will see."

"I was on my way to Paruk's shop. He is expecting me."

"He can wait."

The car ahead was travelling at speed and Aziz was lagging behind.

"Drive faster."

"The dust," Aziz protested.

"Shall I take over the wheel?"

Aziz pressed the accelerator. The dust from the two cars swirled in the air.

"The dust."

"Keep up."

"I can't see."

"Keep up."

Aziz quailed. He was driving at a dangerous speed along a rutted road behind a car spewing dust.

Suddenly the realization came to him that Gool and his associates were the "ambassadors".

"You are the ambassador?" Aziz asked.

"What?" Gool said with such menace that Aziz froze.

"Slow down," Gool said. And as if the driver of the car ahead had been commanded together with Aziz Khan, the two cars slackened speed and came to a stop beside a clump of trees.

"Get out."

"What are you going to do to me?"

"You will see."

"Listen, Muslim brother, look at yourself. You are without a beard."

"Beard? I am handsome enough without one."

"But . . ."

"Stop fooling. Get out!"

"Aziz got out of the car while Gool remained seated. Gool's associates emerged from their car and came towards him.

"Muslim brothers, you are without beards!" Aziz shouted and began to run. "Muslim brothers, you are without . . ."

Gladiators

Mr Rijhumal Rajespery, the principal of the Tagore Indian High School, lived on the first floor of a two-storeyed building. He was a bachelor. His state of bachelorhood was not the result of his insensitivity to feminine allure, but of his positive dislike of all things Indian. He considered Indians to be the "filthiest and most uncouth denizens on the earth's crust". Once when Ebrahim spoke of marriage to him, he answered:

"Are you suggesting that I terminate my single state of man by marrying an Indian Yahoo? The day I marry, I shall marry a white woman."

"Are you ashamed of being an Indian, Mr Rajespery?"

"For your information I am not a common Indian. I am a pure Dravidian."

Cleanliness was his forte and obsession. His suite of rooms — a polished brass plate outside the door blazed: Mr R.A.J. Rajespery B.A. — was carpeted and expensively furnished. His clothing was immaculate. His middle-aged body, consisting mainly of bones, was at all times spruce and smelling of perfume and after-shave lotion. His sparse gently-waving hair was glued to his head; his moustache was the barber's masterpiece. His motor-car, a black

Citroën ("a car in advance of its time") was polished to a mirror's gloss by his white-clad servant Anna.

Though Mr Rajespery's manners were impeccable, he derided our frailties and foibles in sadistic street sermons. "The words 'Thank you', 'Please', 'Pardon me' do not appear in the vocabulary of Indians. You are a mob of unruly Yahoos. I find your manners odious and crude." And he would walk hurriedly away towards his car, open the door, operate the pneumatic suspension so that the car rose from its low-slung position, and drive away with a look of utter disdain.

At school Mr Rajespery spent his time in dealing with "long-haired unproductive louts". He fought an endless battle to have recalcitrant pupils march in military fashion, show eternal respect for superiors, obey instructions and "behave like Europeans". He earned many uncomplimentary nicknames, but eventually the word Yahoo recoiled in vengeance upon him and became permanently his. It was a name that must have flayed him, for schoolboys "Yahooed" from stairs, balconies, corridors and dark recesses and the name reverberated through the streets like some wild call in jungle terrain.

Mr Rajespery was a "dedicated student of the Fine Arts". His artistic pretensions were displayed in canvasses in which a vibrant orange-red dominated his paintings of landscapes — his only subject — where the oil ran in surrealist rivers of fire and destroyed perspective. On occasions he would exhibit his paintings on the balcony. Once he constructed a number of miniature homes, as architects do, with wood, plaster, paper and other materials, and opened the exhibition to the public. In explanation he said: "I have been commissioned by the authorities to plan the new Indian residential suburb of Lenasia and these are models of some of the homes that will be erected." We examined the models with interest. "Please remember it is a solo effort, a solo effort. My only hope and prayer is that the Yahoos won't convert the suburb into a slum. I may also mention that I have been commissioned by my educational superiors to draw up a new syllabus for Fine Arts in schools. Indian children are generally ignorant about art, not to mention a certain primary school principal."

The primary school principal was Mr Rajah who lived on the ground floor of the same building. He was a fat satyr of a man, a lover of the flesh of goats and the flesh of fat women. On several occasions I carried messages from him to certain well-nourished women in Fordsburg. He had five children from his fat wife Halima. He was an extremely affable man and was always ready to take us for a drive in his red Chevrolet ornamented with chrome-plated accessories to various cafés and fruitshops and regale us with confectionery, fruit and cool drinks. "Help yourselves, boys, it's on me," he would say, with the owner looking wide-eyed and pretending to be pleased. We later discovered that the various fruitshops and cafés belonged to parents of children who attended his school and that "It's on me" hardly meant at his expense. His kitchen was well-stocked with provisions, from spiced ox-tongue to trays of choice fruit, and the provisions seemed to increase in quantity when end-of-year examination results at his school were about to be released.

Mr Rajespery and Mr Rajah were enemies. The origin of their antagonism lay in their differing temperaments rather than in some quarrel over a specific matter. One day we were clustered around Mr Rajah who was sitting on a chair outside his doorstep. He was talking to us about Mr Rajespery.

"He thinks he is superior because he lives upstairs and has carpets in his rooms. And all those whites visiting him? A lot of stupid school inspectors. Yesterday I heard him telling Mr Marks that if I so much as looked at his paintings he would have me arrested for it would be 'tantamount to theft'. Those were his words. His paintings are fit for the rubbish heap of an asylum."

We laughed and just then we saw Mr Rajespery going up the stairs to his apartment in the company of a white man.

"Some people always attach themselves to their masters," Mr Rajah said loudly.

Mr Rajespery, smarting at the sarcasm, proceeded to his rooms. We remained with Mr Rajah for some time while he told us anecdotes and cracked jokes, most of them of an indecent kind.

Mr Rajespery and the man came down the stairs. We watched in silence. Good manners demanded that Mr Rajespery accompany his visitor to his car in the street. On his way back Mr Rajah addressed him:

"Stop, Mr White!"

But Mr Rajespery quickly climbed several steps of the stairs and then stopped.

"Some people's manners are putrid."

"Some people use Elizabeth Arden's complexion creams but there is no white result!"

We laughed derisively.

"If you speak to me address me properly, Mr Rajah."

"You can only run after whites."

"I am proud of that. They are civilized."

Ebrahim decided to intervene in the argument.

"Mr Rajespery, the whites are oppressors."

"I am afraid I don't understand you politicians. They are our superiors."

"We Indians have a culture. What have your superiors?" Mr Rajah asked.

"Culture? If you call eating foul-smelling curry culture, eating betel-leaf and spitting all over culture, living in filth culture. Has anyone in India ever invented such a thing as a bicycle, not to speak of an advanced machine like my Citroën? Indians are a lot of unproductive morons. Yahoos!"

And he walked up the stairs to his apartment in triumph.

Mr Rajah felt beaten.

"You boys should not take this lying down. He has insulted you. Don't worry about me. I'll get him some day."

When the fight between the two eventually took place it was by proxy. Anna, slender and tall, represented Mr Rajespery; Elizabeth, fat and short, represented Mr Rajah. The battle had its origins in a squabble which started after a basin of dirty water had been emptied over Mr Rajespery's Citroën. Mr Rajespery came down the stairs, stopped halfway down when he saw Mr Rajah, and accused him of having sullied his car. Mr Rajah retreated to the safety of his doorway.

"Why don't you instruct your servant to empty your filthy water somewhere else?"

"Why do you park your car on the pavement?"

"I will park it where I prefer."

Mr Rajespery's servant stood beside him, dressed like a nurse, and Mr Rajah's servant beside him, dowdy and ugly.

"Anna, did you see that creature empty the dish water?"

"I saw her, master."

"You didn't see me," shouted Elizabeth.

"I did, with my own eyes," answered Anna, placing her index fingers on her eye-lids.

The two women now took up the argument in an African tongue. They spoke menacingly and shook their hands wildly. Suddenly Anna came down the stairs. Elizabeth proceeded towards her and they confronted each other.

They began with a sort of skirmish during which they tried to tear off each other's clothes. Anna's starched cap went flying, the straps of her apron were forced apart, and her blouse was ripped off. She in turn tugged at Elizabeth's dress; the cheap material offered no resistance.

Anna delivered several hard punches to Elizabeth's body. Elizabeth clasped her and the two women fell and rolled along the pavement. They threshed, wrestled, pounded with clenched fists. When they were tired they rested for a while, their hands gripping each other's, their legs intertwined.

The battle had moved a short distance from where it began. Mr Rajespery was left standing on the stairs and Mr Rajah in his doorway.

The two clasped naked bodies were rolling on the pavement again. Suddenly Anna screamed. Elizabeth had her teeth embedded in her arm.

Several people threw themselves on the women and, at length, managed to free Anna's arm from Elizabeth's teeth. Anna lay on the pavement, her arm bleeding. We ran to Mr Rajespery who was still standing on the stairs to tell him of Anna's condition, and that he should take her to a doctor.

"To a doctor? I am a doctor," he said, staring at us.

Mr Rajah stood at his door, his thumbs in his braces, and laughed triumphantly. Mr Rajespery, seeming oblivious to him, descended the stairs, went towards his car, opened the door, entered and operated the automatic suspension. The car rose to its maximum height, then went down, rose again, went down again. Mr Rajah came to sit on the fender of the car, and laughed jeeringly as the car rose and sank. Suddenly Mr Rajespery darted out of the car in a swift menacing movement that shocked Mr Rajah who fell and sprained his ankle, bounded over the steps of the stairs, entered his apartment and locked himself in.

Someone took Anna to a doctor. Fortunately her wound was not serious. But more serious was the state of her master's mind. Next morning he was seen sitting in his Citroën, speaking to himself, shaking his fists at those looking at him, and refusing to come out. Many people came to see him; children milled around his car; and everybody laughed at the sight of Mr Rajespery in his black Citroën, going up and down.

Black and White

Shireen was the daughter of the widow Wadia. She was pretty in a paganish way, with black eyes peering impishly through unruly hair. She wore her skirts daringly short and when she wore trousers they were always so tight that they displayed her well-formed thighs. She was a girl full of gaiety and wit, at times skittishly anarchic and irresponsible, and none of us with whom she engaged in love-making interludes ever came to believe she could be possessed permanently.

One day she said to us:

"Guess what, boys? I am in love."

We laughed.

"All right then, someone is in love with me."

We were eager to know.

"He will be here tonight. Keep a look-out for his motor-cycle."

"Is he one of those cycle-obsessed morons?"

"You are all jealous. He has blond hair."

"A white!"

"Yes, white like cheese!"

"Anyway, he smells it."

We laughed.

We kept a look-out for Shireen's lover that night in Terrace Road. She came to join us on the pavement outside Hassen's Shoe Store, with mock impatience smoked several cigarettes and threw them half-smoked into the gutter.

"He will never come to Fordsburg at night," I said.

"You think he is afraid of people like you?"

"Where did you meet him?"

"In Mayfair."

"In Mayfair! A poor white!" Nizam exclaimed.

"Jealous? Of course I met him in Mayfair and what's wrong with that? A Mayfair white is as good as any other white. He's got white skin, hasn't he? He says he digs me."

Suddenly the roar of a motor-cycle resounded and we saw Shireen's lover approaching. Shireen ran towards him, waving her hands and shouting:

"Hi Harold! Hi Harold!"

We watched him slacken speed and steer his motor-cycle towards the street kerb. Shireen jumped on the motor-cycle's petrol tank and revved the accelerator in triumph, waving at us excitedly.

We went towards them. Shireen introduced us. Harold did not bother to get off his motor-cycle or shake our hands.

He came every Friday evening to meet Shireen. They would go into the doorway recess of Hassen's Shoe Store. Occasionally we watched them from the opposite pavement, and when the passing beam from a motor-car exposed them momentarily, we saw them embracing. He whispered to her incessantly. He was a lean, eager-eyed youth, with a receding chin; he was always dressed in jeans and a leather lumber-jacket ornamented with emblems of motor-cars and motor-cycles. His motor-cycle was a powerful gleaming machine that seemed to compensate in some way for his lack of personality.

As time went on the novelty of having a white lover seemed to wear thin and Shireen began to taunt him. On one occasion she ran to us gathered on the opposite pavement and said:

"Guess what, boys? He wants me to go with him to the mine dumps."

"Mine dumps? What for?"

"To undermine me!"

We laughed raucously, sardonically.

On another occasion she said:

"Must I go with him, boys?"

"Where?"

"To the bushes near the zoo."

"And do what there?"

"Behave like a white monkey!"

We hissed and booed.

"He is a low beast," Idris said.

"Don't call him a low beast," Shireen said in mock anger.

"I said his motor-cycle is a lovely beast."

We gathered around the motor-cycle and chanted: "A lovely beast! A lovely beast!"

There were times Shireen failed to meet him; she was engaged in other love affairs. One night he quarrelled with her as we watched. Then he gave her presents (earrings, a watch, an engraved locket) and insisted she go with him on his motor-cycle. He pulled her by the hand. She resisted at first, then eagerly, willingly, went towards his motor-cycle, but suddenly broke free and ran into the yard. He stood beside his motor-cycle for a few moments, thwarted, defeated. We chuckled sarcastically. He looked at us menacingly, then drove away in a torrent of gaseous noise.

Shireen told us that she had had enough of Harold and had decided to break with him. A prolonged love affair was oppressive to her penchant for ever-varying love encounters with males. In order to achieve the final separation she decided to spurn him in front of an audience, and we were a ready audience. She rehearsed with us her plan of action a day before.

When Harold arrived that Friday evening we clapped our hands.

"The hero is here!" Shireen shouted.

"From the gutters of Mayfair!" Nizam screamed.

Harold looked at us without saying a word. He got off his motor-cycle and Shireen went towards him. We watched the two go into their usual meeting place. After a while Shireen came running towards us grouped on the opposite pavement.

"Boys, give us a kiss! Boys, give us a kiss!"

And we kissed her.

"I belong to everybody," she declared, facing Harold. "To everybody, you understand. That is, to blacks only, black boys only. Whites not allowed."

She burst out laughing. She had routed Harold. He remained in the recess, caged, humiliated. Then Nizam did a foolish thing which was not part of Shireen's plan. He went towards the motor-cycle, shouted, "Here goes!" and pushed the machine with his leg. It crashed on the street; glass shattered. When the reverberations of the impact died away we remained silent as though something ominous had occurred. We were annoyed with Nizam. His action extinguished in a moment the exquisite pleasure we were deriving from Harold's painful humiliation in our suburb. We felt we had had enough and went away.

I saw Shireen standing beside the fallen motor-cycle, in the light of the street lamp. Then she crossed the street and went towards Harold, presumably to apologize to him.

A little later we heard a scream followed by the roar of a motor-cycle. We ran towards the shoe store and found Shireen lying huddled in the doorway recess. She was crying and had blood on her mouth.

The Commandment

Moses lived in the yard. He was well over seventy years of age — his matted hair a bluish grey — yet his body was surprisingly resilient and strong. About ten years earlier he had been engaged by Mr Rehman to look after his many children. Before that he had worked for many years as a builder's assistant. In a mushrooming city he had helped to build homes, skyscrapers, apartment blocks and roads: pushing wheelbarrows, excavating, operating drills, blasting.

Moses enjoyed special status and privileges not given to ordinary servants, such as being allowed to eat at the kitchen table. It was his mastery of the Gujarati language (swear words and all) that elevated him. So complete was his mastery that those who heard him speak Gujarati for the first time were dumbfounded and thought that some Indian spirit had taken possession of him. In fact some people had approached Hajji Musa to explain the phenomenon, but he had dismissed them with the cryptic declaration that some things were "too deep" for common people to know and those who tried would "perish by evaporation". When not looking after the children of his employer, Moses did all sorts of odd jobs for us, such as going to the shops for a trifle or collecting our dry-cleaning. He was generally liked and the children loved him.

And then, one day, came the order that Moses should leave Fordsburg. According to the order Moses was contravening the law in three respects: firstly, he had no right of domicile in an area inhabited by Indians, Coloureds and some Chinese; secondly, he was no longer a productive labour unit; thirdly, he had no document to prove that he had been born in Johannesburg. The order stated that he was an "alien" and that he should "go forthwith for resettlement" to his "tribal homeland".

At first Moses was bewildered, but the police came several times to warn him (and warn Mr Rehman that he was harbouring an alien and faced prosecution) and he came to understand the import of the order.

Its first effect on him was that he began soliloquizing in Gujarati. "They say I must go home. Home? Yes. Transkei. And do you know what I will find there? They tell me there is a city, with real streets and real buildings. There is also a hospital for me . . ."

As Moses went on speaking, the children would gather around him, and sometimes they burst into laughter when he cracked a joke about "home". He would wander into our homes and utter his lament and everyone felt sorry for him.

When the period given in the order had expired, the police came again and told Moses that if he did not leave willingly, he would be jailed and transported to his "homeland" at the state's expense. Mr Rehman was given a stern warning. The time allowed was extended by a month; if after this he was still in the yard the law would take its course.

At the prospect of his enforced removal the old man's soliloquies became interminable and at times he would shout hysterically: "They tell me I will be happy there. There are big cities there. The air is fresh too. My chief is waiting for me. O Chief, I am coming, O Chief . . ."

Everyone tried to think of a way to save him from the "homeland": some were for concealing him; others for disguising him; others for taking him away to some place of safety. But all ideas remained ideas. Mr Rehman was his employer and nothing could be done that would not involve him as well. He did not have the heart to tell Moses to go before the police arrived. He preferred to face the consequences.

Unable to save him, people started giving Moses presents, old clothing and money. He accepted those gratefully, and spent the money feeding the children with ice-creams and sweets.

During the final week Moses no longer slept but paced all night in the yard, talking, talking, and sometimes banging on a tin drum until our nerves became brittle. And then a queer thing happened to us. We began to hate him. Vague fears were aroused in us, as though he were exposing us to somebody or something, involving us in a conspiracy — he spoke our language — threatening our existence. Indefinable feelings began to trouble us. Of guilt? Of cowardice? We wanted to be rid of him as of some unclean thing. Suddenly everyone avoided him and the children were sternly told not to go near him. Even Mr Rehman began to feel our hostility.

"I am going to my homeland," he went on and on. "I am going to see my chief and all my people. There are cities there! There are parks there! There are hospitals there!

And there are no cemeteries there!"

When the police arrived on the appointed day they found Moses — hanging from a roof-beam in a lavatory in the yard.

Red Beard's Daughter

Of all Red Beard's daughters Julie fetched the highest price in a marriage transaction — but she played her father a trick on her wedding-day and he never got his money. He had three other daughters who were already married. Julie was not beautiful, though her complexion was fresh and her hair long. Her father was called Red Beard because his beard was always dyed with henna. His looks gained an added fierceness from the redness of his lips and mouth through his constant chewing of *paan* (betel-leaf). He had never worn a Western suit in his life; he was either to be seen in a *koortah* or in a long coat and matching trousers made of the finest English cloth. When he was dressed, smelling of *attar* and with a red fez on his head, he looked like some sort of gnome. In fact he was a mild, good-humoured man who loved jokes. He had never remarried after the death of his wife, but the four liabilities she had left him he turned into assets by setting a price on them.

Red Beard received a proposal for the hand of Julie from a certain Mr Ben Areff, a shopkeeper in a distant country town. He had heard of Red Beard's practice of setting a price on his daughters, but that was no deterrent as he was a fairly wealthy man. He sent his emissaries and Red Beard agreed to bestow the hand of his daughter at the price of one thousand rands. The emissaries then wanted the date for the engagement to be fixed, and Red Beard said that they could come after two weeks and drink the "engagement sherbet" as was the custom.

Julie was happy that she was going to be married and though she was teased a great deal by her friends and neighbours about the semi-yokel who had bespoken her, she kept her sweet temper. On the appointed day she was engaged — but Mr Ben Areff did not present himself. He sent a representative who said that he was ill with influenza and had been advised by his doctor to stay at home.

After a week Julie approached her father with a request.

"I should like to see Ben Areff before . . ."

"See him? What for?"

"I . . ."

"All men are the same," Red Beard said fiercely.

"Please."

"No."

Julie, frightened, left the room. Red Beard sat down on the settee, crossed his legs, took a *paan* from a nearby tray, and began to chew. Julie's request had stung him. However, after a while his anger subsided and he thought that perhaps his daughter's request was reasonable. He, too, began to feel curious about Ben Areff's appearance. Had illness really prevented him from coming to his engagement?

The next day Red Beard telephoned Ben Areff and after inquiring about his health invited him and his emissaries for lunch on the coming Sunday.

Ben Areff and his emissaries came. When Red Beard saw the man he was shocked, but said nothing. One of the emissaries explained: "Mr Ben Areff is the son of his late father's second wife. You know in the country . . ."

"I understand," Red Beard said, calming himself again. He thought for a while, then said: "This is going to make things difficult. You know what modern girls are. They are inclined to be fussy."

"You are the father," the emissary reminded him.

Ben Areff, who was wearing sun-glasses, now took them off. He was a man of average height and looked very diffident. He wasn't the sort of man to be envied. At home neither in an Indian world nor an African world, he was a derelict socially.

"I am the father," Red Beard answered, "but you know times have changed. Tell me, has Mr Ben Areff proposed marriage to other girls?"

"Yes," the man answered, rather reluctantly.

"I see," said Red Beard. "Well," he continued thoughtfully, "this alters the whole picture. Mr Ben Areff is different (you understand), but if the price is right I'll see what I can do."

The man spoke to Ben Areff and told him that it was best for him to talk to his future father-in-law.

"Please tell me how much you want?" Ben Areff asked.

Red Beard answered without hesitation:

"You can see I have no kind of work in life. I had a shop once. Give me two thousand rands in cash and I shall be satisfied."

Ben Areff asked the principal emissary (a fat man) to go out with him and they had a long discussion. A group of women looked at the two men and among them was Julie.

She had been ordered by her father to remain in a neighbour's house until she was sent for, but she had disobeyed.

Ben Areff and the fat man re-entered the house and told Red Beard that the sum of money he wanted would be paid. The emissary then wanted a date to be fixed for the wedding, but Red Beard shrewdly declined, saying that he required time to speak to his daughter.

"Don't rush things. You know what girls are today."

After lunch Ben Areff and the emissaries left. Later Julie entered the house and her father said to her: "He will make a good husband for you."

"I won't marry . . ."

"What?" Red Beard screamed.

"I saw him."

"You saw him! And what is wrong with him?" he demanded.

Julie began to weep.

"Don't you question the appearance of any of Allah's creatures," he scolded. "He is a good man. He will look after me when I am old. Do you want to see me die of starvation?"

Julie ran out of the room.

The emissaries came again and a final agreement was reached. Red Beard — a gritty bargainer now — was to receive, in addition to the cash sum agreed upon earlier, a sum of twenty rands a month for the rest of his life.

The wedding day was fixed. Julie again expressed her opposition to the marriage, but her father's verbal outburst silenced her. The wedding preparations went forward. Julie stiffened towards everyone — including her sisters who had come to help — as though they were part of a conspiracy to marry her off. But a week before the wedding-day her mood changed; she looked happy and everything went smoothly. It seemed that she had accepted her lot.

The wedding-day arrived — but of Julie there was no sign. She had disappeared during the night. Red Beard cursed and screamed while everyone hunted for her. She had gone and left her father to face the bridegroom and the guests.

Ben Areff and his party arrived at the appointed hour. People watched him emerge from the car in the company of his relatives bearing gold jewellery and other gifts for the bride. His best man was carrying two garlands. They approached and stopped outside the house.

Red Beard was lying inside, breathing heavily as though felled by a blow. A few people took on the responsibility of telling Ben Areff that his bride had fled.

When told of Julie's perfidy, Ben Areff looked mortally embarrassed and humiliated. He stood there as if not knowing what to do. Then, he turned to his best man, took one of the garlands and hung it on the door-knob. The action fractured the tension and in some way restored his dignity.

The garland hung on the door-knob till evening. By then the flowers had withered.

Film

Nothing, since the time of the beard controversy, had shaken Muslims as much as the imminent release of the film *The Prophet* on the Johannesburg cinema circuit. Though the film had received early publicity, it had not yet been seen by anyone, not even by Hermes Films, the syndicate that had bought it in America. The film was to arrive shortly by Pan American jet from Hollywood. The anger of devout Muslims was aroused and I found myself, working as a freelance journalist at the time, in the thick of the issue. A day did not pass without individuals and representatives of religious groups urging me to inform not only the cinema syndicate but the "entire world" that the film was "sacrilegious" and "blasphemous" and that its screening would "not be tolerated".

The directors of Hermes Films approached the religious objections to the film in a secular way and stated that any decision could only be taken, in the rational order of things, after the film had been seen at a preview to which they would invite Muslim religious organizations. This response only served to leaven the anger of Muslims and the Islamic Academy convened a Muslim Council to deal with the matter. The Muslim Council, after a day of deliberation, decided to detail their objections in a letter to Hermes Films and gave a copy to the press. The pith of the letter read:

"You, the directors of Hermes Films, have invited us to sin by seeing the film. How can we, believers in the sacred Law of the Almighty, sit down with you in a den of iniquity — you will agree that cinemas are places where scenes of revelry, nudity and lewd acts are screened daily — and view something that blasphemes our Prophet Mohammed? Tractors will not pull us there, never mind oxen.

"Lest you are ignorant of the Law of Islam on picture-making, let us apprise you that all pictures of animate objects are banned, whether of pencil, paint, crayon or celluloid. Our Prophet said: 'Every picture-maker will be in the fire of Hell.' Our Prophet had foreseen the time when picture-makers, and the hosts of godless others involved in the film industry, including your good selves, would want to corrupt the virtuous people of the earth, and placed a strong unequivocal injunction against pictures. It is even reported by his contemporaries that he said: 'Angels do not enter a house in which there is a dog or a picture.' So do not presume to tell us that it is rational to see something before it can be condemned. We don't have to see something that is damned from the beginning.

"You will now appreciate your own temerity in asking us to sin by viewing the film. Anyone involved with this film will be consigned to the fires of Hell even if he is an angel in every other respect."

I went to interview Mr Winters of Hermes Films on the reaction of his syndicate to the letter. He was a big man, pale in complexion, with bronze hair cut in a fringe over his forehead. He was sitting behind a walnut-wood desk in his office on the eighteenth floor of Twentieth Century Centre.

"You will appreciate," he said, leaning forward, with his grey eyes twinkling under bushy brows, "that my company operates strictly on a commercial basis. All other issues are irrelevant. The film has been bought for a hundred thousand rands and we intend to release it for screening."

"You do not think the objections have any validity?"

"None. The film, we are informed, is historically true."

"Are you certain there is nothing offensive?"

"Nothing. The Prophet is portrayed as a hero."

I recorded his statements in my notebook and prepared to leave.

"By the way," he said, coming with me to the door, "you can state in your report that cinemas are very democratic places and that no one is compelled to go to them."

The press report of the interview outraged Muslim conscience. The film became the topic of conversation and the theme of every sermon at every mosque. The Muslim Council was summoned again and this time an aggressive tone was added to its deliberations. The Council finally decided on the types of action to be taken against the cinema syndicate if they carried out their intention to release the film: protest resolutions would be adopted by Muslim groups throughout the country and telegrams sent to the syndicate; international Muslim organizations and all Muslim governments would be urged to lodge strong protests; demonstrations would be held. As the issue was now beginning to look grave and required daily attention, an Action Committee of five men headed by Molvi Haroon was elected.

One incident marred the unanimity of the proceedings of the Muslim Council. A Mr Mohammed proposed a resolution that a telegram should be sent to the Prime Minister urging him to ban the film under the Censorship Act. Molvi Haroon immediately objected and, pointing a warning index finger at Mr Mohammed, said: "The entire matter has nothing to do with politics." Mr Mohammed retorted: "Molvi Haroon, you should not think I am one of your pupils." Molvi Haroon replied: "I wish you had been, for you would then have experienced how I deal with those who are insolent." Mr Mohammed countered with: "You think I am an inhabitant of Lilliput!" Fortunately for Mr Mohammed, Molvi Haroon had not heard of that country, and the dispute ended.

The upshot of the meeting was that Hermes Films found themselves receiving an avalanche of letters, telegrams, cablegrams and protest resolutions. I telephoned Mr Winters and asked him if there was any change in his company's attitude and he replied curtly: "My company is not prepared to communicate with fanatics. Our intention to release the movie still stands."

The Action Committee responded: "We are determined to eliminate this plot of the enemies of Islam. We shall reduce to ashes Twentieth Century Centre and any cinema screening the film even if it means human sacrifice on our part."

I telephoned Mr Winters and asked him what his company intended doing. He informed me that a meeting of the directors would take place the next day and if I came up immediately after the meeting he would give me their reply. I went the next day and while I was being whisked in the lift to the eighteenth floor it occurred to me that this would perhaps be the last time I came there as, on the next day, if Hermes Films did not capitulate, the building would be gutted by fire. I waited in the reception room — among ferns, cyclamens and begonias — for the crucial decision.

When Mr Winters entered the room looking crestfallen I knew his company had capitulated. He told me: "My company is prepared to settle the dispute. We don't want to give Muslims the trouble of setting fire to Twentieth Century Centre and we don't want to be held responsible for giving them the opportunity of committing suicide. They can have the film for a hundred thousand rands and hold a ceremonial burning if they wish."

On being informed of the decision the Action Committee replied briefly: "We regret we are unable to accept the offer of Hermes Films as it is too expensive."

It seemed that the whole issue would now enter the doldrums of the bargaining table and the promise of the fire-cracker fuse fizzle out, since Hermes Films made no further overture. Then the film was advertised for screening at the Pantheon Cinema and the fuse flared up again.

The Action Committee hurriedly summoned a plenary session of the Muslim Council to decide on collective action. The meeting began on a stormy note when Mr Mohammed suggested that the Council in organizing resistance seek the assistance of political groups. "The film is an insult to people who are not white. Our fight against the film is a fight for freedom." Pandemonium broke out. A dozen voices accused Mr Mohammed of introducing politics into religion. An Action Committee member shouted: "At the last meeting you wanted the film banned and now you talk of freedom. You are nothing but an opportunist trying to take over the Council." "You're a liar!" Mr Mohammed roared and rushed forward to grapple with the speaker. But he fell over a chair as several men attempted to intercept him. Mr Mohammed's fall had the effect of calming everyone's tempers and Molvi Haroon went on to harangue the meeting. "The Prophet says in the Koran: 'Verily, the life of this world is but play, amusement, mutual pride and the accumulation of wealth and sons.' Now is politics not part of the life of this world? Is politics not amusement, mutual pride and the accumulation of wealth? Ibn Abbas reported . . ." Mr Mohammed jumped up from his seat and shouted: "Why leave your five sons out?" There was pandemonium again.

The meeting ended with a declaration that trumpeted a call to arms:

"We Muslims proclaim to the enemies of Islam that the choice is between the film and our lives. Either we live and the film dies, or the film lives and we perish. The accursed progeny of Satan are operating an international conspiracy to discredit our Prophet.

"Will Muslims rise in a Jihad to defend the honour of our Prophet? The first answer has already been given by our protests. We shall finally answer with our blood which will dye the surface of the earth red.

"We call on all Muslims to join us in a march on the Pantheon for the purpose of incinerating the cinema and its owner.

"May Allah continue to guide us."

On a Monday afternoon I went to Red Square where the demonstrators gathered. There were about a thousand men from all over the country. Some were dressed in white robes, some in Arab garb with burnouses, some sported embroidered silk turbans. They were all bearded. Molvi Haroon, looking very distinguished in a saffron-coloured turban, would lead the procession into the heart of the city and personally light the flame that would set the cinema ablaze. The Action Committee rallied the men — two standards with green flags emblazoned with the Islamic moon and star were raised aloft — and the demonstrators were about to set out when the security police arrived.

An officer came up to Molvi Haroon and a few others who were standing apart and asked them courteously if they would permit him to read a proclamation.

"What proclamation?" Molvi Haroon asked.

"Let me read it then you will all know at once."

The Action Committee conferred together and decided that no harm would be done by allowing the proclamation to be read. In any case they were not involved in politics.

The officer motioned with his hands to everyone to come close and read: "You are hereby informed on this the 10th day of March at 2.13 p.m. by me, Captain Martinus Paulus Reichman, that in terms of the Riotous Assemblies Act no meetings of persons for the purpose of public demonstrations may be held."

When the Captain had finished Molvi Haroon smiled at him ironically and said, "This is a religious gathering."

"Are you trying to tell me that you are holding a religious gathering in Red Square on a Monday afternoon? I am giving you and your people exactly fifteen minutes to disperse, otherwise my men will charge."

The Action Committee held a quick meeting and then Molvi Haroon addressed the demonstration, who all sat down on the ground, in Urdu. He told them that the infidels were trying to lure them into politics but they would not suceed. There was a conspiratorial crusade against Muslims, but their eventual triumph was as certain as the triumph of Saladin. Nothing would deter them from setting fire to the Pantheon Cinema and its owner. They should all find their way in ones and twos, using devious routes, into the city centre and gather outside the cinema.

The demonstrators felt dispirited. The appearance of the police, with guns in shining holsters, the menace of the truncheons and batons swinging playfully in their hands, was enough to cow the boldest, and many of them, instead of finding their way to the cinema, found their way home. They were law-abiding citizens and did not want to get involved in politics (anything of interest to the security police was political). However, the Action Committee and ten others reached the Pantheon. I had preceded them in my car and waited for them to arrive. They gathered outside the cinema, a huge granite structure with a red neon sign flashing above its five entrance doors: *The Prophet*. Around massive pillars were posters in glass cases advertising the film.

The group found themselves jostled by the pedestrians, by the people entering the cinema, and by those examining the posters. Several curious onlookers gathered to stare at the white-robed men with ferocious beards. Some people congratulated them and expressed the hope that their presence would make the film a success (they thought that the group's presence was a gimmick by the owner of the cinema to attract the attention of the public). Others wanted to know where they came from and if they were real Arab sheikhs. Children holding their mothers' hands shouted: "Mummy! Look at their beards! Mummy! Look at their beards!" The noise of the city exploded all around them and they began to feel lost. After a while a doorkeeper in maroon uniform with gilt buttons and yellow braid came up to them and told them to move on as they were obstructing the pavement, which had become unusually crowded with people trying to enter the cinema. "And by the way," he said, "this cinema is for Europeans only." The group looked at the infidel in contempt and said nothing. The doorkeeper went away, shrugging his shoulders. He came back in a short while, looking upset.

"The manager wants to know if you are Arabs or other Easterners?"

No one replied. Molvi Haroon smiled faintly.

"I say," he shouted, "don't you understand English? Are you Arabs or Indians or some other race?"

No one answered. More people began to gather.

I was standing near the group, so he turned to me.

"Can you tell me who these people are?"

"I can't tell," I said, preferring to keep my professional neutrality.

He addressed the group again.

"I say, the manager wants to know. If you are Indians he knows the law. If you are Arabs he doesn't and will phone the lawyer to find out. Will one of you speak?"

They gave the man a stony look.

"Speak! Speak!"

Throwing up his hands in frustration he went into the cinema. Soon he returned with the manager. More people had gathered around to witness the entertaining incident that was developing. The manager approached the group.

"Gentlemen, could you please identify yourselves."

The group stood like statues. They were not going to talk

to a man who was part of an anti-Islamic conspiracy.

"They just want to make trouble," the doorkeeper said irascibly.

"Not so fast, Valentino," the manager said gently, turning to the spectators.

"Can anyone help, please. Who are these gentlemen? What do they want?"

No one ventured an explanation. Besides, the men looked so fierce, with hatred smouldering in their eyes like ancient Assyrian warriors, that they were afraid to question them. But a lady, dressed in bottle-green slacks, with a string of beads around her neck, said to the manager:

"Why do you want to interfere with them?"

"I am not interfering. I am only trying to be helpful."

"They don't need any help. Go back into your cinema. I am sure they don't want to enter your whites-only cinema."

"You black bitch!" the doorkeeper shouted. "Who are you to tell us?"

"Quiet, Valentino!" the manager said.

The lady, who was tall and lithe, took a step towards the doorkeeper and dextrously smacked him across the face. "Don't speak to me in that way," she said.

"Bitch!" he screamed, lunging at her, but several people got in his way and the manager thrust his hand accidentally into his face. The doorkeeper swore and tried to kick the lady, but instead kicked someone else who kicked back at him.

"Stop! Stop!" the manager pleaded desperately. "It is only a small matter."

People came running across from the opposite pavement. Cars came to a standstill and began hooting. The demonstrators found themselves pushed back towards the entrance doors of the cinema. People began to take sides. Some were for the lady, others for the doorkeeper. Tempers began to flare. The manager went on appealing for calm but nobody seemed to be listening to him. A fist bludgeoned the doorkeeper's face, scuffles broke out and suddenly everyone was fighting.

The police arrived and several shots were fired into the air. The reaction was almost immediate — the fighting stopped as though Doomsday had come. The police charged and the rioters ran helter skelter, seeking refuge in shops, restaurants, pharmacies, hairdressers' salons and in the cinema.

I was standing beside the demonstrators who were huddled together in a niche in the porch of the Pantheon Cinema, unable to move because of the press of people, when the manager succeeded in making his way to where we were.

"Gentlemen, come with me, please. I don't want you to be hurt."

Molvi Haroon and his group were so shocked and bewildered by the tumult they had caused and the sudden arrival of the police that when the manager appeared, urging them to go with him, they felt that a saviour had come to lead them to a place of safety.

"This way, gentlemen," the manager said, taking Molvi Haroon's hand, pushing others out of the way, leading them into the building. I followed. He shepherded us through an inner door and giving us over to usherettes with torches quickly disappeared.

The auditorium was thickly carpeted and overhead faint stars were shining in an indigo sky. We sank into plush velvet seats. On the panoramic screen a procession of Arab horsemen was approaching a desert city. It was met at the entrance gate by the chieftain who led the way to his palace where the riders dismounted. They entered a splendid room where a feast lay spread. While the handsome "Prophet" and his party were feasting, flutes began to play and dancing girls in diaphanous jade silk glided in among the guests . . .

Obsession

One of Gool's associates was Milo, a short, stocky, well-dressed man who would come to Fordsburg in his white convertible Chrysler. As he drove past, he would greet the Indian women walking along pavements or standing on balconies, but none of them ever bothered to return his greetings.

He was a master at snooker and seldom suffered a defeat in Gool's premises in High Road. One day he said to Gool while surveying the billiard table: "The Indian women are lovely, especially in their saris . . ."

And he bent over the table and smacked the ball with the cue. It rebounded from the end of the table, colliding with another that careered straight into the net at the opposite end.

"So you are taken by the mysterious East, eh?" Gool said, chalking his cue.

"Beauty!" Milo said, moving to the other side of the table.

"They're expensive, unlike your women who are bought with cattle."

"Expensive?"

"Gold."

Gool thrust his stick at the ivory ball; it shot from side to side, failing to strike a red renegade on the edge.

"Gold for an Indian woman . . ." Milo said softly, steering three balls one after another into the net. "Gool, any good Indian film showing today?"

"Not a bad one at the Lyric."

Milo looked at his watch and said: "Time for two more games."

He gathered the balls and arranged them in the centre of the table.

Going to the Lyric Cinema had a double attraction for Milo. There was firstly the attraction of the female cinema-goers. He would gaze at the richly-attired women, smelling of exotic perfumes, their eyes glittering in the foyer lights, hair either coiffured or hanging in tresses, and saris sensuously exposing midriffs. Sometimes he would be given a seat beside a woman. In the crepuscular light he would glance surreptitiously at her profile. Then there was the attraction of the film itself. Though he failed to understand the language or the plot, he feasted visually on the gorgeous film stars, their garments taut against their bodies, and jewellery embellishing their necks, wrists and ankles.

Yet, after the film show was over and the women had passed him by as another cipher in the world of helots, a feeling of depression would constrict him. He would drive his car homewards, pass by drab barracoon-type houses, go through muddy roads skirted by dirt and poverty, and look at the women dressed in dun coarse skirts and shapeless smocks. When he reached home he would survey his wife with latent scorn as though she were an Amazon, his mind still ablaze with the feminine world of the cinema. And when he went to bed at night kaleidoscopic images of Eastern women would invade his mind, and a sense of injustice at the scheme of things, and of his own unblazoned place in it, would overwhelm him.

Medina House was a mansion, Eastern in design, form and ornamentation. One entered it from Terrace Road. There was a high wrought-iron gate flanked on either side by a wall six feet high with spikes running along the top. A flight of steps led to a portico, the columns embossed with leaves and lotuses. A large double door, the upper half consisting of mosaic glass, gave entry into a hall with several doors: one opening to the stairs that led to the upper floor of the mansion with its latticed balcony; another leading into a large living-room where a model of the Taj Mahal was prominently exhibited, and the adjoining dining room; and another to the basement room where the Darsot family's jewellery was kept in a large green safe.

The Darsots had two daughters, Noorunisha and Khalida. Noorunisha was the elder. She was a modest-looking girl with long black hair which she plaited into two pigtails. She was naturally shy and her parents did not have to tell her not to talk to males. She had had several proposals of marriage, but her father had rejected them on the grounds that the families of the suitors were not of his financial and social standing.

Milo sent Belinda, a girl friend, to seek work at Medina House. She was refused at first, but after several applications Mrs Darsot was impressed by Belinda's eagerness to serve her, and engaged her as housemaid. Belinda soon acquainted herself with the mansion and its contents and gave Milo all the particulars. Milo decided that the best time to enter Medina House would be at about ten in the morning when Mrs Darsot and her daughters would be alone. To gain entry into the mansion he devised a plan. He obtained a van and had the following words printed on the outside: *York Safe Co. Ltd.* With two others he drove up to the mansion and rang the bell at the gate. When Mrs Darsot came Milo said that he had been sent by his firm to deliver a small safe. Mrs Darsot, seeing the men in their work clothes and the van of the firm in the street, unlocked the gate. Milo and his men carried in a crate (containing pieces of scrap iron). Immediately they were inside the mansion they locked the door, rounded up everyone at gun-point and herded them into one room.

When Milo saw Noorunisha he was mesmerized. Prior to Milo's entry she had been preparing to go out shopping with her aunt and cousin who would be arriving to fetch her. She had had a bath, dressed herself in an elaborate gold-inwoven sari of black silk, combed her hair, and had just completed darkening her eye-lids with kohl. Controlling himself, Milo demanded all the money and jewellery that was kept in the safe in the basement room. Mrs Darsot agreed to give him everything. But Milo, his eyes fixed on Noorunisha, ordered the girl to take the keys and lead him to the room.

In the basement room he took the keys from her and opened the safe. The jewellery was in velvet-covered boxes. He opened a box, took several pieces and examined the filigree handiwork. Then he took a gold necklace smouldering with rubies and turning to Noorunisha — a hieroglyph of fear — placed it around her neck. Next he selected two earrings and hooked them to her pierced lobes. He lifted her arms and adorned her wrists with bangles and her fingers with rings. Finally, he walked around her, admiring her. Before him stood a woman miraculously come down from cinema screens, in appearance like Nargis herself, his favourite film star.

Thanking his gangster gods, Milo took Noorunisha's hand.

One of his partners came rushing down the steps. He saw Noorunisha decorated with jewellery and Milo kissing her hand.

"Milo . . .? What . . ."

Milo awoke from an Eastern night's dream.

"Go . . . back," he said.

The partner quickly removed the jewellery from Noorunisha and stuffed it into his pockets, saying:

"Come! Quick! There is knocking at the door."

He grabbed Milo by the arm and the two men rushed up the stairs where they were joined by the third partner. The three, guns in hand, then opened the door and rushed out — past two shocked women — ran down the steps, jumped into their van and drove away.

In the street Noorunisha's cousin had parked his car behind the van. He had been waiting for his mother and sister who had gone off to fetch her when he saw the three men emerge from the gate and hurriedly get into the van. Realizing that they were robbers he gave chase, but after a while lost track of them. He returned to Medina House where he found everyone unhurt, and hurriedly telephoned the police.

In the speeding van Milo's partner said to him:

"What made you do that?"

"Do what?"

"Putting all that jewellery on the girl."

"Did I?" Milo said, accelerating the van towards Main Reef Road.

"Wasn't there any money in the safe?"

"No."

The van rounded a bend, tyres screeching, and sped towards Soweto.

"Look!" Milo said.

There was a police road-block ahead.

Gerty's Brother

I first saw Gerty in a shop in Vrededorp. Vrededorp, as everyone knows, is cleft in two by Delarey Street; on one side it is colonized by us blacks and on the other side by whites. The whites come over to our side when they want to do their shopping, and return with a spurious bargain or two. I saw her in a shop in the garishly decorated Indian shopping lane called Fourteenth Street. I had gone there with my friend Hussein who wanted to see a shopkeeper friend of his. I think the shop was called Dior Fashions, but of that I am not quite sure because shop follows shop there and this one didn't strike me as being in any way fashionable. Anyway, that is where I saw her. My friend spoke to the shopkeeper — a fat dark man with a darker moustache — and I just looked around and smoked a cigarette.

I sat down on a chair and then I noticed two figures darken the doorway and enter the shop, a girl and a boy. The shopkeeper spoke to the girl and then suddenly laughed. She laughed too, I think. I wouldn't have taken any further notice of the group as I was seated at the back of the shop. But then the shopkeeper switched to Gujarati and spoke to my friend. I heard him say that she was easy, though one had to be careful as there was the usual risk involved. Hussein replied that he was keen and wouldn't like to waste much time about the matter. I think the shopkeeper introduced him to her at this stage. Then I heard him tell Hussein that he was going to organize a dance at his place on the following Saturday evening, that he was going to invite Gerty, and that if Hussein were interested he could take her away from his place. All this he said in Gujarati, rather coarsely I thought.

Later, when Hussein and I had climbed into his Volkswagen and were on our way to Fordsburg, he informed me that to soften her before the party on Saturday he had bought the girl a frock. He asked me how I liked her and I said she was all right as far as I was concerned, though, of course, I had not been near enough to see her properly and size her up. But I said she was all right and he felt very satisfied at having bumped into a white girl. He told me that she lived in Vrededorp, "on the other side", and that she seemed to be very easy. He said that when he had done with her he would throw her over to me and I could have her as well. I answered with a vague "Let the time come". He then said something about "pillar to post", and laughed as the car tore its way through the traffic into Fordsburg.

Saturday night I was at my landlady's, stripped to the waist because of the heat, reading an old issue of the *New Statesman*. There was a knock on the door and somebody asked for me and entered. It was Hussein, all dressed up with bow tie and cuff-links and gleaming shoes that were out of place in my spartan room.

"Where to, my dandy friend?" I asked admiringly.

"To the dance party. I thought you would be ready. You promised to come with me."

I said I had forgotten, but that I would be ready in a minute. I dressed quickly, but didn't care to put on a white shirt or a tie. I wasn't very particular about what I wore and I think it pleased my friend because my appearance was something of a foil to his, and set off to advantage his carefully put-together looks.

We set off in his Volkswagen for Vrededorp and in a few minutes the car braked sharply in Eleventh Street in front of the house of Hussein's shopkeeper friend. We were quite early and there were not many people present. Hussein's friend was happy to see us and he introduced us to those who were there. There were some lovely-looking girls in shimmering coral, amber and amethyst-coloured saris and others in more sober evening dresses.

After a while Hussein asked to see the shopkeeper privately, and I think they went out to the front verandah of the house. When they returned I saw that Hussein was not pleased about something or other. Other girls arrived, all gaily dressed and very chic and charming, and I was beginning to look forward to a swinging evening. The girls offered me tea and cake and other tasty things to eat and I didn't refuse as my boarding-house wasn't exactly a liberal establishment. All this time my friend Hussein was walking in and out of the room, and was on the look-out whenever someone knocked on the door and entered the house. The party got going and we danced, ate the refreshments provided and talked euphonious nonsense.

I was just getting interested in a girl, when my friend interrupted me and said that he wanted to see me urgently. I followed him and we went to the verandah. Someone had switched off the lights and I saw two figures standing there, a girl and a small boy. He introduced her to me as Gerty. He then took me aside and asked me if I could drive the two of them to the Zoo Lake immediately and leave them in the park for a while, and if I could keep her brother company while he saw to Gerty's needs. As it was a risky business he didn't want the others in the party to know. He would like to get done with it before joining the party.

I said I didn't mind and the four of us got into the car. I drove to the Lake. It was a lovely night in December and we breathed in the luminous wind of the city streets as the car sped along. Hussein and Gerty sat in the back seat. They didn't say much to each other, but I guessed that they were holding hands and fondling. Gerty's brother sat beside me. He must have been seven or eight, but I didn't take much notice of him. He was eating some cakes and chocolates that Hussein had taken from the house. I dropped the pair in a park near the Lake. Hussein asked me to return in about an hour's time. The park was a darkness of trees and lawns and flowers, and it occurred to me that it made no difference if one slept with a white or a black girl there.

Gerty told her brother that he mustn't worry and that she was all right and that he should go with me for a while. Before I drove off he asked me what they were going to do and I said they must be a bit tired and wanted to rest, but that did not sound convincing. Then I said that they had something to discuss in private and the best place was in the park. He agreed with me and I started the car. I didn't feel like driving aimlessly about for an hour so I drove towards the lake. I asked the boy what his name was and he said Riekie.

I parked the car under some pine trees near a brightly-lit restaurant. There were people dining on the terrace amid blaring music, others were strolling on the lawns or resting on the benches. I asked Riekie if he would like an ice-cream and took him to the restaurant and bought him one. We went down to the water's edge. The lake is small with an islet in the middle; a fountain spouted water into shifting rays of variegated light. Riekie was fascinated by it all and asked me several questions.

I asked him if he had ever sat in a boat. He said he hadn't. I took him to the boat-house and hired one. The white attendant looked at me for a moment and then at Riekie. I knew what he was thinking about but I said nothing. He went towards the landing-stage and pointed to a boat. I told Riekie to jump in, but he hesitated. So I lifted him and put him in the boat. He was light in weight and I felt the ribs under his arms. A sensation of tenderness for the boy went through me. You must understand that this was the first time I had ever picked up a white child.

I rowed out towards the middle of the lake, and went around the fountain of kaleidoscopic lights. Riekie was gripped by wonder. He trailed his hands in the cool water smelling of rotting weeds and tried to grab the overhanging branches of the willows along the banks.

It was time to pick up Hussein and Gerty. Riekie looked disappointed, but I said I would bring him there again. At this he seemed satisfied and I rowed towards the landing-stage.

Hussein and Gerty were waiting for us. They got into the car and we returned to the house in Eleventh Street.

The party was now in full swing. There were many girls and I didn't waste much time. My friend stuck to Gerty; if he was not dancing with her, he was talking to her. And by the time the party ended at midnight Riekie had fallen asleep on a sofa and had to be doused with water to wake him.

We dropped Gerty and her brother at a street corner on our way to Fordsburg. Hussein had rooms of his own in Park Road, situated in a small yard at the end of a passage. A tall iron gate barred the entrance to the passage. There were only three rooms in the yard. Hussein occupied two and the other was occupied by a decrepit pensioner who lived in his room like some caged animal that no one ever came to see.

At first Hussein was afraid to tell Gerty where he lived. There was the usual risk involved. But I think eventually he came to the conclusion that in life certain risks had to be taken if one was to live at all. And so Gerty and her brother came to his rooms and she took on the role of mistress and domestic servant and Riekie became the pageboy.

Gerty and Riekie were very fond of each other. The harsh realities of life — they were orphans and lived in poverty with an alcoholic elder brother — had entwined them. Hussein didn't mind Riekie's presence. In fact the boy attached himself to him. My friend was generous, and besides providing Gerty with frocks for summer, he bought the boy clothing and several pairs of shoes. Riekie was obedient and always ready to run to the shops for Hussein, to polish his shoes or wash the car. In time his cheeks began to take on colour and he began to look quite handsome. I noticed that he wasn't interested in boys of his own age; his attachment to his sister seemed to satisfy him.

Riekie would often come to my landlady's in the company of Hussein, or my friend would leave him there when he had some business with Gerty. If I was in the mood to go to the movies I would take him with me.

And then things took a different turn. Hussein came to understand that the police had an eye on him, that somehow they had come to know of Gerty and were waiting for an opportunity to arrest him in incriminating circumstances. Someone had seen a car parked for several nights near his rooms and noticed the movements of suspicious-looking persons. And he was convinced the police were after him when one night, returning home late, he saw a man examining the lock of the gate. As he was not in the mood for a spell of prison, he told her that she should keep away from him for some time, and that he would see her again as soon as the air had cleared. But I think both of them realized that there wasn't much chance of that.

There wasn't much that one could tell Riekie about the end of the affair. My friend left it to Gerty, and went to Durban to attend to his late father's affairs.

One Sunday morning I was on my way to post some letters and when I turned the corner in Park Road there was Riekie, standing beside the iron gate that led to my friend's rooms. He was clutching two bars with his hands, and shouting for Hussein. I stood and watched as he shouted. His voice was bewildered.

The ugly animal living in the yard lurched out of his room and croaked: "Go way, boy, go way white boy. No Hussein here. Go way."

Riekie shook the barred gate and called for Hussein over and over again, and his voice was smothered by the croaks of the old man.

I stood at the corner of the street, in my hand the two letters I intended to post, and I felt again the child's body as I lifted him and put him into the boat many nights ago, a child's body in my arms embraced by the beauty of the night on the lake, and I returned to my landlady's with the hackles of revolt rising within me.

Ten Years

Yasmin, a girl of about fifteen, was in her bedroom seated on her bed, sobbing. After she had returned from the court in the afternoon, she had locked herself in her room, refusing to allow her father or anyone else — her aunts and cousins, hordes of other sympathizers — to enter the room.

It was now past six in the evening. The street lights in the narrow smoke-filled streets of Fordsburg were glowing. Yasmin's father, Mr Adam Suleiman, the veteran Orient Front politician, was in the lounge of their small house, reading the evening paper. For the second time now he was reading the report of the trial, the final summing up of the case by the judge, the verdict, and the sentences passed on the five men found guilty of sabotage. Their photographs were prominently displayed, but he focused his eyes on one face only — his son's face, passionless like a mask, carved in deep shadows.

"Ten years, ten years," he whispered feebly, and he felt, with a painful finality, the closing of a shutter somewhere inside him.

The arrest and trial of his son Amin had racked him. The protracted, involved court proceedings, the endless discussions with the counsel for the defence, the expense, the anxiety — these had corroded his health and mental composure. He looked like an ascetic, an ascetic who had failed to find the promised bliss.

At seven his eldest son Ebrahim was to arrive from Durban. There was some comfort in having another son. Although he would no longer have his favourite son near him, he hoped that Ebrahim would decide to stay with him and be a buttress to him in the years of anguish that lay ahead.

Mr Adam Suleiman's political experience included the rigours of prison life. He had been imprisoned several times during his long, politically active career; every time the Orient Front had embarked on a passive resistance campaign against some discriminatory law or other, he had been in the forefront. The campaigns had ended without achieving anything much to speak of. But now in retrospect he felt thankful: he would be closer to his son's anguish during his long period of incarceration.

At seven Ebrahim arrived. Father and son greeted each other, but rather coldly. Ebrahim sat down on a chair, and after a few moments of strained silence, jolted his father by saying, "So he had to join the saboteurs. I suppose he became desperate."

Mr Adam Suleiman scanned his son's face; he looked there for some softness, some mellow sympathetic quality. But on Ebrahim's astringent face there was only implacability and bitter scorn. There was no trace of pity for a brother imprisoned for ten years.

"I don't understand what you mean," the father said in a timid voice.

"Don't you?" Ebrahim asked with ironic emphasis.

"No, I don't."

Ebrahim produced a packet of cigarettes from his pocket and, with his dark bony fingers, lit one.

"So you don't grasp what I mean? Must I clarify to you the stupidity of his action and the stupidity of your encouragement — the crass imbecility of it all. Blowing up pylons and all that!"

"There is no point in talking about the past. Your brother is in prison."

There was anger within the father, but anaemic and muted. He hated his son just then for smoking nonchalantly as if nothing had happened. And Ebrahim had not even cared to inquire about his sister. She was still in her room, but no longer crying.

"And why should I not talk about it all? Are you trying to forget the past? Do you expect me to forget the time when you told me to leave this house because you could not stand my politics and my ideas? You forget the quarrels in this house."

"I have not forgotten them. But please forget the past at the present moment. Have you no feelings for your brother?"

"Is it my fault — the ten years? Or his own? Or yours perhaps?"

"My fault? What do you mean? In what way am I responsible for his imprisonment?"

"I suppose I must enlighten you. You seem to have a short memory. Do you forget your unreasoned defence of the stupidities perpetrated by the Orient Front and your unfatherly rages when I refused to be your flunky and follower?"

"Oh, forget the past, my son. I cannot bear to think of it."

"And do you forget that you told me to leave this house

when you were afraid that Amin was beginning to see the absurdity of your politics and was on the point of joining the People's Movement?"

The father did not answer.

"And now that Amin is in prison and you need me you have sent for me. I suppose you think I have no kind of human dignity and self-respect; you can pick me up and throw me away as you will."

Mr Suleiman remained silent.

"Do you admit that you were wrong in your politics, and that you wronged me by ordering me to leave this house?"

Mr Suleiman did not reply. There was an inner resistance to admitting this. He feared that his son would quickly seize upon the admission in order to make satirical invasions into the past.

"You do not admit because to face reality is too much for you. You supported the Orient Front in its time (I need not remind you that most of the leaders have now absconded from the country) and the few remaining supporters — like my brave brother Amin — are in desperation blowing up the doors of a post office here, a pylon there, or a pillar or two of some public building. The Herrenvolk laugh at your childish actions and gather you with ease into their nets. But what can one expect from fools of the first order? Need I remind you of what happened to your passive resistance campaigns? You called me a traitor, a coward. And what did you achieve? Nothing. No, perhaps not nothing, but a kick from the Herrenvolk jackboot and a taste of prison life."

"Perhaps you are right. But you seem to forget that we were brave and dared, while you sat, critical, inactive, afraid."

"Yes, but what about the futility of your actions? You seem to forget that Amin has been given ten years. Ten years for daring, for being brave as you call it. Action without the possibility of achieving anything — that is not audacity but stupidity and rashness."

The father bowed his head.

"And you encouraged Amin to join the band of desperate men. You are responsible for his imprisonment. Yes, you can now go and scribble, as you used to do, on public buildings: 'Down with tyrants', 'Down with the Group Areas Act', 'Freedom is around the corner' and so forth. Such scribbling may soothe your conscience, make you feel that your case is exalted, that you are contributing to the liberation struggle. But all your life you have fed yourself on delusions. My mother — you dragged her from one prison to another on your senseless passive resistance campaigns. Her illness did not matter to you — the cause was more important. At her death your grief was a travesty; you gloated at what people said about her being a martyr, a woman who had dedicated her life to the cause of freedom. You were blind to the obvious insincerity of their words. And what has happened to your philosophy of non-violence, the Gandhian principles that you and your Front professed to uphold? Passive resistance! A contradiction in terms, that is what it is. Political suicide and political madness, the way of the weak and the cowardly. And when passive resistance failed after the Herrenvolk courts had kicked you enough in the guts, you and your Front turned in panic to perform ineffectual puerile gestures — blowing up pillars and pylons. Just as little children, unable to punish a parent who frustrates them, resort to breaking up their playthings. You have always lived in a world of delusions, with Utopia to be purchased around the corner."

Mr Adam Suleiman wilted under the blast of accusatory words. He felt defeated and humbled, his life crumbling within him. He would have infinitely preferred a spell in prison to the venomous tongue of his son. At a time when he ardently needed commiseration, the futility of his whole political life was forced on him.

And then his daughter's bedroom door opened. She stood before them, her long black hair dishevelled and flowing over her green dress, her eyes reddened by crying. She was like some figure in a tragedy, lacerated by the political passions that were a part of her family.

Ebrahim rose, went towards her, touched her head with his hand — and then promptly left the house.

venomous tongue brought up
points father didn't want to
face about himself.

Labyrinth

"Say good-bye, say good-bye to papa," Gool said to his three-year-old daughter. She laughed as he tickled her.

"Where you going, papa?"

"To see friends, Nazli."

He tickled her again and she laughed again as his wife came up to him. He handed her the child. He kissed them both and then went out of the house at the rear. He entered his sports car standing in the driveway, a red Farina Spider, and drove to the street edge. His wife and child were waving at him from the door and he waved back. He looked along both sides of the street, turned left and stormed away.

He drove to High Road.

A game of billiards was in progress.

"Any news?" he asked Faizel who was chalking his cue.

"None."

And Faizel continued playing.

There was a time, Gool remembered, when everyone there would have greeted him eagerly. Now there was a mood of sullenness enhanced by the uninterrupted clicks of colliding billiard-balls.

Gool went over to Hamid, touched him on the shoulder and took him aside.

"Everything quiet?"

"Everything quiet."

"Keep the guns loaded."

"They won't come in here."

"No, but keep the guns loaded."

When the billiards game was over Gool was offered a stick. He declined. He sat down at a table and poured some liquor into a glass from a decanter. As he sat drinking he reflected on their estrangement from him. He had been unable to counter successfully a challenge that had confronted him and his failure was leading to the psychical disintegration of the gang. "They are deserting me," he said bitterly to himself as he saw them clustered around the billiards table in silent preoccupation with the game. His agony was that of a leader who finds himself rejected. Their rejection was not on a level of clear consciousness, but rather a subtle instinctive movement away from him as his leadership no longer offered them security.

Trouble had started when a new gang, The Spears, visited the various gambling clubs "protected" by Gool and offered superior "protection". A few timorous ones among the club proprietors had accepted the new rulers; the brave ones who dared resist found themselves beaten up and their coffers ransacked.

The action of The Spears represented a crisis in Gool's life. He had lorded it over others for so long that his sovereignty seemed eternal. A few individuals, in earlier years, had tried to oppose him and been silenced without much trouble. But the arrival of The Spears brought him face to face with an organized rival body. Yet it was not so much the actual physical challenge that shook him but the fact that it was possible. Physically audacious, he could oppose threat with threat, fist with fist, and bullet with bullet. But rationally and emotionally, he could not accept the possibility of a body of men deliberately banding together to subvert his rule. And neither could he accept the harsh and bitter irony of his situation: The Spears had appeared on the gangland scene at a time when, having loaded his bank coffers, he felt secure for life. At this mellow hour of repletion, their appearance enervated him and dulled his retaliative faculties. Yet while they existed he could not look the world in the face and meet it on his own terms.

Eventually he had decided to have it out with his rivals as he could no longer bear the humiliation. He made an ostensible peace offer. He sent a message: if they would come to High Road he would be prepared to make an arrangement with them. The Spears, feeling flattered at Gool's apparent capitulation, accepted the offer and four men turned up to confer with him. The conference soon degenerated into a battle of foul words, fisticuffs — and bullets. Gool intended killing one or two of his antagonists on his own premises (he would plead self-defence as a motive later). But the ruse did not work. The Spears escaped with injuries.

It was during this mêlée that a bullet fired by Gool shattered the head of an alabaster statuette of Apollo and sent it crashing to the floor. The death of the god triggered an ominous reverberation through him, like seismic disorder, and in the moment's hesitation that followed his adversaries escaped. He picked up the shattered pieces and put them in a cardboard box which he left on the table-pedestal where the god had once stood. The next day he threw the box and its contents in the garbage can in the backyard.

Gool had acted unwisely in making his peace overture, for it implicitly contained his fears (though it displayed his cunning). His response and its consequences were personally disastrous for him for they fissured the bond that tied him to his gang. Had he been able to summon the selfless audacity of his former years and flung himself into the contest boldly, even at the risk of having his gang annihilated, his men would have followed him and perished gladly.

Akbar entered. Gool called him over.

"Brandy?"

Akbar sat down on a chair, but declined to drink.

"Have you heard anything?"

"No."

"They are not planning anything?"

"I haven't heard."

That the confrontation would come Gool knew. After the failure of his tactical defensive manoeuvre, his adversaries had retreated, but would soon show themselves. Akbar had spoken to friends all over the suburb, even posted spies. On the information gained, he would parry the enemy.

"Shall we go to the Avalon this evening?"

"Fine."

"Let's go for the tickets now."

"Going to the Avalon," Akbar said loudly to the billiards players.

Faizel joined them.

Gool drove his car to the Avalon Cinema. He parked near by and Akbar went to get the tickets. Gool kept his engine idling. Akbar came back.

"The cashier says he wants money."

"Tell that fat pig since when do we pay."

Akbar went back.

Since the advent of The Spears his status in society had slipped from its apogee. He sensed this from the attitude of people, in the way they spoke to him. A certain intonation had been elided from their speech. But he had not encountered the truculent arrogance displayed by the cinema cashier before. Had he transferred his allegiance? He realized that some people were secretly relishing his inability to annihilate his rivals, and others waiting anxiously for the final confrontation.

Suddenly a black Chrysler appeared beside Gool's car and levelled guns began spouting bullets. Gool drove away at high speed, dashed past a red traffic light, rounded several corners daringly, mounting the pavements with screaming tyres, passed a stop sign without slackening, and steered his car towards the Main Reef Road. He accelerated the Spider as it weaved through the traffic, and looked into the rear-view mirror to see the pursuing car. He shouted to his companion on the back seat: "Faizel! Faizel!" Faizel lay slumped, then groaned and Gool shouted again as he pressed the accelerator, narrowly missing a pedestrian crossing the road. His pursuers overtook several cars by hooting fiercely and they were now behind him, hooting. "Bastards! Bastards!" Gool cried as his car engine thundered. There was a string of stationary cars ahead of him. A red light! He swerved his car to the left and sped along the gravel side road. The Chrysler still followed him. "Swines! Swines!" he shouted, overwhelmed by their tenacious devilry. The light turned green as he reached it and he swerved in front of a car to get on the tarmac. He must get off the Main Reef Road and head towards the mine dumps, the golden mounds of sterile sand that lay on his left. Among the web of roads at Crown Mines he would be able to elude his pursuers.

He turned off the Main Reef Road. They were still following him closely. Then he saw the faces of his pursuers in the rear-view mirror: intent, grim, menacing. He turned to the right and sped down an incline, skirting a sand pyramid. His car flashed along an arc in the road, then he was over a bridge and among an avenue of trees. The road turned left, then left again. The hooter of the car behind burst into sustained tumultuous bellowing. "Swines! Swines!" The sound stampeded in his flaming brain. A gang of helmeted miners looked at him in a cinematic succession of faces. He was in a labyrinth of arcs, tangents, radii, perimeters, alive with hideous bellowing, screaming, thundering. A sooty monster loomed and passed, siren shrieking, with gnashing pistons. A huge black door barred his way, then metamorphosed miraculously into blue ether. Faizel made a final effort to resurrect himself from the blood-stained seat at the rear, put his hand on Gool's shoulder and collapsed with a cry. The touch, like a macabre caress, and the death cry unnerved Gool. He turned his car into a sand road — the road rushed towards him then treacherously dissolved. The red Spider careered into a mantle of dust, slithered and slewed, with its engine roaring, suddenly rolled over several times and plunged down an incline, scattering sprays of yellow dust into the air, and, coming to rest at the foot of a cypress tree, exploded into an inferno.

The Notice

The time came when houses were being expropriated in a section of Fordsburg and Indians pressed to go to Lenasia, a reservation some twenty miles away. When Mr Effendi's house was expropriated, he knew that the official would soon come with the usual six months' notice. But Mr Effendi decided to evade formal acceptance of the notice for several reasons: firstly he had been coerced into selling the house; secondly, he was not happy to live in a reservation outside metropolitan Johannesburg; and thirdly, the houses in the expropriated section, according to newspaper reports, were not going to be demolished until the government authorities had finally decided on details of the Oriental Bazaar that was to be erected, and this would take two or three years.

It was easy for Mr Effendi to evade receiving the notice for he was a commercial traveller. Whenever the official came his wife would say: "Mr Effendi he not home. He in country."

"And when will he come home?"

"Well, he traveller. He busy man."

And the official would depart and return on another day. But he never found Mr Effendi at home, for he always returned, whenever he did, at night and left at an early hour in the morning. At last the official became desperate as his seniors were beginning to believe that he was failing in his duty. He decided to call on Mr Effendi at night.

"Who dere?" his wife asked.

"Mr Hill. I want to speak to your husband."

"He not home. He still in country."

"I want to enter the house and see."

"You can't."

"I shall call the police if you don't let me in."

"Au-right, I open. Wait, I go dress."

She went to her bedroom for a while and then returned to open the door. She was a well-nourished woman in a pink gown with her plaited hair liberally oiled. The official entered the lounge and then went into the adjoining bedroom. He saw a form covered with blankets.

"Is that your husband in bed?"

Mrs Effendi looked abashed.

"I only woman and sometimes I lonely woman. Dat not my husban but friend."

She smiled and coyly looked away as though embarrassed by the confession of marital infidelity. The official was taken aback. He walked into the lounge and Mrs Effendi followed him.

"I only woman, you understand. My husban always in country."

The official smiled. And as an idea came into his mind, the disappointment he felt in not finding Mr Effendi at home evaporated. He went towards the door.

"You are a clever woman, Mrs Effendi. Enjoy yourself. Good night."

Mrs Effendi closed the door, went to her bedroom and

saw her husband — a hairy, fleshy, big-boned man — emerging from under the blankets.

"A stupid official! A stupid official!" he boomed between intervals of mocking guffaws. His pleasure at tricking the official was spiced by the satisfaction of defeating, though in a small way, those who had expropriated his house.

The next day the official came again. He spoke in such a friendly way that Mrs Effendi invited him into the house and offered him coffee.

"You know Mrs Effendi," he said, settling down in an armchair, "Indians are not all bad people. They have these big shops in Market Street and they give a lot of credit."

"Is dat so, Mr Hill?"

"Yes, I am beginning to like them."

"Sometimes Indian people not so good. My husban sell dem goods and den dey don' pay. Derefore he all de time in country."

"That is true. That keeps him busy. And that keeps you busy too," he added with a wink.

"You are a good man, Mr Hill, if you keep it a secret."

"Don't worry. I can hold my tongue."

When the official left, Mrs Effendi felt that she had him well under control and as long as this was the case she and her husband would be able to lengthen their stay in Fordsburg.

And then the official called again one night.

"I have to carry out my duty," he said apologetically as he stepped into the lounge. Mrs Effendi let the official in as it was late and she did not expect her husband back. The official placed his bag on the table, sat on a chair and pointed at the bedroom door with a smile.

"Is he in?"

"No, he still in country."

"I mean . . . you know who."

"Oh," she said laughing. "No, he no come tonight. He stay wit wife."

"Oh, he is a married man," the official said with emphasis. He laughed merrily. "I like you, Mrs Effendi. You are a clever woman."

"All Indian women clever," Mrs Effendi thanked him, smiling at his gullibility.

"Yes, they are very clever."

Mrs Effendi excused herself and went to the kitchen to make coffee. The official now removed his jacket and lit a cigarette. When she returned with the coffee he thanked her and said: "You know what I have done for you, Mrs Effendi? I have told the office that Mr Effendi has gone to India for a visit."

"Really, Mr Hill? Do we stay longer here?"

"Yes. It is a risk. But I am doing this only for you."

"I very glad Mr Hill."

"Remember, only for you. Not a word to anyone."

"Thank you, Mr Hill."

Mr Hill drank his coffee. Then he rose from his chair and boldly went to sit beside Mrs Effendi on the settee. She was shocked, tried to rise, but Mr Hill had his arm around her shoulders. However, after a brief struggle, she managed to free herself and went quickly to the kitchen.

He was unperturbed by Mrs Effendi's unwillingness to succumb. Perhaps she needed a little time to adjust to his transformation from an official into a Romeo. He had the night to himself and decided not to hurry matters. He saw a bowl of fruit on the table and helped himself. He munched an apple while gazing at a silver-framed picture of the Taj

Mahal. "Beautiful! Beautiful!" he whispered as a feeling of being involved in some Eastern romantic adventure — with harems of princesses, tambourines, sherbet and all that — took hold of him (he had had two double brandies in the bar shortly before his arrival). Soon a houri, clad in silk and glittering with jewels, would appear before him (he had seen such things happen in films) to offer him her dusky charms. Then he ate a peach, two bananas and some grapes. After that a sense of delicious euphoria filled him. It was a sultry night. He removed his tie, undid several shirt buttons revealing a cadaverous torso, lit a cigarette, stretched himself out on the settee and adjusted the cushion under his head so that he was more comfortable.

It was while the official was lying on the settee, waiting for his black-eyed houri to join him, that Mr Effendi returned home after being delayed on a country road by a minor technical fault in his car. Mrs Effendi had locked herself in the kitchen, wondering whether she should remain in her house or seek refuge in that of her neighbour.

Mr Effendi was surprised to see the lights burning in his house, but thinking that his wife had fallen asleep, opened the door using his own key. He was shocked to see a man sprawled on the settee. After a moment of bewilderment he realized who the man was. So the man had trapped him! But what business did he have to lie on the settee in his house, obscenely displaying the front of his torso? Did his wife permit him? Another man in his house while he was away! In a paroxysm of rage he rushed out of the house to call his assistant Charles — an ex-boxer still in fine fettle — who was unloading the bags from the car in the street. He shouted to Charles that there was a "dog" in the house who must be "killed".

Mr Hill quickly ran to the table and from a file in his bag took out the notice.

Mr Effendi and Charles stormed in.

"You are supposed to be in India!" Mr Hill shouted, waving the notice and retreating to the bedroom door.

"India!" Mr Effendi said, coming to a sudden standstill.

"Yes. Look at this notice. You can stay longer here."

"India . . .? Stay longer here?"

Mr Hill went up to Mr Effendi and showed him the notice. He pointed to the words at the bottom of the page: "Gone to India for a visit."

"It true," Mrs Effendi said, coming to stand beside her husband (after watching apprehensively from the kitchen door). "No more hiding away. Mr Hill do us favour."

"Oh! Oh!" Mr Effendi burst out laughing. "So you have tricked your seniors at the office. Wonderful! Wonderful!"

Mr Hill laughed too, but at his own cleverness in foiling an irate husband.

"Come sit down, Mr Hill. Let's have coffee," Mr Effendi said.

"Thank you," Mr Hill said, placing the notice safely into the bag and looking at Mrs Effendi going towards the kitchen.

Mr Moonreddy

Everyone in Lenasia, a township on the perimeter of Johannesburg, considered Mr Moonreddy to be a gentleman. He was a small, mild-tempered man with glossy black hair. He was very proud of his hair, and every morning when he got up and dressed with meticulous care, it was his hair that received fastidious devotion. There was an invariable ritual he followed in its grooming. He would fill the wash-basin with warm water, pour in a spoonful of Dettol or other antiseptic, pour into the hollow of his left palm a pink shampoo and briskly work up a thick lather on his head. He would then wash off the soapy froth and dry his hair with a clean towel and an electric hair-dryer. After that he would rub into his scalp expensive hair oils (Mr Moonreddy was very careful in the selection of hair preparations: "Only the best," he would say with a golden-toothed smile); he would then comb his long hair backwards and with deft fingers set the waves. Finally, he would shower his head with a sweet-scented spray to keep his hair firmly in place for the day. And, before setting out on the long walk to the station to take the train to Johannesburg where he worked at an hotel as a waiter, he would glance at himself in the mirror, and smile approvingly.

Mr Moonreddy was a bachelor and lived with the widow Moodley and her ten-year-old daughter in the area mock-humorously called "Dry Bones" in Lenasia, on account of the rough-and-ready, monotonously homogeneous, rectangular houses and the dusty, rutted roads. The widow Moodley was a spry little woman of about forty, pleasant, gossipy, very clean, with a strong penchant for maroon-coloured saris. Her hair was always neatly gathered in a bun at the back of her head, with a comb or two to keep it in place. Mr Moonreddy's first requirement as far as housekeeping went was cleanliness, and he often boasted that the widow Moodley was one of the few women who kept the customs of the "dirty Tamils" out of her home. The widow's daughter was a weak-eyed girl, but very industrious, and Mr Moonreddy would occasionally bring her a delicacy, such as a grilled lobster, from the hotel where he worked.

That Mr Moonreddy was a waiter was no fault of his. He was convinced that he had been cut out for a better vocation in life, but that he had been the victim of "unpropitious circumstances, unpropitious circumstances, gentlemen". He uttered these words in the local bar one day in the company of some teachers who frequented the place. The "unpropitious circumstances" happened to be the poverty of his parents. They had slaved in the sugar-cane fields of Natal, and they had found it hard, with their low resources, to keep their only son in school. As a consequence he had left after Standard Four ("Year after year I topped class, and my teacher said it was real tragedy that I leave") and his education had come to an end. Later, after a few years, an "inauspicious period" set in with the death of his parents; he was left to fend for himself. He became a "waiter by profession" and moved from Natal to Johannesburg.

"Gentlemen," he said to the group of teachers over whisky and soda, "you see me, Mr Moonreddy, a self-made man not educated like you, not belonging to intellectual class, but a waiter. Yet a waiter of distinction."

"A waiter of distinction," someone said in a voice tinged with an ironic undertone. "Let us drink to him."

They swilled their whisky with evident satisfaction. One of the teachers offered to buy another round of drinks. Mr Moonreddy stood up and said, " No, gentlemen, you not buy me drink. Let it never be said that I cannot buy teacher colleagues drink." He placed his hand in his trouser pocket and produced a wad of notes. The teachers looked at the money enviously, for they were a poorly paid lot.

"I am fully aware of the financial circumstances of gentlemen teachers. Allow me the pleasure." And he flourished the notes and called the steward.

"Steward, come here, hurry up!"

The steward, a lazy, thin fellow, shuffled up, and Mr Moonreddy ordered whisky and soda for all.

One of the teachers, seeking a bit of amusement, inquired slyly: "Mr Moonreddy, when the whites at the hotel call you, do they show any kind of respect?"

Mr Moonreddy was outraged. He eyed the man for a moment with glazed, tipsy eyes.

"Look here, man. I am not any Tom or Dick. I am Mr Moonreddy of Lawrence Hotel, you understand?"

"And I am Mr Ram of Republic Bar," said the steward, coming up with the drinks.

"Mr Moonreddy, don't talk to him. You are a born gentleman," someone said in an attempt to pacify him.

But Mr Moonreddy was not easily soothed. He could not weather deprecatory remarks; they harrowed some rawness inside him. He swallowed the liquor in one swig and stared at the empty glass as though it had offended him.

The teachers moved off to play a game of billiards. Mr Moonreddy sat meditatively for a while in his chair, then rose, went to the barman, bought a double whisky, drank it while standing, and went out.

Outside the bar there was the odour of rain in the air. The lights in the few shops shone weakly. Mr Moonreddy went homewards, swaying and lurching along. When he reached Mrs Moodley's door, it began to rain.

Mr Moonreddy's hours of duty at the Lawrence Hotel stretched from about eleven in the morning to ten at night, and he usually took the last train to Lenasia. In this train a number of other waiters rode with him. He rarely condescended to speak to them in a friendly way, and whatever conversation existed was of a cool, distant kind: he would offer them cigarettes or borrow matches, briefly comment on the weather or make a curt remark about the drunk white guard. As the train journey was short, Mr Moonreddy's reserve never really caused any offence. As soon as they reached Lenasia station, they went their several ways.

One night as Mr Moonreddy reached the widow Moodley's door he heard the fierce howling of dogs down the road, and then the prolonged, high-pitched, agonized wail of a dog, its body torn by the pack. Mr Moonreddy stood outside for a moment, his figure enveloped in shadow. An infinite sense of pain and bitterness gushed over him; the cry of the dog seemed to find some accord in his soul; it triggered off reverberations of pain. And when he entered the house and crept into bed, he felt a sort of unhappiness he had never experienced before.

Three nights later he again heard the cry of a dog and he again experienced the anguish, as though his very body was being attacked by the vicious brutes. He stood in the road, undergoing this violent experience, rent by canine teeth. And when the dog's cries ceased, Mr Moonreddy was surprised to find himself in a quiet road, with the houses looming around him, and the coolness of tears on his cheeks.

And when, on subsequent nights, he again heard the cry of a dog his feelings underwent a subtle change. There was still the feeling of fellowship with the animal, of sympathy, but an element of pleasure crept into it, of *schadenfreude*, a peculiar insidious kind of pleasure. It seemed as if he experienced a state of catharsis, a purging of pressures within. If he happened to be in bed and heard the cry, he would jump out and fling the window wide open, so as to capture within him every note of anguish, and listen as though he were entranced by the score of some terrible symphony.

A month later, as the widow Moodley was busy with her household chores, there was a knock on the door. When she opened the door she found a young man who informed her that he had been instructed to deliver a dog for Mr Moonreddy. She was puzzled. "I can't see what he want to do with a dog," she said. The dog was tied to a pole in the yard.

Mr Moonreddy cared for his dog as he had cared for no one else in his life. He fed it with the choicest of meat; from the hotel he would bring fried chicken. Mrs Moodley and her daughter were not amused by Mr Moonreddy's fad of feeding his dog food that was suitable for human consumption, and she was tempted to appropriate some of the money he had given her to buy various "pets' delights".

Early in the morning Mr Moonreddy would give his dog exercise, taking it into the veld for a run. He would encourage it to run after rabbits and wild meercats. Although the dog never managed to catch them, Mr Moonreddy would watch enthusiastically through a pair of binoculars. He spent a great deal of time and effort teaching the dog certain commands, and especially instilling hatred for other dogs. On the way home after the morning's expedition, Mr Moonreddy would encourage his dog to attack other dogs along the road, but he would not relax the leash; he felt satisfied with the dog's fierce tugging and the eager willingness to obey him.

One night, after he had returned home, he took his dog and furtively went out. It was a dark night. There was a refreshing breeze. He passed along the roads of "Dry Bones", skirted the shopping centre, and entered the area where the wealthier class of Indians live. He stood under a tree on the pavement and with eager eyes scanned the street. Then he saw a shadow moving towards him at a trot, and his heart beat with wild elation. His nervous fingers glided over the neck of his dog as the words stumbled out of his mouth. "Go! Go! Kill!" He removed the leash and the dog bounded away towards the running shadow; when the shadow came under a street lamp Mr Moonreddy saw that it was a little dog. Instantly his great Alsatian was upon it. The little dog let out a howl, and then a multitude of sharp cries as the fangs gored into the flesh. Mr Moonreddy stood under a tree, clutching a branch, bathed in sweat, tears running down his cheeks, overwhelmed by a complex feeling of pleasure and pain.

While Mr Moonreddy stood under the tree, he was unaware of a man who came out of his house and threw several stones at his dog. It was only when there was complete silence for some time and his dog was brushing against him, that he regained a complete sense of his own identity. When he had sufficiently recovered, he went home.

Early next morning he went into the yard and — the discovery stunned him — his dog was dead. There was a scarlet band of congealed blood near its ear. An involuntary scream escaped from his lips, a scream that brought the widow and her daughter running from the house.

Mr Moonreddy choked; his eyes welled with tears; words stuck in his throat as he pointed helplessly at the dog and at the two females. The widow and her daughter froze at the accusing finger. They fled into the house. Later they heard Mr Moonreddy entering his room, closing the door and locking it.

The Visitation

1

Mr Emir Sufi was an undersized man who had grown obese over the years because of his penchant for sweetmeats. He was a wealthy man, owning several apartment buildings in Fordsburg. His daily life revolved around three pastimes: women, driving one of his motor-cars — the Jaguar was his favourite — and visiting cinemas. Besides his wife who lived in Orient Mansions in Terrace Road, he kept a concubine in each of his apartment buildings. His motor-cars (he replaced the old ones whenever new models made their appearance in dealers' show-rooms) were usually parked in the spacious basement of Orient Mansions. All his cars were nut-brown in colour; all his suits were shades of brown. He was essentially an unassuming man. One never saw him in public places in the company of his women as he firmly believed that home was the proper place for them, their company only to be enjoyed in the privacy of bedrooms; but his belief was knotted with the fear that exposure would unleash in undisciplined men curiosity, envy and hate. Blessed with all he needed, he led a quiet, dignified life.

To Gool, the gangster, Mr Sufi presented himself as mellow prey. He needed what Gool termed "protection", and so he found himself included in the select group of merchants and landlords who enjoyed Gool's patronage.

With Mr Sufi the payment of the monthly "protection fee" to Gool was a social ritual; by having it so, he preserved his dignity. He would be at Orient Mansions on the last day of every month. Fawzia, his daughter, would prepare all the delicacies required for the occasion. About eight in the evening a bell would ring and Mr Sufi, standing nervously on the balcony, would go towards the wrought-iron gate that gave access to the landing and the stairs. He would open the gate, welcome his visitor by shaking his hand, and lead him along the balcony towards a double-door — its upper half gleaming with stained-glass lozenges — that gave entry into a large sitting-room which was lavishly furnished and mainly used for guests. Mr Sufi and his family occupied the entire top floor of Orient Mansions, consisting of the parlour, six bedrooms, a living-room, a large dining-room, a well-equipped kitchen, several bathrooms, a reception room for tenants and an office.

On these occasions, while pouring tea and offering delicacies to Gool, he would talk about films and film stars, motor-cars, the weather, cricket and soccer, but never asked Gool any personal questions. After half an hour Fawzia would enter the room with a silver tray on which lay an envelope. Mr Sufi would take the envelope, stand up, shake hands with his visitor, give him the envelope as though he were conferring an award, and lead him out. He would unlock the gate and shake Gool's hand once more before he departed.

Gool would make his way down the unlit stairs, holding on to the railing to give him anchorage should he miss a step. If there was one thing Mr Sufi was doggedly courageous about it was his refusal to have the stairs illuminated, not even for the gangster's sake. All the stairs, foyers and corridors of his apartment buildings — most of them three-storeyed structures, rather old and in need of renovation — were unlit. He was obsessed by the idea that a continuously burning lamp was not only a waste of electricity — in his personal creed waste was allied to nihilism — but a fatal drain on his bank account in the form of municipal charges. Should any of his tenants complain of the difficulty of using stairs in the dark he would, weathering a squall of inner turbulence, dismiss the complaint with the curt declaration that the grave, too, was a murky place.

Mr Sufi's relationship with Gool was restricted to the monthly visit. Should he see him in the street, at the mosque or in the foyers of cinemas, he would try to avoid him, but if the meeting was unavoidable, he would lift his hand in recognition, say a word or two and depart. He carefully avoided shaking Gool's hand in public as he did not wish to give people the impression that he was on friendly terms with the man.

Gool was of average height, tawny in complexion, with leaf-flat glossy black hair and a fastidiously trimmed moustache. He was always sprucely dressed in a suit, even when summer temperatures were unrelenting. He was reputed to be a wealthy man. His main sources of revenue were the gambling clubs in Fordsburg, Pageview, Newtown and Mayfair. Once a month he received a harvest of "protection fees" from the various club owners. He also collected "fees" from affluent individuals during social visits like his monthly call on Mr Sufi. At times he engaged in commercial dealings, but his true acumen was displayed in activities of the type described as "back door trading". On occasion he played the role of peace-maker among feuding families and was liberally "rewarded" by the parties involved for restoring peace.

Over the years Gool had subtly integrated his activities into the life of the community and developed his methods into an art. There was nothing of youthful vainglory about him; neither did he display the uncontrolled instincts of a desperado nor the overt cupidity of a run-of-the-mill gang leader. Refined in manners, judicious and crafty — usually restrained, he was capable of uncoiling in an occasional display of swift, calculated brutality that took his opponents by surprise — he was feared and respected. At times he took up the cause of the weak and the poor — he redressed wrongs and dispensed charity. He had been to jail for a brief spell, but that was for taking part in a passive resistance campaign organized by the Orient Front. His gang was not known by any spectacular name, and therefore did not project an image of lawlessness and savagery. His own name stood for his gang's. If someone said, "I shall call Gool," or "Gool is with me," he meant a gang. Gool so completely overshadowed his gang members that to many people he seemed imbued with superhuman power.

One evening Mr Sufi's relationship with Gool underwent a profound change. Gool made his usual visit but did not depart after receiving the envelope.

"Your sweetmeats are delicious, Mr Sufi. Does your daughter make them?"

Gool sat down on a chair and took a red sweatmeat encrusted with pistachio nuts. Mr Sufi, nervous at the inquiry, sat down as well.

"She is a lovely girl," Gool said, biting into the delicacy.

Mr Sufi looked at his guest with trepidation.

"How are your other women getting on?"

"They are well," Mr Sufi replied feebly, stretching his hand on a sudden impulse to take a chocolate-coated éclair. He crushed the éclair and the cream frothed over his fingers. He stuffed it into his mouth.

"Here is a serviette," Gool said with a smile, and offered him one.

Mr Sufi wiped his fingers and mouth.

"I'm expecting a phone call here. Any minute now," Gool said, looking at his watch.

Mr Sufi's body stiffened as though something fatal were about to happen. His mind reeled with the menacing possibilities of the prearranged telephone call. Was there a plot to kidnap him? Or Fawzia? Or was Gool's gang going to ravish his concubines while he was held captive in his own home? Or was Gool trying to implicate him in a murder?

The telephone rang and Mr Sufi jumped up from his seat.

"Frightened you a bit," Gool said, standing up and going towards the telephone.

"Yes . . . Hullo Akbar . . . Have they arrived . . . Send them to Orient Mansions . . . Top floor . . . I am waiting."

While Gool was talking over the telephone, Mr Sufi drank some tea to calm himself. Gool came back and said:

"You know, I thought of you this morning when I was told they were bringing a consignment of lamps. 'Who else,' I said to Akbar, 'but my friend Mr Sufi would have use for them? I always have difficulty in using his stairs in the dark.' "

"Lamps?"

"Yes, sometimes I get unusual things and then I think of

my friends. You have so many flats to light up."

He smiled and pointed to the cigar-case. Mr Sufi hurriedly gave him one.

"You'd best tell your daughter to open the gate. They will be here any moment. Have you an empty room?"

"Unfortunately not in this building."

"This room is large enough. Tomorrow you can have them stored somewhere else. We could easily move some of the furniture. Come, let's get busy before they come."

Gool stood up, but paused a moment.

"The lamps could be left on the balcony if you wish."

"No . . . this room will do," Mr Sufi said, fearing the exposure of "back door" goods.

With a show of eagerness, puffing and looking florid, Mr Sufi helped Gool shift the settee, armchairs and display cabinet.

Feeling faint, he told Gool that he was going to tell his daughter to open the gate, and left the room. He hurried to the bedroom, was relieved to find his wife not there and sat down on the dressing-table stool to assuage his agitation. He heard footsteps and, quickly grabbing a comb from the dressing-table, began to rake his balding cranium. A moment before his wife entered the room he realized his folly and put the comb down.

"Tell Fawzia to open the gate quickly. They are bringing some goods."

His wife left, perplexed at finding her husband in the bedroom while Gool was still in the house.

Mr Sufi returned to the visitors' room and was about to sit down when Fawzia came in and announced that the goods had arrived.

"Please tell them to bring the lamps here," Gool said.

"We have made room."

Fawzia left and after a few minutes five men in single file with boxes on their shoulders marched into the room. Gool directed the arranging of the boxes.

"How many?" Gool asked one of the men.

"Fifty."

"Bring them all up," he ordered. He opened one of the boxes, removed some of the plastic foam covering, carefully extracted a bulb and unwrapped it.

" 'Apollo' . . . Lovely name . . ." Gool mused, examining the picture of a statue of Apollo on the wrapper. "Beautiful . . . Some sort of Greek god."

"Yes," Mr Sufi said, glancing at the picture without sharing Gool's aesthetic pleasure. He did not even attempt to recall, from his school days, who Apollo was.

More room had to be made. The furniture was packed closer, the carpets rolled up. The boxes were stacked to the ceiling. At last those who had brought the lamps left and Gool too took his leave.

On the stair landing Gool paused for a moment.

"A lamp is a wonderful thing, Mr Sufi. But it has a strange habit of blowing out at night when the shops are closed. Now your flats and stairs will never be without lights. Your tenants will be grateful. Good night."

And he descended into the gloom of the stairs.

Mr Sufi's life-pattern had been shaken: he felt as though he had been sucked into another world. But slowly, in the silent darkness of his bedroom, he came to himself and realized what had happened. Gool had converted his best parlour into a warehouse containing thousands of lamps. Thousands! He made a quick arithmetical calculation. If each box contained two hundred lamps and there were fifty boxes, then he now possessed ten thousand. He shivered at the thought of the vast number. What was he going to do with so many? He could not give them to his tenants for — besides the fact that such impulsive benevolence would give rise to suspicion and questions — his tenants replaced burnt-out lamps at their own expense. And as for lighting the stairs, foyers and corridors of his apartment buildings after so many years of eclipse . . . If the police arrested the thieves . . . He pulled the blankets over his head. God! If Gool had wanted more money he would gladly have given it to him. What had he done to deserve this affliction?

Perhaps he could take several boxes at a time in one of his cars and throw them over a precipice somewhere. The thought filled him with hope and he threw the blankets off. He pressed the bedside lamp button and found, by a queer trick of fate, that the lamp failed to go on. He pressed the button several times in desperation. The lamp was burnt out. He thought of Gool's parting words (how prophetic!) and a spasm of fear gripped him. He felt his body oppressed by the darkness. He covered himself with the blankets. Gradually his fear thawed. It was perhaps a fortunate accident that his bedside lamp had failed, for what would people have thought of him if they had seen him carrying boxes into his car like a servant? And he would have had difficulty carrying the boxes down the unlit stairs. Perhaps he should leave the lamps where they were. If the police came he would tell them the truth.

When his wife came to bed he pretended to be asleep, and the pretence mercifully extended into reality.

Next morning he told his wife to lock the visitors' room and let no one in. In future the family's private living-room would be used for guests as well.

But throughout the next day Mr Sufi was troubled. The lamps had been obtained illegally and therefore he could neither use them nor dispose of them. He decided to appeal to Gool over the telephone. He would tell him that although he appreciated the lamps he had unfortunately nowhere to store them. He would be glad if he could arrange to have them taken away.

"You need lamps all the time," Gool answered.

"The danger . . ."

"What danger, while I'm around?"

"Please Gool, tell those who brought the lamps to take them away. I will pay them."

"Mr Sufi, the lamps are a personal gift from me. Every night lamps blow out and in no time you will need some more."

As Mr Sufi replaced the telephone a lamp seemed to blow out within *him*.

A fortnight later Mr Sufi, emerging from a cinema and going towards his car, was caught in a thunderstorm. He rushed into a nearby café. Gool, who was sitting at a table in the company of a lady, saw him and called him to come over.

Mr Sufi was shocked to hear Gool's voice above the din of the storm. He looked towards a dimly-lit recess and saw Gool and the lady. Controlling his agitation as best he could, he went towards them.

"Come and have some coffee. Sit down," Gool said.

"I am in a hurry . . ."

"Sit down and relax. Hurry kills."

Gool poured coffee and passed the cup to Mr Sufi.

"Gloria," Gool said to the lady, "have you met my friend Mr Sufi?"

"I have heard of him," she said, extending her hand to him across the table. She was a dusky woman, her face plastered with heavy make-up, her hair a thick sorrel-coloured mane.

"You are so handsome!" she exclaimed, admiring Mr Sufi's crescent-shaped sleek eyebrows and his liquid dark eyes fringed with long, almost feminine eyelashes.

Mr Sufi blushed and Gool said laughingly, "Look at him, blushing like a schoolboy! No one would think he is an emir with a harem."

"You are also very rich," Gloria said emphatically, leaning over the table.

Mr Sufi looked embarrassed, but Gool rescued him, saying, "She loves picnics. She is a wonderful cook. You must join us some day."

"Yes, I will," Mr Sufi said, hoping that he would never have to go with them.

"Mr Sufi," Gloria said, "you will make a wonderful cook's assistant. I shall insist that you help me."

"You and Gloria will make a pretty pair," Gool said. "By the way, are the lamps coming in useful?"

"Yes," he answered, drinking coffee and trying to hold the cup still in his hands.

"What lamps?" Gloria inquired.

"Lamps to light up his apartment buildings."

"How wonderful!" Gloria sang.

Mr Sufi forced a smile, but inwardly he was riled that Gool should have mentioned the lamps in the presence of Gloria. Soon everyone would know about them.

"Replace all the old lamps with new ones," Gool said,

"and at night your buildings will look like those in New York."

"Or San Franciso!" Gloria said, clicking two fingers. "By the way, one of my friends stays in your building in Lilian Road. Do you know Hanif?"

"Yes," Mr Sufi said, looking out of the window without bothering to recall the man. The storm had abated. "You must excuse me now. I have to go."

Gool extended his hand to him and so did Gloria who said, "Don't forget to visit me sometime. Gool will tell you where to find me." And she blew him a kiss.

2

As the end of the month approached, Mr Sufi's fears began to swell. Gool would come on his usual visit and what explanation would he give him for having left the lamps in the visitors' room? What would Gool say to him when he found the stairs and the foyer unlit? And what if Gool had received more lamps and decided to give them to him? Should he order the housemaids to store all the lamps in a spare bedroom and later, after Gool's departure, have them brought back? What if the police arrived while the lamps were being moved? His only defence would be lost. Mr Sufi was still undecided when the last day of the month arrived. Before the day ended he would have to do something. But he was saved when Gool telephoned and said, "Mr Sufi, I am unable to come this evening as I have an important matter to attend to. Can you come to High Road now?"

"Not at your place Gool . . . you understand . . . I could

meet you anywhere else."

"Then meet me in fifteen minutes at the corner of Fox and Loveday Streets down town. Bring your cheque book with you."

Mr Sufi felt so relieved that Gool would not be visiting him — he would have another month to decide what to do with the lamps — that he decided to give Gool twice the usual fee.

When he reached the appointed place, Gool was waiting for him. There was another man with him. Mr Sufi had seen him many times before in Gool's company but had not met him. Gool shook hands and introduced him to Akbar. Akbar was tall and lean with a sharp-featured face; his sparse long hair was combed backwards and lay curled over his coat collar.

"Mr Sufi has enough lamps to light up the city," Gool said to Akbar above the din of the traffic. Akbar laughed.

"Come, I have a small business deal," Gool said, placing his hand on Mr Sufi's shoulder. "The place is not far from here. We can walk."

They crossed two streets and entered an arcade. Mr Sufi could hear his heart thumping. They were somewhere in a labyrinth where garish neon signs signalled frantically and hideous rock music pulsated from loudspeakers.

Gool stopped at a chemist's window and said:

"Look!"

A three-foot marble statuette of Apollo stood among bottles of ladies' perfumery and toilet preparations, garlanded with magenta ribbons.

"Beautiful. Do you recognize him?" Gool asked.

Mr Sufi looked without answering.

"I was correct. That's the Greek god. Don't you remember

the picture on the lamp wrapper?"

"Yes," he answered. But, preoccupied with the business deal Gool had spoken of, he made no attempt to recognize the similarity.

"That's Apollo. I wonder why they named the lamps after him? Perhaps he had something to do with light."

Gool admired the statuette, then walked on.

They walked into a quiet street. Mr Sufi found himself in a motor-dealer's showroom standing before a red sports car with a retracted black hood.

"Here she is," Gool said. "A beauty."

Mr Sufi looked at the sports car as though mesmerized. It was a vibrant scarlet, its body sleek, low-slung and missile-like in design. He walked around it and read the gilt letters below the manufacturer's emblem at the rear: Farina Spider. Exotic sports cars had always fascinated him, but he had stoically curbed the temptation to buy one as he felt that a sports car would not accord with his image of dignified affluence.

Gool opened the door on the driver's side, got in, opened the passenger's door and asked Mr Sufi to get in.

"Just the thing. Beautiful and fast. Feel the seats. Lovely and soft. Do you like it?"

Mr Sufi's hand glided over the upholstery.

"A little expensive," Gool said, "but what's a little expense between friends? And it will do my image good," he added with a suppressed chuckle.

The salesman came up and Gool said to him:

"We'll take this beauty now. Get the papers ready."

"What's the price?" Mr Sufi asked timidly, his heart lying in the carpeted well where his shoes rested.

The salesman told him.

He took his cheque book from his pocket, hastily signed a page, handed it to the salesman, told Gool he had to take his wife to a doctor, got out of the car and left the premises.

For the first few moments he felt happy at his escape, even though his happiness had been gained at an exorbitant ransom. But later, when he reached his car and drove into Fordsburg, he felt bitter and angry with himself. He should have asserted his manhood, defied the gangster's blackmail. He regretted he had not opposed Gool many years ago when he had first come to him and slyly proposed, during a friendly conversation, the "protection" he offered to certain selected individuals who, because of their status and wealth, presented themselves as easy prey to the wicked and the covetous. He should have taken up arms against that proposal. Now he was placed in a defensive position. Still, he had the power to parry the blow. He could instruct the bank not to honour the cheque. He could even go to the police and inform them of the lamps. There was nothing to stop him. Only in the cinema world did criminals triumph over good men. He turned his car in the direction of the police station. But a red traffic light interposed, an omen of disaster. Didn't he know that Gool was a master, that he manipulated the police? Didn't he know what would happen to him if he attempted to implicate Gool in a crime? Didn't he know that several times Gool had been brought to court, but invariably walked out a free man, free to revenge himself on his enemies? He drove homewards, oppressed by the presentiment that the sports car was a prelude to further blackmail.

On his way home he passed Nirvana Mansions, one of his properties in Crown Road. His concubine Olga lived in the

building. Torn by rage and helplessness at being plundered
by Gool of a part of his wealth — so vital to the functioning
of his urban soul — he desperately craved some diversion
to forget his loss. He turned his car and drove back to
Nirvana Mansions. He parked at the entrance of the
building and hurried up the stairs.

Olga opened the apartment door. She was wearing a
tangerine dress, a red scarf and a yellow apron. She had
been in the kitchen where she was preparing lunch. Mr
Sufi shut the door violently, and surprised her by gripping
her waist and leading her to the bedroom. "The food will
burn," she said, but he took no heed and, entering the
room, flung her on the bed.

Later, Olga freed herself, hurried to the kitchen and
found it filled with acrid smoke.

Mr Sufi fell asleep. He woke in the evening and had a
bath. Feeling physically refreshed — though the money
spent on Gool's Spider still gnawed at him — and very
hungry, he sat down to have supper with Olga. Feeling
restless after supper, he decided to go with Olga for a drive
to the Zoo Lake. She dressed, applied make-up and
adorned herself with jewellery.

They reached the Zoo Lake and parked near some huge
oak trees along the bank. The dark water lay tamely before
them, its stillness occasionally broken by a waterfowl or
the splash of water against a rock. The stillness of the lake
reminded him of the lamps, the journey to the motor-
dealer and his own state of inner devastation. He remained
silent, longing to confide in Olga, to say, "I have a problem.
What shall I do?" But he had never made confidantes of his
concubines. Besides, it would have been a reduction of his
manhood to seek help from them.

He drove back to Fordsburg, though Olga would have liked to walk with him along the lake's banks.

In the apartment Olga undressed. She was a well-shaped woman, her skin the colour of tawny sand. Her glossy mass of bronze curls matched her eyes perfectly. Her entire appearance was one of mellowness and earthy richness.

"You are troubled, Emir," she said softly, sitting down beside him and taking his hand in hers. It was with stoic self-restraint that he refrained from telling her of his burden.

"I shall be all right," he said. "A tenant made me angry."

"Tell me what happened, and perhaps you will feel better."

"Not tonight," he said. "The night will be spoilt by talking about him."

3

A succession of bills began reaching Mr Sufi's address: bills for clothing, liquor, cigars, petrol, household articles, furniture, billiard tables. At first he refused to believe that the purchases had been made by Gool and was angry with the shopkeepers, assuming they were at fault. He rehearsed, again and again, what he would tell them: "There is a mistake somewhere in your accounts department. This could lead to a loss of business prestige, you know." He alternated between fits of rage and helplessness. Finally, in resignation, he sat down at his desk, wrote out cheques, addressed the envelopes, and went out to post them. At the post office he found more bills in his post box. It galled him that the bills were not temporary business phenomena but would come for as long as Gool lived. In order to replenish his plundered bank account — the Spider cost twice as much as his Jaguar — he increased the rent of his tenants. They objected. Some vacated their apartments immediately; others threatened to leave if he did not reconsider his decision. He remained adamant, saying that maintenance charges had risen.

He decided to "divorce" his concubines. The decision was a painful one, but because of his changed relationship with Gool, he could no longer go on maintaining them, nor enjoying them. There was a night when, stretched out beside Abeda, he had been reminded by the bedside lamp of those other lamps — and, drained of all potency, had risen and fled. To buttress his decision he reasoned that concubines were not rare jewels; he could dispose of them and keep them again when his former life-pattern was restored. And should his concubines no longer be available, he would keep others. The bounty of Allah would always provide men with women. He felt glad that the bond between him and his concubines had been based on the barter system: he provided each one with an apartment and keep in exchange for erotic pleasure. He therefore had no scruples in ending the bond. Yet not wishing to forfeit his women totally (their presence on his premises would keep gossips quiet) he generously offered to let them stay on as tenants at lower rents. All except two left, fearing use without keep.

Both decisions — to increase the rent and "divorce" his concubines — were largely determined by a surrender to fear and panic. The first brought him into conflict with his tenants, the second drove him into emotional isolation, forcing him to search within himself for resources to fend off Gool.

At the end of the month he waited as usual for Gool's visit, but Gool failed to arrive. Mr Sufi was bitterly disappointed. He wanted to enter the visitors' room together with Gool to verify a belief that had fixed itself in his mind during the past week; the belief that the lamps did not exist. Lamps! Surely, he rationalized, they were part of the fairy world of Aladdin? Or an illusion woven by Gool? Perhaps he had begun to study magic and the creation of the lamps was a playful demonstration of his power. The strange and sudden manner in which things occurred that night — the prearranged telephone call, the arrival of five marionette-like helots with boxes on their shoulders, the seemingly infinite quantity of boxes, the conversion of his parlour into a warehouse — pointed to the unreality of the lamps. If he entered the room with the magician Gool, the truth of his belief would be vindicated.

For another reason he would have been happy to see Gool. By talking with his tormentor, or by virtue of his physical presence, Mr Sufi would find some comfort for his fractured being. But Gool was craftily keeping away. Since Gool had taken him under his "protection", he had never, except last month, failed to pay his visit. Perhaps he was ill, or arrested, or killed? But he knew intuitively that these suppositions were idle: the man led a hero's charmed life. And as the minutes passed, Gool's absence began to weigh on him and he yearned for the times when Gool unfailingly arrived to have tea with him.

Later that evening the bell rang. Mr Sufi hurried to the gate to welcome his belated visitor, but found two men who said they had brought five more boxes of lamps.

Pale with disappointment and the sudden collapse of his belief in the non-existence of the lamps, he allowed the men to leave the boxes on the balcony. When they left he told his wife to instruct the housemaids to store the lamps in the parlour.

Mrs Zuleikha Sufi was a plump, fair-complexioned, grey-eyed woman, devoted to the rearing of her daughters and satisfying her husband's domestic needs. Considerate and kind, she gave away money to servants, children, beggars and charities. Over the years she had looked upon her husband's desire for other women as part of his manly privilege, sanctioned by religion, and though she had maintained no relationship with them, she had never hesitated to pay a clandestine visit to any of them if she learned of illness or death in their families. She was grateful that her husband had never married any of his women or had children by them. Even the recent "divorce" of his women she considered as falling within the ambit of his privilege. She neither questioned his motives nor regarded his action as something to be pleased over. Perhaps her husband felt that he was getting on in years and wished to stay at home and give her more children. If that was his intention, she was happy; she had always longed to give him a son. Now that he was home every night it would not be long before she fell pregnant.

Zuleikha soon learned that her husband was no longer the same man whose quiet presence had once ruled her life. He was subject to starts and depressions, he found fault with the food, was irritated by talk, by the tinkle of cutlery. She was afraid to question him. She had noticed these changes since the night the lamps had arrived, but she felt it would be impertinent to tread into a man's world by asking questions. She went about her household duties quietly, trying to please him in every way she could. Even when, unable to unburden himself to her, he relegated her to another bedroom, she accepted it calmly, unlike a wife who had always shared her husband's bed.

Emir Sufi's relationship with his family had always been a loose one. Preoccupied with his pleasures outside the home and his role as a landlord, he had relinquished his family to the periphery of his life. He had fathered four girls and their rearing was left to his wife. He thought that providing them with the usual necessities of life was his principal duty. He was a stranger to the joy of playing with his children, of taking delight in their beauty and innocence, even of spoiling them with over-indulgence. In fact, the birth of the girls had been a sharp disappointment to him. He felt that his wife, by not producing boys, had diminished his masculine status and reduced his image in society. But that was not all. The girls were also liabilities; eventually they would be the instruments of the dispersal of his wealth; and more, the extinction of his name. Consequently, his daughters had not been given the love and devotion of a father.

The arrival of five more boxes of lamps shook Mr Sufi; they were a reality that implicated him criminally. He felt outraged. He went downstairs and climbed into his Jaguar.

He drove about the streets aimlessly, but shunned the neon-lit area of the cinemas and the gay crowds. Then he steered his car through quiet streets in search of solace. He passed through Park Road, turned into Lovers' Walk,

Avenue Road, Lilian Road, Park Road again. Then he drove to Crown Road.

He parked his car in a pool of shadow under a plane tree and rested his head on the steering wheel. Where could he find solace? He thought of the mosque. He drove to the one in Newtown; when he reached it the muezzin's call for prayers erupted from the minaret. He parked his car, but remained seated, immobilized by indecision. He had never attended evening prayers at the mosque (having confined himself to the formality of attending noon prayers on Fridays) and the small devout congregation would be startled to see him. They would guess that a troubled mind had driven him there. Several men in black cloaks and white skull-caps passed along the pavement and he watched them until they disappeared through the gates of the mosque. He started his car and drove to the Lyric Cinema.

He entered the cinema without looking at the posters and without the usual box of chocolates in his hand. The film turned out to be Bergman's *The Virgin Spring*. The evil atmosphere of the film terrified him and he fled.

He drove about the streets again. When he passed Kashmiri Flats he stopped. His friend Abu-salaam, who owned the building, lived there. It occurred to him that perhaps Gool had also given Abu-salaam some lamps. In fact Gool might have given lamps to all the landlords under his "protection". If he knew this he would have the consolation of being involved with others. He parked his car and hurried up the stairs, but he stopped when he saw the stairs illuminated. He looked up at the lamp as though he had seen it for the first time. His eyes filmed with tears and the lamp seemed to splinter.

Abu-salaam was about to have tea and was happy to see his friend. He was in his dressing-gown and looked very relaxed.

"How are you, Emir? I haven't seen you for some time."

"I was passing by and thought of visiting you before going home," Mr Sufi explained.

"It's not time for bed yet, but I relax better in my night clothes," Abu-salaam said, handing Mr Sufi a cup of tea.

"How's business getting on?" Mr Sufi asked.

"A little slack for this time of the year, but one can't make money all the time," he answered, relishing his tea. Abu-salaam owned a clothing factory.

Mr Sufi found himself overwhelmed with envy. The man looked so blithely contented that he could not help saying:

"I shall send you several boxes of lamps tomorrow."

"Lamps?"

"Yes, I obtained some very cheaply at a sale."

"Thank you, but I have enough in stock to last a long time."

Elation filled Mr Sufi. His friend could only have received them from Gool. He eagerly waited for him to confess. But Abu-salaam went on sipping tea.

"I am giving you the lamps free."

"Why do you want to give them away? You have so many flats to see to and your stairs always seem to be without lights."

A squall of acrimony and discord beat within Mr Sufi. Not only was there an accusing reference to his stairs, but his charitable overture was spurned. For a moment even his vision was affected and Abu-salaam appeared physically distorted. Enmity welled up within him and he struggled desperately to curb the words that spilled from his lips:

"Has Gool given you lamps?"

"Gool given me lamps? What a curious thing to say. Did he give you the lamps?"

"No," he said, hastily swallowing the tea and rising from the armchair.

"Where are you going? I'm just beginning to enjoy myself."

"I must go," he stammered and left hurriedly.

4

As the days passed Mr Sufi sought refuge in cinemas from his inner torment and constant preoccupation with himself. Cocooned in a twilight world, he felt safe while watching comedies, adventures (ancient and modern), love stories and science fiction. He shunned films whose titles suggested personal suffering. Of course there was always the danger of running into Gool. But he made certain of not meeting him by circling the cinema in his car first to establish that Gool's Spider was nowhere in the vicinity.

One Friday evening Mr Sufi went to the Avalon Cinema. While he was examining the posters outside, Riad, one of his tenants, came up to him and said:

"How are you, Mr Sufi? Would you like to come in?"

"Are they showing a comedy?"

"No. We are having a live show. There are some beautiful girls on stage."

Mr Sufi went towards the ticket office.

"No, you don't have to pay. Come with me."

And he led him towards the entrance door and into the foyer.

"Are you the new manager here?" Mr Sufi asked.

"No. But let me introduce you to some friends first," Riad said as they approached several men.

Riad introduced them to Mr Sufi, and then had an idea.

"I think I will introduce Mr Sufi to the audience and give him the honour of crowning Miss Venus and awarding the trophies."

Mr Sufi was puzzled but Riad went on to explain:

"We are all members of the Spartan Gymnasium. We are having our annual contest, but this time we have also arranged a stage show. Come inside and have a look."

Riad led Mr Sufi up the stairs and they emerged into the heart of the auditorium. They were ushered to seats.

A blues singer was singing into a microphone in her hand. As she swayed she revealed long legs through a black satin dress slit down the sides. The band played at the foot of the stage.

When she had done the audience applauded. She sang another song and Mr Sufi began to feel at ease and looked forward to enjoying himself.

The next item was a dance called "The Cat Walk", performed by a man and a woman and suggestive of a furtive love encounter. Then followed an acrobatic display, a judo demonstration, a eurhythmics performance and finally several rousing folk songs from the Cape.

Then a banner was brought on stage and pinned to the rear curtains. The banner read: "Miss Venus Contest".

"You are going to enjoy this," Riad said.

Martial music resounded and simultaneously a group of bikini-clad women marched on to the stage. Mr Sufi found his whole body in delightful effervescence at the sight of the lovely array of female flesh, ranging from the sheen of ebony to porcelain white.

"Have a closer look, Mr Sufi," Riad said, and handed him a pair of opera glasses.

He raised the glasses to his eyes and gave a sudden start as the women plunged across his vision. They walked across the stage, their limbs moving in unison, their arms gently swaying, their heads held erect. Then they assembled for everyone to admire and applaud them. The curtains were drawn and when they reopened a beam of light revealed the figure of a single woman. She smiled, turned, walked several steps, looked at the judges below her in the front seats, then walked smartly away, the light pursuing her. The spectators applauded and there was some whistling by men. Another woman entered and the display went on. Fifteen women had entered the contest and Mr Sufi kept his connoisseur's eye fixed on them, his entire body braced by the spectacle.

When the last contestant left the stage Riad said:

"Come, you must crown our Miss Venus."

"No, some other time."

"It will only take a second. I will stand beside you. Please come."

Mr Sufi's refusal had been uttered out of politeness and a wish not to dislocate prior arrangements, but when Riad insisted he agreed, as the opportunity of crowning a beautiful woman might not come to him again.

The two men mounted the stage, in the middle of which a tinsel-decorated throne now stood. A judge passed to Riad a slip of paper on which was written the name of the winner. Riad announced her name. Miss Venus entered and

Riad placed a scarlet cloak over her shoulders and handed her a staff. She sat down on the throne. Mr Sufi found a crown of artificial jewels thrust into his hand and he went up to Miss Venus and crowned her. Music and applause proclaimed the coronation of Miss Venus and cameras flashed on all sides. Then all the other contestants came on stage and Mr Sufi found himself corralled by a bevy of gorgeous women.

Suddenly all the lights were switched on and the stage was crowded by members of the audience, congratulating Miss Venus. Mr Sufi was rudely pushed aside. He found himself at the rear of the stage, an insignificant figure banished by a jubilant horde. Riad looked for him, found him at last, and took him by the arm.

"Come, let us return to our seats."

Soon everyone left the stage and another banner was brought which read: "Mr Apollo Contest". This banner was pinned over the first banner.

The word Apollo reverberated painfully within Mr Sufi; he thought of fleeing. But he had already enjoyed so much of the show without having paid that he felt it would be discourteous to leave. Besides, the entrance door might be closed and he might find himself trapped in the foyer. The lights on the stage were now extinguished and the banner was in shadow. Then a disc of light illuminated the front of the stage.

A contestant appeared in the disc and began to display the muscles of his body. When he had finished he was greeted with a burst of applause.

"He is one of the finalists," Riad said. "We had the elimination contest at the gymnasium yesterday. Two more and then the winner will be selected."

The next contestant appeared and he went through the same ritual of muscle display. Then the third one came on. He seemed to be the favourite to win as he was greeted with loud applause.

When he had gone all the lights were switched on and the word Apollo seared Mr Sufi's eyes.

"Come," Riad said. "You must award the trophy to the winner."

"No," Mr Sufi protested.

"Come. Afterwards you can meet Miss Venus."

He accompanied Riad as though impelled by some mechanism within him. Everyone applauded the two men as they ascended the stage. Riad addressed the audience.

"Ladies and gentlemen, in a few minutes I will announce the winner of the Mr Apollo contest. In the meantime, I want to introduce you to a patron of the Spartan Gymnasium, Mr Sufi. He is not only a well-known man, but a man who has shown the keenest interest in the perfection of the human body, in health, strength and beauty which are our mottoes . . ."

Mr Sufi, a short corpulent figure in the glare of the stage lights, failed to discern the hundreds of faces in the dim auditorium looking at him ironically. All he saw was a cinematographic blur.

". . . in what we all have in common, whether rich or poor, learned or ignorant . . ."

One of the judges came forward to the foot of the stage and handed to Riad a slip of paper. At the same time the three contestants entered and Riad signalled to one of them to stand on a small wooden dais, and to the other two to flank him.

"Ladies and gentlemen, I take pleasure in announcing

the winner of our Mr Apollo Contest, Brutus Gabo."

Mr Sufi found a large trophy in his hand and he went forward to give it to the winner. Mr Apollo took the trophy and shook Mr Sufi's hand. Mr Sufi winced at the pain of crushed fingers while camera flashlights attacked him from all directions. There was loud applause, but some men in the front rows, perceiving the physical variance between the two men, burst into laughter. He heard this mocking undercurrent of merriment and felt a gust of profound loneliness, misery and insignificance sweep through him among all those people.

As during the Miss Venus Contest he found himself pushed to the rear of the stage by a crowd and it was while he was trying to recover from his ordeal that Riad took him by the arm.

"Come, you can meet Miss Venus now."

Riad led him to a glass-panelled office in the foyer of the cinema.

"Sit down, Mr Sufi. She will be here in a few minutes. Tomorrow you can come to the gymnasium and take her out for a drive. She is not a difficult girl . . ."

After a while three men entered and shook Mr Sufi's hand, one of them again sadistically crushing his fingers.

"I am Apollo," Brutus said, seeing that Mr Sufi failed to recognize him. In his suit he did not look as big as he had appeared on the stage where the light had accentuated his muscle contours. The other two men were the defeated contestants, Julius and Anthony.

The crowd leaving the cinema was beginning to thin. Then Mr Sufi saw Miss Venus approaching. She still wore her crown and cloak. She was accompanied by two women still in their bikinis and by the men he had met in the foyer when he arrived.

Miss Venus and the other two women were introduced by Riad to Mr Sufi. Miss Venus kissed Mr Sufi and sat down on a chair beside him. Riad addressed him:

"Mr Sufi, we have been honoured by your presence and I want to express, on behalf of the members of the Spartan Gymnasium, our gratitude. As a patron, you will appreciate . . . (Miss Venus stretched out her hand and placed it gently on Mr Sufi's lap) . . . that there are the usual expenses in holding contests, not to mention the requirements of our gymnasium — and that a donation will be highly appreciated."

Mr Sufi took out his cheque book, wrote out a page and handed it to Riad.

Riad smiled. Miss Venus withdrew her hand. Everyone thanked Mr Sufi and took leave, Mr Apollo once again using the opportunity to crush his fingers. He was left alone with Riad. Riad escorted him out of the office to the cinema door.

"Good night, Mr Sufi. I have some clearing up to do."

Riad shut the door behind him.

Mr Sufi stood on the pavement beside his car for a while, a lonely figure in the feeble light of a street lamp outside the deserted cinema.

5

The conviction that Gool had given lamps to all the landlords under his protection took hold of Mr Sufi's mind. There was no reason for Gool to give them to him only. He

was surely aware of the advantage of distributing the lamps
to all. If only Mr Sufi could establish his belief he would
have the consolation of being part of a group. Should the
police start investigating he would not be the only one to
be implicated. But there was an abyss for him to cross.
None of those who enjoyed Gool's protection ever spoke of
it; nor did they enquire of another, nor confess to another,
any dealings with him. There was a tacit contract to remain
silent. But it was vital for his mind's peace that he establish
his belief and in this only Abu-salaam could help him. Had
he not mentioned that he had enough lamps in store to last
a long time?

Mr Sufi visited Abu-salaam again. He had no clear idea
how he would elicit the information. He hoped that at
some point in the conversation he would be able to
ambush Abu-salaam and get a confession from him; or that
Abu-salaam would inadvertently say something that would
constitute clear proof; or that a jest would contain the
kernel of an admission. He called upon his friend at about
the same time as on the previous occasion, hoping to find
him in the same relaxed mood.

When he knocked on the door, Abu-salaam's wife
opened it.

"Abu is in the bathroom, but he should be out in a
minute. Sit down."

He sat in an armchair and waited, but his friend seemed
to be in no hurry to come out of the bathroom. He smoked
several cigarettes and was a little surprised that Abu-
salaam's wife did not come to keep him company. She
seemed to have disappeared as he did not hear her moving
about.

When at last Abu-salaam appeared in his bathrobe,

looking flushed, Mr Sufi said:

"I may be going to Durban next weekend. Do you want to come?"

"Why should I?"

There was something curt about the question, but he decided to ignore it.

"It isn't pleasant going alone on a long journey," Mr Sufi said.

"I shall never go with you!" Abu-salaam said, sitting down on the edge of a settee with his elbows on his knees and looking scornfully at Mr Sufi.

"I thought . . ." Mr Sufi began in a tremulous voice.

"You thought many things! Tell me what you meant the other night when you asked if Gool had given me some lamps?"

A pulse of joy passed through Mr Sufi. So the man had received some lamps from Gool!

"I didn't mean . . ." he protested gently.

"You didn't mean? What! Weren't you trying to suggest that I was receiving certain supplies in my factory . . .? What were you trying to find out?"

Mr Sufi felt a frigid gust sweep through some void within him. He realized that Abu-salaam had commercial dealings with Gool and had not received any lamps.

Pointing an accusing finger at Mr Sufi, Abu-salaam went on:

"You will soon go and tell everyone . . . of my private business affairs. Why can't you keep your mouth shut and not talk of things that should not be mentioned . . . You . . ."

"Why don't you hit him!" a voice screeched near Mr Sufi. He saw an apparition in a green dress.

A horde of words from Abu-salaam ambushed and attacked him.

"Just what did you mean? You think I don't know you were trying to get me involved . . . Even now coming at night . . . trying to take me to Durban . . . Why did you come then looking so upset . . . You were trying . . ."

Unable to answer, cowering in his armchair, his vision captive to hallucination, Mr Sufi looked at the woman near him for help and to his horror saw her undergoing a demon transformation.

"Hit him!" she screeched again.

A furious green-winged harpy swooped upon him.

He found himself in the street, his body miraculously intact. He recalled the aggressive harpy, and a warrior who desperately tried to fend her away from him, at the same time pushing him towards the door which he was unable to see.

6

After several months had passed Gool telephoned Mr Sufi.

"I am coming to fetch you in a few minutes' time. Some friends of mine want to meet you."

As soon as Mr Sufi put the telephone down fears began to rack him. He was now going to appear in public with the gangster. His involvement with Gool was to become more firmly spliced. Perhaps he would introduce him to men who were wicked, more ruthlessly demanding. He waited for Gool on the balcony like a prisoner, restlessly pacing up to the gate and retreating to the furthest end. He desperately hoped that something would prevent Gool from reaching him, a collision with a bus or a sudden fissure in the road. But Gool came. Feeling numb, he accompanied him down the stairs. The sports car was parked in the street and a group of people were standing there, admiring it. Mr Sufi hesitated.

"Let's go in my Jaguar."

"It's too hot in a closed car."

Gool opened the door of the Spider for Mr Sufi. He climbed in without daring to look around and see whose eyes were focused upon him. Gool got in, started the Spider and drove off at speed.

"You must have missed me," Gool said, smiling. "I was away in Durban."

"Yes," he answered feebly, his mouth filling with a blast of air that painfully distended his gullet for a second. Then he was seized by the illusion of the streets, the buildings, the lamp-posts receding on a swift, noisy conveyor belt while he sat in a stationary car, and was therefore not surprised when Gool's premises in High Road came to a halt beside him.

Gool opened the car door for Mr Sufi and they went inside. There were several policemen in uniform seated around a table, drinking liquor.

"Gentlemen, meet my friend Mr Sufi. He owns half of Fordsburg."

The policemen rose from their seats and shook hands.

"Brandy," Gool said, handing Mr Sufi a glass. He took it mechanically.

"Mr Sufi, if you are ever in trouble, these friends will stand by you."

They all drank to Mr Sufi's health and happiness and bit

into oriental dainties.

"You are not drinking, Mr Sufi," Gool reminded him. "Would you prefer wine?"

Mr Sufi took the liquor at one gulp, and then began to cough violently. Gool offered him his handkerchief and poured more liquor into his glass.

The policemen were thirsty and drank without restraint. One of them quipped that dealing with crime was a "thirsty business", and Mr Sufi was surprised to hear himself say that "some people have a thirst for crime", at which Gool laughed uproariously and slapped Mr Sufi's back with gusto.

"We are all in business together," Gool said. "You collect the rent, I collect fees and they collect fines."

Everyone laughed, except Mr Sufi who saw no connection between their respective vocations in life.

"But there is a difference," Gool went on, addressing Mr Sufi. "You receive, I pay. There are the boys, their families, the lawyers — and let us not forget our friends here."

"Yes, yes," Gool's friends chorused.

They ate and drank some more. Then Gool took them all to look at his premises. He showed them the expensive new furniture he had recently acquired. Then he invited everyone to the billiards room. Several men were playing, but when the party arrived they laid down their cues and stood aside.

"Gentlemen," announced Gool, standing beside Mr Sufi with his hand on his shoulder, "Mr Sufi donated this new billiard table to our club." He clapped his hands and everyone followed suit. "On behalf of all, I thank him. And I take this opportunity to say that we shall stand by him through thick and thin."

They all applauded.

"Let me play a game with you," Gool said to Mr Sufi.

"I am not used to this," Mr Sufi protested, feeling unsteady on his legs. Gool led him to the edge of the table while Akbar gathered the balls. One of the men offered them two cues.

"Mr Sufi, you must hit the ivory ball with the cue," Gool said.

Mr Sufi looked at the ball — which tantalizingly divided itself cell-wise into twins — bent over the table, drew the cue back and thrust at the target. The cue failed to touch the ball and everyone laughed.

"That will do," Gool said, coming to his rescue. Everyone fell silent. Gool took his position at the table and bent over, telling Mr Sufi to stand behind him and hold the end of the cue. Mr Sufi obliged and Gool smacked the ivory ball straight into the grouped balls. They fled to the edges of the table.

Everyone applauded.

The policemen decided to leave and Gool and Mr Sufi went outside with them to say good-bye.

"I think you need some freshening up," Gool said to Mr Sufi after the policemen had gone. "Let's go for a drive."

As the sports car wove through the streets Mr Sufi felt that shocked and disapproving eyes were observing him as he sat beside a notorious criminal. When Gool stopped outside Broadway Cinema and said, "I want to get a few tickets for this evening," he felt even more exposed. It was towards the end of the matinée show. His fear was abruptly realized. The doors of the cinema opened and people came flocking out. Several men recognized him and greeted him. In desperation he looked for the gadget in the car that operated the hood, but failed to find it. Gool returned, but stood beside the Spider and talked to several people. They looked at Mr Sufi. Then Gool got in and drove away.

The car flashed across a highway straddling the city and Mr Sufi began to panic. For the first time he conceived the possibility that Gool might kill him. He might drive him to some lonely spot in the country and there enact one of those gruesome crimes he had seen on cinema screens.

Gool drove to the Zoo Lake. He parked the car under some willows. Before them spread an idyllic view: a mirror of water on which boats and ducks were gliding. Gool lit two cigarettes and gave Mr Sufi one.

"Mr Sufi, you know you owe me a cheque."

He produced his cheque book from his pocket.

"Here's a pen," Gool said. "But you will have difficulty in writing it out. Let me help you."

He handed Gool the cheque book.

"I hope you don't mind; I am adding two little zeros to the usual sum. You know how many payments I have to make."

Mr Sufi, beginning to feel restful after the panic that had seized him earlier, did not object. Gazing at the placidness of the lake he saw no reason to agitate himself because Gool wished to add two little zeros. In fact he felt grateful to Gool for graciously sparing his life.

Gool returned the cheque book to Mr Sufi and got out of the car.

"Come, let us get a boat."

Mr Sufi went with him to the boathouse where Gool hired a boat from the attendant. He jumped into the boat and taking the oars asked Mr Sufi to join him. He hesitated. A clot of words declining the invitation stuck in his throat.

"Hold the oar and jump in."

Gool held out an oar to him, but Mr Sufi decided to clamber into the boat unaided.

They glided swiftly over the lake, ducks and swans flapping their wings frantically to get out of the way. There was an islet in the middle of the lake and the boat cut towards it, past other boats loaded with gay young men and women. A vapour, faintly smelling of rotted lake plants, rose from the surface of the lake and Mr Sufi saw within its depths a muddy night. A thrill of fear pulsed through him.

"It's lovely, isn't it?" Gool said, holding the oars above water for a few seconds.

"Yes," he answered, involuntarily dipping his hand into the lake. The rush of the cool water filled him with dizziness.

The boat reached the shore of the islet and seemed to Mr Sufi to have been stopped by some unheard lake's *fiat* from below. And to his amazement, the islet, with its willows, acacias, flowering shrubs and varieties of bird life, began to circle on its own axis. He sat petrified, clutching the plank of his seat. Suddenly a gale seemed to blow into his face, dispelling the hallucination, and the boat's prow raced towards the boathouse.

Gool jumped out of the boat as it reached the landing-stage near the boathouse and held out his hand to his passenger, who took it gratefully and climbed out.

"That was lovely," Gool said, breathing in deeply and flexing his arms. "Let us take a walk now."

They walked along the lake's margin, the western sun flaming low down in the sky. Gool pointed at some water-fowl among reeds and then, kneeling on a flat rock near the bank, drew Mr Sufi's attention to tiny yellow fish. They walked on and stopped on a small bridge that crossed a rivulet flowing into the lake. A large fish broke the calm waters, and they watched the expanding water rings until they disappeared.

"Beautiful. That's nature," Gool said.

They neared some oaks. (These were the same trees near which Mr Sufi had parked his car many nights ago, his heart filled with a longing to confide in Olga sitting beside him.) As they reached the oaks loud raucous cries — like barbaric laughter — erupted. Several hadeda ibises rushed into the orange and red sky. Mr Sufi was shocked. The cries seemed to herald an attack on him by Gool. Darkness covered his eyes as he looked up at the trees. He felt himself losing his grip on life.

"They are loud, aren't they?" Gool said.

He heard Gool's voice in the distance, as though through a tunnel.

Gool had moved away from under the oaks to watch the flight of the birds. He shaded his eyes with his hand and watched them fly away towards the sun's flaming corolla and melt into gold. He then returned to Mr Sufi who was recovering from the shock.

"These trees are very old," Gool said. "Sometimes I wish I was a tree. Then the older I'd grow the deeper my roots would sink into the earth."

"Yes," Mr Sufi said, feeling inspired by Gool's appreciation of the oaks. "They are beautiful."

And he touched the trunk of a tree and felt the rough strong bark. Gool's implied confession of human frailty restored within him the tranquillity that had been so sharply fractured by the ibises.

"We must go home now," Gool said, and they returned

to the car.

When Gool's Spider stormed into Fordsburg it was dusk.

In the sanctuary of his home Mr Sufi was filled with elation. He considered it a miracle that he could still be alive after being alone with Gool. His elation extended into the evening and he was gripped by an expansive, charitable mood. He went downstairs to Mr Das Patel's café on the ground floor of Orient Mansions and, sitting down on a chair which the café owner hastily provided, began to talk animatedly with several people lounging there. Mr Das Patel plied his landlord with refreshments.

"Mr Das Patel," Mr Sufi said, "give everyone here some refreshments and a box of 'Black Magic' chocolates . . . at my expense."

The café owner went around offering refreshments and chocolates. Several schoolboys entered and Mr Sufi told him to provide for them too.

"Never neglect students, Mr Das Patel. They are our bright stars."

Mr Sufi sipped a fruit drink. Everyone was surprised at his transformed personality. They had never seem him in a convivial, generous mood before.

"By the way, boys," Mr Das Patel said. "Yogi Krishnasiva he come out of prison soon."

"When?" several voices wanted to know.

"Let me see." He went to a calendar hanging on one side of a glass case full of cakes. "I count every day since he go jail, but I make sure now." He turned the pages of the calendar.

The Yogi was a well-known figure who lived on the second floor of Orient Mansions. About a year before he had been arrested under the Immorality Act for making love to a white woman. He had been tried and imprisoned.

"In six weeks exact," Mr Das Patel said, coming from behind the counter. "Dey make him real yogi in jail, boys. Hard bread and water. He not get white cake dere!"

Everyone laughed at the innuendo.

"Tell me, boys," Mr Sufi said, "I have been puzzled by the meaning of the name Gool. You are educated. You should know."

"You should ask Gool," one of them said, but Mr Sufi answered stiffly: "It is no joking matter. My enquiry is connected with no one. Do you know the meaning of your own name, whatever it is?"

The boy thought it best to shake his head.

"Gool means rose in Persian," another ventured.

"Fancy calling a man a rose!"

Everyone laughed.

Mr Sufi, taking delight in his schoolmasterish role, began to question the boys again but they seemed ignorant of the meaning of the word. Then one of them who had been thoughtful for some time shouted:

"I've got it! Gool is an Arabic word for an evil spirit preying on corpses. One reads about them in Eastern stories."

Mr Sufi's hand, holding a bottle of fruit drink, trembled and his face flushed.

"No," he shouted. "You are being stupid!"

The boy looked ashamed and Mr Sufi, supported by his anger, was able to regain control of himself.

"Must I tell you the meaning of the word? It is short for 'goolam' and you should know the meaning of that word."

"Slave," the boy said hesitantly.

"Yes, slave," he said laughing, forgiving the boy and

forgetting the "ghoul" of Eastern stories.

"Yes, isn't it curious. And does any one of you know why a name like that should be given to a son? Because of the superstitious belief that it would keep away evil invoked by the envious."

And he laughed again in an unusual hysteria-tainted voice.

That night as he climbed the stairs of Orient Mansions the words "slave" and "Gool" seemed to drum rhythmically in his brain with every step he took. He stopped on the dark stairs, pondering on the significance of the singular irony that a man named slave was the master of his life. Was it the deliberate intent of some mischievous force to bewilder and poison his reason? In a rational world a man such as Gool could not exist. Perhaps he was an agent or embodiment of some occult evil . . . Yes . . . there he was, standing on the second floor landing, surrounded by a livid aura . . . He was coming down towards him step by step . . . He was a ghoul!

The demon sprang upon him and was grappling with him, while explosions of raucous laughter erupted from demented lips.

He fell on the steps and awoke from his nightmarish hallucination, his ears still ringing with reverberating laughter. Fear seized him as he lay on the cold steps, until, gathering some superhuman energy within him, he rose and rushed up the stairs. When he reached the top floor landing his wife and Fawzia were at the gate.

"There was someone," he said, trembling.

"We heard laughter," his wife said, opening the gate and quickly locking it after her husband had entered.

Several people from the second floor came hurriedly to

the gate with torches and enquired if anything was wrong. They had heard horrible laughter.

"There was a madman," Mr Sufi said, trying to regain his self-possession.

"I saw him going down . . ."

"Saw?"

"Well . . . there is some light from the stair-window."

"Did he try to harm you?"

"No . . . I am all right . . . Goodnight."

Mr Sufi went to lie down in his bedroom while his wife prepared some tea for him. In the illuminated, comforting atmosphere of his bedroom he soon forgot the experience on the dark stairs. The overwhelming fact that he was alive prevented him from probing into the nature of his experience and filled him with a rising euphoria so that when his wife brought his tea he said he would have some cake as well.

While having tea and cake it occurred to him that he was now presented with the opportunity to have the stairs lit — the madman would be his excuse — without having to succumb to humiliating pressure from his tenants. Since Gool had given him the lamps he had on several occasions tilted with himself, but had not found the courage to take this step. The practice of saving on the cost of electricity had become an obsession with him. He had also feared that lighting the stairs could lead to his arrest. For instance, a tenant might learn that lamps had been stolen from some warehouse or factory and link the theft with the sudden illumination of the stairs. But, he reflected, the lit stairs of Orient Mansions would not set a precedent. He would never agree to any requests by tenants in his other buildings to have their stairs lit.

Next morning he took six lamps from a cupboard in his office and told one of the housemaids to fix them in light-fittings along the stair walls. The lamps in his parlour he would never use.

7

For weeks Zuleikha had been preparing to attend the wedding of a relative in a distant country town. She had been to the dressmaker who had meticulously sewn the dresses for herself and her daughters. Fawzia was the eldest. She was eighteen years old, very elegant, with plaited thick black hair that usually fell over her right shoulder. Her face was serenely beautiful with dark eyes flashing beneath sleek eyelashes and kohl-blackened eyelids. Salma, the second eldest, was twelve years old. She looked like a dusky Egyptian. Then came Nazreena who was four years old and Ruwayda who was three: they looked so much alike with large glaucous eyes and brown hair that one could mistake them for twins.

Fawzia was to be a bridesmaid and her dress had been sewn according to specifications. Mrs Sufi had visited many shops before purchasing the gifts for the bride and bride-groom, gifts that had stirred her girls into a flurry of excitement as they were given the task of wrapping them and tying them with coloured ribbons. In fact for Fawzia it was a special occasion: it was at weddings that men who wished to marry scrutinized young women and marriage proposals often came soon afterwards.

So for Mrs Sufi the wedding was not only a festive time,

with her husband joining the family — something he rarely did otherwise — but an event that could lead to Fawzia's marriage. She wanted her daughters to look beautiful, as indeed they were, and she sent them a day before to the hairdresser's to have their hair elaborately curled and perfumed. And she had her own hair attended to by the hairdresser at home.

On the morning of the wedding day Zuleikha and her daughters rose at an early hour and dressed themselves. Her husband was up also; he was in the bathroom, and though she felt some anxiety about his health (there were days when he did not look well) she refrained from asking him if he was well enough to take them in the car. She would have been able to bear the disappointment of not attending the wedding: not so her daughters. But her anxiety about his health dissipated when he came to breakfast dressed in his new suit, especially ordered from the tailor for the occasion, and looking fit.

Mother and daughters happily went down to the basement where the cars were parked and Mr Sufi followed them after locking the gate. He was going to take his family in the new Mercedes which he had recently bought and, anticipating that a great deal of talk would centre on the car, he felt something of the delight weddings had always given him.

On the way Mr Sufi's thoughts began to wander from the delights of the wedding. By now everyone must have heard of his changed life and of his new companion. Among the guests there would certainly be people from Johannesburg and they would spread the news, if they saw him, to others. In fact, they would say, they had recently seen him with Gool riding brazenly in the Spider through the city streets.

Slowly panic began to swell in him, and the car which had sped along swiftly began to decelerate gradually. His wife and daughters were unaware of the tumult in his mind as they were used to his reserve. Yes, talk about the Mercedes might lead to talk about the expensive Spider he had bought for Gool. Others might even daringly say that he had been forced to "divorce" his concubines as Gool and his gang had ravished them.

Disturbed by these reflections, Mr Sufi became the prey of wilder imaginings. Thieves might break into his residence while he was enjoying himself at the wedding and mischievously decide to telephone the police and inform them of the lamps stored in his guests' room. He could not . . . He suddenly swung the car off the road and stopped under a tree. He placed his hands on the steering wheel and rested his head on them with a sigh.

"What's the matter?" his wife cried, alarmed.

"I am not feeling well."

"We must get home quickly."

"The wedding!" Fawzia cried.

"Fawzia!" her mother said angrily, looking back. She saw the disappointed faces of her daughters.

"I'm sorry, Mummy," Fawzia said penitently.

Zuleikha saw a house along the roadside. They were about thirty miles from the city.

"Let me go and get help," she said, opening the door of the car.

"No, don't go," her husband said feebly.

"Perhaps there is someone who could help by driving us home."

"I will manage," Mr Sufi said. He started the car and turned it in the direction of home.

Zuleikha watched her husband with anxiety. She remembered his experience on the stairs and regretted her selfishness in not having asked him in the morning if he was well enough to take them. Her daughters sat silently, tears welling up in their eyes. Although concerned about their father, they could not banish the disappointment they felt in not going to the wedding: days of joyous preparation and expectation came to nothing in an instant.

Only when Mr Sufi reached home did the disappointment he had caused his wife and children register in his consciousness. He felt wretched.

Zuleikha helped her husband to bed and, despite his protest that his illness was temporary, telephoned the doctor. She also telephoned her relatives and told them they would not attend the wedding.

The doctor found nothing physically wrong with his patient, but did not say so. He prescribed some sedatives.

8

When Mr Sufi came to hear of Yogi Krishnasiva's release from prison, he decided to pay him a commiserative visit. The Yogi had always been a model tenant and though many people had derived amusement from his fall — especially politicians who despised him for declaring that if one possessed inner liberty political liberty was unnecessary — he had felt sorry for him, for he too was strongly attracted to women. But there was another reason why he wished to visit him. He felt that the Yogi's theoretical insight into the instability of life had gained a practical dimension by his penal experience and that he was now a much wiser man. If he were able to confide in the Yogi regarding his own problem, he would certainly receive advice that would help him.

The Yogi's mother opened the door. She was a bulbous woman whose flowing sari's heroic attempt to conceal her shape failed around her midriff where the flesh came out in rolls.

"Thank you for coming to see my son. You know what people are. They all hate him. Sit down."

"I want to speak to him."

"He has changed."

"Changed?"

"Yes, he won't speak to anyone. And he has given up walking."

"Given up . . ."

"Come and see."

He followed her. She opened a door, let him in and closed it. The curtains were drawn and the room was faintly lit by a flame-bud burning on an altar table in a clay bowl, before a brass figurine of the dancing god Shiva. Several incense sticks bloomed and smoked from a small porcelain vase.

He looked for the Yogi but saw no form seated in the usual meditation posture. Scanning the room, he saw what looked like two upright cobras — as though some petulant charmer had transfixed them. His eyes followed the length of the cobras to the floor and there he saw two eyes staring at him. He sat down on the carpet and looked at the Yogi, convinced that as soon as he recognized his landlord he would bring his feet down. But the Yogi remained poised on his head. To assist the Yogi into recognition he every now and then tilted his head, and when that failed resorted to chanting his name several times, mantra-wise.

He realized that he would have to be patient. The Yogi could not remain in an inverted position forever. While waiting he reflected on some of the beliefs that were part of the ascetic way of life. There was the belief that life was an illusion. Why was this so when everything pointed to its reality? If he accepted this axiom, then by the necessity of logic, he would have to regard Gool as a dream figure and all his fears as groundless. But the Yogi's fall demonstrated the falsity of this belief; he had tried to deny the reality of life and life had caught up with him. There was also the belief that the souls of men entered into beasts and birds. If he had a choice he would have liked to be a bird, preferably a falcon, for then he would have sway over two kingdoms, the terrestrial and the ethereal. Was reincarnation and its related doctrine of karma possible? Could he have been a gangster in a previous life and was he therefore in this life, by the demands of retributive justice, condemned to experience the pangs of a victim? But there was a fatal flaw in this belief, for how could one expiate meaningfully if one had no idea of the wrong perpetrated in a previous incarnation? Or was suffering just a case of occult mischief?

They came upon him unexpectedly, two horrid cobras that locked themselves in a pincer-grip around his neck. He tried to rise — out of a nightmare — shouted mutely for help, dragged them across the floor, gasped, moaned, and fell against the door. That saved him.

The Yogi's mother opened the door and threw herself on the two men. She eventually succeeded in freeing her landlord's neck from her son's coiled feet. Mr Sufi, thankful, hurried out of the room without hearing her apologies.

9

One day Mr Sufi went to collect rent from a Mr Rahim who was consistently late in his payments. When he presented himself at his door Mr Rahim, in an irate mood, said:

"Are you not rich enough? Must you increase the rent?"

His words seemed to be a prearranged signal, for immediately he uttered them several doors were flung open and Mr Sufi found himself surrounded by a host of tenants and their children.

Mr Sufi, though he abhorred tenants who made him wait for long periods or tried to evade payment, had always been delighted that there were a few tenants such as Mr Rahim who never paid their rents when due, for it gave him the opportunity to visit them. He had found Mr Rahim — a small, wiry, lean-faced man with brown, restless protruding eyes — a delightful fellow and had always marvelled at his ability to devise plausible excuses for not paying on time. He would open the door and hobble on one leg, moaning with pain; or appear with his neck swathed in bandages; or emerge from an inner room, his entire body covered with a blanket, pleading in a deep voice that his body if exposed to light would, according to the best physicians, disintegrate. What Mr Sufi was unaware of were the curses he levelled at him after he had left.

"You know you have to pay," Mr Sufi said.

"Yes, but what I don't know is that I have to pay more."

Mr Sufi quailed. He looked at the other tenants and was met by menacing scowls. They pressed closer to him and he felt suffocated.

"You can leave if you don't want to pay."

His words struck at the instinct for shelter in the hearts of his tenants. Several voices assaulted his ears.

"You are a greedy pig!"

"You will die and leave all your money!"

"Bloodthirsty landlord!"

And before he could make his escape he found his face slapped by Mr Rahim. He was stunned. The crowd was stunned as well and fell back, for Mr Sufi was no ordinary man. This gave him the opportunity to withdraw.

The incident disturbed him for many days. Never had tenants been so outrageously rude to him. And he felt especially bitter against Mr Rahim. Many times he had made no demand on Rahim when he failed to pay his rent on the due date. Occasionally he had even condescended to have tea in his poorly-furnished flat. Humiliated now, he could not even have the man prosecuted: the rehearsal of the incident in court would trigger bad publicity for him. He could easily have Mr Rahim assassinated by Gool, but that would knot him permanently to Gool. He raged and brooded, and eventually his anguish precipitated the idea of killing Gool. For was he not the prime cause of his humiliation? Because of Gool he had increased the rent and because of him received the slap on his face.

He spent several hours seeking a moral justification for his idea. Considered in abstraction, it was against all laws, whether those of nature, society or religion. But if the character of the intended victim was taken into account then his idea was ethically sound. Many of the films Mr Sufi had seen ended with the annihilation of villains by heroes who suffered no subsequent conscience-pangs. As for being arrested for murder, surely the police would exonerate him — congratulate him, in fact, for having saved society from a demon.

Having buttressed himself internally, he then gave his attention to translating his idea into action. Should he hire some desperadoes to waylay Gool and stab him in a quiet street, or should he have him run over by a car? After some thought, the hiring of others seemed to him the action of a coward (even films made this explicit enough) which would diminish him in his own eyes. He had to undertake the act himself if it was to be endowed with any nobility. Should he use a knife or a gun? The knife was associated with the common murderer, the masked thug (cinema screens were full of them). The gun was the best weapon. Besides eliminating the victim swiftly and almost painlessly it was the weapon used by civilized men everywhere in their struggle against criminals.

Where should he kill him? In front of his family at home? This did not appeal to his ethical sense. When he was alone with Gool, say at the Zoo Lake? He dismissed this idea, as murder in such a setting would be strongly suggestive of malevolent premeditation. The best place would be at his premises in High Road: murder there would be in keeping with the character of the gangster's lair.

He was faced with an initial difficulty. He did not have a gun, and a law prevented "non-whites" from purchasing or possessing one. He could perhaps obtain one by paying some white man ten times the price for parting with the weapon illegally, but this did not appeal to his business sense. He was on the verge of abandoning his idea when the thought leapt to his mind that he could buy a gun from Gool and kill him with it. He chuckled at the thought. Surely this would be consummate revenge for him? Not only would he feel compensated for the pain the man had inflicted upon him, but he would also be the instrument of retributive justice. Filled with elation, he rehearsed the murder in his imagination. He would go to Gool's premises, buy a gun by offering him a large financial bait, shoot him through the head and leave. He would then go to the police and tell them he had killed him in self-defence with his own weapon.

He went in his car to High Road, but passed Gool's premises without stopping. He returned there, but again failed to stop. Tormented by indecision, he drove through the streets aimlessly. After an hour he gained sufficient courage. He went back to High Road and parked his car behind the Spider. His intention was now diluted with the thought that there was no harm in visiting Gool and that he need not act should circumstances be unfavourable.

"What a surprise!" Gool said, shaking his hand. "But you look troubled. Come, sit down."

Gool took a decanter from a cabinet and poured liquor into two glasses.

"This will cheer you up," Gool said, handing him a glass.

Mr Sufi, while sipping the liquor, considered whether he should make his request or wait till the next day. But Gool was alone and the liquor was warming: he felt he should not postpone matters. He asked Gool about his family's health and then got the words out:

"I need a gun."

"Gun?"

Gool looked at him quizzically and then smiled.

"Please don't tell me you want to kill yourself."

The reference to suicide alarmed him.

"No, no. I need it for self-protection."

"Who is threatening you? Tell me and tomorrow we will attend his funeral," Gool said, pouring more liquor into the glasses.

Mr Sufi could not help smiling. Tomorrow he was going to attend Gool's funeral.

"I must have a gun. Here's a cheque."

"You know it's expensive and illegal."

He took out his cheque book and pen. He felt certain that Gool's greed would overcome him. He was prepared to write out any sum Gool wanted for he would not live long enough to take it to the bank.

"It will take a few days to get a gun for you."

"I need a gun now. My tenants are threatening me," he blurted out.

"Bastards! Who are they?"

He was forced to relate the incident involving Mr Rahim. When he ended his story he was surprised to see Akbar and several men enter the room. He did not know that Gool had touched an alarm button under the table.

"Akbar, will you visit Mr Rahim in Liberty Mansions in May Road and tell him to stop playing with Mr Sufi."

Akbar and the men left.

"Now, that will settle things. In future leave the business of rent-collecting to me and you will have no further trouble."

"I must have a gun," he said in desperation, frightened at Gool's intention to collect the rent. He wrote out a cheque recklessly for a very large sum and handed it to Gool.

Gool looked at the cheque indifferently. Then he went towards a cupboard, took out a gun, and returned with it to Mr Sufi. He withdrew the magazine and showed him the cartridges by spilling them in the palm of his hand, then reloaded the magazine, slotted it, and handed him the gun.

Suddenly fear of using the weapon he held penetrated his consciousness and he was seized by nausea, dizziness, and the paralysing realization that if he killed Gool his gang would avenge him.

"You are not well," Gool said. "I think you should go home and rest."

Gool took the gun and escorted him to his car. He returned and replaced the gun (which contained blank cartridges) in the cupboard. The cheque was on the table; he folded it and put it in his wallet.

Mr Sufi went home, swallowed several aspirin tablets and crept into bed. When he awoke in the evening his wife told him that Mr Rahim had been waiting several hours to see him.

Mr Rahim had brought the money. His face was bruised, his eyes swollen and dark.

"I am very sorry . . . The others put me up to it . . . I am grateful to live in your building . . . I have children . . ."

Mr Sufi understood his terror and a feeling of pity burgeoned within him, pity that had never entered his relationship with his tenants — for it had always been a firm tenet of his that a sympathetic landlord would not remain in possession of his properties for long.

He took the money, counted it, then put some back into the envelope and handed it to Mr Rahim.

"You needn't pay the increased amount."

Mr Rahim, surprised by his magnanimity, left the building a bewildered man.

At the end of the month Gool called Mr Sufi over to High Road.

"Today is rent-collecting day. Let us go together."

He had forgotten about Gool's intention to become his rent-collector. He was now filled with dismay, for not only would his tenants see him associating openly with Gool, but the gangster would require a fee for his service.

"Gool, the rent is usually paid to my book-keeper in Mint Road. Only after the seventh of the month does he give me a list of those who have not paid."

"I see. Then on the eighth I'll go with you."

He left, feeling thankful. If Gool had proposed that in future all rent was to be paid to him at his premises, he would have had to agree. He regretted that he had thought of killing Gool. He had always abhorred violence (apart from the entertaining variety in cinemas) and he wondered what demon had given him the idea.

Gool's intention to be his escort threatened to deprive him of the pleasure of what he considered to be work. He would visit the tenants who had failed to pay; listen patiently to their excuses; assert his authority over them by reminding them of their negligence and irresponsibility; at times complain of the expense of maintaining his properties and the exorbitant rates and taxes he paid; or sternly remind them that failure to pay could have serious legal consequences. The few days a month he spent collecting arrear rents provided his conscience with the anodyne that he worked as everybody else did.

On the eighth of the month the book-keeper sent him

the usual list and Gool telephoned to say that he was ready to be his escort.

He was expecting only Gool to accompany him, but when he reached High Road Akbar and Faizel also seated themselves in his car. Exposing himself in public with Gool was bad enough, but to be seen in the company of his companions was certain to bring about a total collapse of his respectability. Moreover, he found sharing the same motor-car with them morally disgusting.

They did not experience much trouble collecting outstanding rent. Most of the tenants had the money ready. A few who did not have the money, seeing their landlord's new associates, apologized profusely and promised to pay before evening. One tenant in Fairmont Mansions who promised to pay before evening was Mrs Hansa whose husband was a commercial traveller. She appeared at the door clad in a flimsy night-dress with her morning-gown flung over her shoulders. She had been combing her hair and attending to her make-up. When she saw the men she gathered her gown closer, exposing the outlines of her lithe body. She was a fair woman, with almond-shaped eyes, a delicately moulded nose and fleshy lips.

"I am sorry about the delay, Mr Sufi. My husband should be arriving from Durban this afternoon. I shall send him over to pay before evening."

She smiled pleasantly at the men.

"Forgive us for troubling you," Gool said chivalrously.

"No trouble," she answered, smiling radiantly at Gool.

"Mr Sufi," Gool said. "I think we can rely on her."

The men took their leave. After collecting the rent from one other tenant, Gool said to Akbar:

"Will you go on with Mr Sufi? I will meet you all later in the car."

Gool went up a flight of steps and knocked at Mrs Hansa's door. She was now dressed. She was wearing a flounced black skirt and a pale yellow blouse. A string of blue beads encircled her neck. Her black hair cascaded over her shoulders.

"Mr Sufi wants you to make some tea for us, please," Gool said, surveying her with admiration.

"With pleasure."

"If you don't mind I will wait for them here."

She led Gool into the lounge of the flat.

"Sit down. I won't be long with the tea."

"Wait," Gool said, holding her by the wrist. "Surely your husband is not returning today, is he?"

"How do you know?" she said, laughing.

"A guess," Gool said, flashing a smile and tightening his grip on her wrist.

"Let me get the tea ready."

"Forget the tea. Come, sit down, and tell me more about the man in Durban."

Mr Sufi, Akbar and Faizel waited nearly an hour in the car for Gool. When he arrived he was smiling broadly.

"She's a mermaid," he said, getting in. "Knows how to wriggle."

Mr Sufi was puzzled. But when Gool went on to say, "The one in the gown is a jolly tenant," he realized whom he referred to and what he meant. He started the car and Gool laughingly advised him:

"You should get rid of that book-keeper agent and do the rent-collecting yourself."

Faizel made a rude remark and Akbar and Gool laughed

loudly. Mr Sufi was riled by their behaviour. In his attitude towards his tenants he had always been morally correct, taking no advantage of the women while the men were at work. Even his own women had been acquired according to custom and religious sanction. Gool's adulterous mating with Mrs Hansa in Fairmont Mansions was a gross, monstrous transgression he could never exonerate. He felt he was in the presence of rotting offal.

"He is a sly one," Gool said, looking at Mr Sufi. "Keeps a woman in every mansion."

"Like sailors who have one in every port."

They laughed.

"Mr Sufi, you have not introduced us to any of your pets."

"I no longer keep them. Only two are left and they are tenants."

"You must introduce us to the two that are around."

The car stopped in front of Nirvana Mansions.

"The next mermaid is yours, Akbar," Gool said, opening the door of the car.

"She will know how to wriggle," Akbar answered, in confident expectation of making a catch.

There was only one family in Nirvana Mansions who had not paid their rent and Mr Sufi led the way to the flat. It was the same flat in which Olga had lived previously. As he walked along the corridor he felt a poignant sense of loss mingled with yearning.

The knock on the door brought forth Mrs Hafiz, a middle-aged, homely sort of woman dressed dowdily. Akbar's face showed disappointment. Mr Sufi asked for the rent. She said her husband was inside and he could speak to him. They entered the lounge. Mr Hafiz was relaxing beside a radio, reading a newspaper. Two small girls were playing with dolls in a corner of the room. Mr Hafiz, without rising from his chair, asked the guests to sit down.

"We haven't much time," Akbar said curtly, looking offended.

"I have come to collect your rent, Mr Hafiz," Mr Sufi said.

"I am out of work at the moment, but I have been promised a job next week. I shall pay at the end of the month."

"Mr Sufi cannot wait," Akbar said, becoming angry.

"If you don't mind, I am speaking to my landlord."

"Mr Hafiz . . ."

It was a swift lunging movement by Akbar that left Mr Sufi stunned. Akbar grabbed Mr Hafiz, seemed to lift him out of his armchair, and punched him on the face with a crunching blow. Faizel rushed at the man as he fell back into the chair and attacked him. Mrs Hafiz, standing in the doorway, screamed and ran towards her wailing children.

"Stop! Stop!" she screamed frantically, clutching the children.

"That's enough," Gool said, intervening. "Cheeky swine! Let's go."

Mr Hafiz lay on the floor, blood flowing from his mouth and nose. Mr Sufi, shocked by the suddenness of the violence, stood in disbelief, fearful, horrified, his mind still a chaos of whirling fists, faces, bodies, blood, and hysterical cries. His legs trembled uncontrollably. He tottered to the bathroom, put his mouth under the tap, drank some water and splashed some over his face.

When he rejoined his companions they were going out of the door. Mrs Hafiz and the children were weeping. People had gathered in the corridor, but the four men passed through without looking at them.

"Shocked you a bit," Gool said to Mr Sufi in the street, placing his arm over his shoulder.

Gool looked unperturbed, as though nothing had happened.

"One must never be soft with tenants," he added.

Gool had stated the principle which had shaped Mr Sufi's attitude towards his tenants, a principle whose lack of compassion he had now seen exemplified in the raw, aggressive, blind violence of the gangsters. And that the violence should have occurred in the apartment where he had luxuriated in Olga's tropical bed inflated the enormity and horror of it. He had been a strict landlord, exacting every cent owed to him by tenants, at times invoking the aid of the law in evicting them, but he had never dreamt of behaving violently. He had kept his moral perspective clear. The experience in Nirvana Mansions fused into a consciousness already anguished and distended by the bizarre tenor of his life since his involvement with Gool.

"We all need a drink," Gool said, looking at Mr Sufi.

They adjourned the quest for rent and returned to High Road for refreshments. Later, they continued the quest. But for Mr Sufi the charm of what he had considered to be work was completely subverted so that when Gool began collecting the rents — and put the money into his own pocket saying, "In future send me the list and leave the rest to me" — he conceded helplessly.

The disenchantment brought into sharp definition his parallel relationship to the gangsters. He and they lived parasitically off others, spending their lives with playthings — billiards, women, motor-cars — and eternally seeking entertainment in cinemas. He and they had never accomplished a day's work, work that contributed to the sum of man's creative labour. His money-minting properties had been acquired through inheritance; the income of the gangsters was a sort of inheritance received from those who were weak and fearful.

As the quest for rent progressed he was nettled by guilt and constricted by a desire to return to Mr Hafiz, to find out if he had recovered, to apologize, comfort his wife and take the children into his arms. A band of Mongols had swooped upon an innocent family and ravaged their domestic peace. He began to fear for the safety of his own family. His small daughters also played with dolls. He yearned to be with them, a feeling that had not come to him when he had spent nights with his concubines. Then the iron gate was protection enough. His imagination lit up with garish realism times when tenants were being evicted and he stood by looking at them indifferently as they were hustled with their belongings out into the street, the children looking bewildered among the furniture and household articles, the shelterless parents standing near him with appealing crestfallen faces.

When Mr Sufi returned home at five o'clock in the afternoon, he felt his ordeal had ended. But with the approach of evening Gool came to fetch him.

"We are having a party to work off today's nasty business. Come, there will be lovely women."

He accompanied Gool, a prisoner. As they descended the stairs Gool said:

"It is a pleasure to go down lit stairs."

"Yes," he answered, looking at the burning lamps. He skipped a step and stumbled. Gool, with a swift gesture, held him.

"Even lit stairs can be dangerous."

As Mr Sufi stepped into the foyer, passed through the doorway, crossed the pavement and seated himself in the Spider, Gool's admonitory words echoed abrasively within him; they seemed to hold some oracular meaning. But the thought-annihilating thunder of the starting car, the recoil of his body as the car hustled through the street, the swift succession of shop-front pillars, denied him any possibility of the grace of insight.

On the way to High Road Gool said:

"The more women at the party, the merrier it will be. Let's get some of yours."

"They are tenants," he protested feebly.

"All the better. Let's round them up."

Mr Sufi directed Gool to a building. When the car stopped, he said he would fetch a former mistress. He returned with Sadia after pleading with her that he wished to take her to a party and had no other intention. When she objected that she didn't want to be "tricked or used", he had reminded her of his honesty. As Sadia came up to the car, she hesitated. Gool quickly emerged from the car, addressed her gallantly and, opening the door of the Spider, had her seated before she could change her mind.

At the next building Mr Sufi had no trouble. Marina, much to his consternation, said:

"Any time is party time. After all, I am free."

Her sardonic words were spawned by the remembered bitterness of a broken relationship. They evoked within him a time when she was bound to him and he was free to take pleasure with any of his women.

When they reached High Road, they found men and women in a gay mood. Gool introduced his companions.

To Mr Sufi's gratitude, Gool made no mention of his former relationship with Sadia and Marina; he mercifully spared him the embarrassment the revelation would have caused and the curiosity it would have aroused. Gool invited everybody over to the bar which was situated in a corner of the dining-room. Drinks were served. Mr Sufi was glad to observe that Sadia and Marina drank orange juice. Soon supper would be ready.

"Sit beside Eve," Gool said to Mr Sufi as they moved towards a table laden with food for gourmets.

Eve was a tall woman in a shining black dress that concealed her scraggy figure. Her face was plastered with make-up, her dark eyes were adorned with fiercely blackened brows and she wore a three-tiered wig.

"I love landlords," she said. "They are so cute."

She laughed so loudly that Mr Sufi marvelled that a voice so herald-like could issue from her wafer-thin lips.

"Ladies and gentlemen," Gool addressed the company, "enjoy yourselves. But before you begin I wish to thank, on everyone's behalf, our patron and friend, Mr Sufi, for his presence."

Everyone applauded and Eve brushed her partner's cheek with a kiss. Her lips were moist with wine.

Mr Sufi scarcely enjoyed his supper, or rather Eve's supper, for she persisted in taking morsels of food from her plate with her fork and stuffing them into his mouth (much to the amusement of those nearby). When her plate was empty she took his plate and began to feed him with what lay in it, so that by the time supper ended he was feeling thoroughly bloated and uncomfortable. To add to the meal's agony he had tried to keep watch on Sadia and Marina and had been needled by jealousy when he saw them enjoying themselves immensely in the company of Gool and Akbar.

After supper they all went to the lounge for coffee, cigars and party chit-chat. Gool lit a cigar and put it into Mr Sufi's mouth. Then he sat down on a settee and placed his arm around Sadia, and Mr Sufi, sitting opposite him, found his lap to be the seat of the mirthful Eve who, besides obstructing his view of his former concubines, wriggled annoyingly in his lap and presented him with the problem of keeping his cigar away from her dress.

Later, dancing began. Mr Sufi had never danced in his life. Despite his protests Eve took him on the floor. He shuffled awkwardly, tramped on her shoes, stumbled. Eve held him, her face a smirking mask. Gool danced with Sadia and Akbar with Marina floated gracefully past him, the gentle light from the lamps playing on their faces.

Eve took Mr Sufi to the bar. "You need another drink to loosen up," she said. Gool and Sadia arrived after them. Gool ordered wine for Sadia. Mr Sufi watched unbelievingly as Sadia took the glass of wine and put it to her lips. She had been one of his favourites, plump, petite, learned in religious mottoes. Now she drank wine like an infidel.

When they rejoined the dancers, Mr Sufi was appalled to find that a saturnalian atmosphere was beginning to prevail. Several women had removed some upper clothing, displaying their bare backs and shoulders. What he had seen on cinema screens was a reality before him. The music swelled into a tempest and he found himself, as Eve drew him among the frenzied dancers, overcome by a madness, a fermentation within. The swift pulse of the music penetrated him, and he jigged and jived and capered and shook, urged on by the demented, serpent-like Eve.

During pauses in the dancing Eve took Mr Sufi to the bar for more drinks. When he could no longer hold a glass with steady fingers, she led him to a bedroom. His mind swollen with discordant images and his ears throbbing with wild music, he was unable to satisfy her. She left him, cursing, to seek another partner. Overcome by fatigue and stupor, he fell asleep.

He awoke when several hands lifted him and deposited him on the floor. He heard voices and opening his eyes saw in the livid light that entered through an open window Gool's form above that of Sadia on the bed. Nausea and horror seized him. They seemed to be enacting a brutalized, gross parody of his former erotic life. A painful pressure began to constrict his head; he tried to lift himself; he seemed to be fighting against a macabre darkness. Then, abruptly, his consciousness blew out.

He awoke to the sound of a piercing voice, a voice within him, though its source seemed external. He touched his face, his body, the floor, trying to establish his existence in a particular time and place in the presence of two slumbering bodies entangled on a bed a few feet away from him.

With effort he rose and moved towards the door. He found himself in a larger room. In the pale light that pervaded it he saw bodies lying on the floor and on several couches. The room's distorted perspective revealed to him a distant purple door. He stepped warily past entwined bodies. Inadvertently stepping on an outstretched hand that shrieked "Swine!" he found himself catapulted head foremost against a wall. He reached the door, and opening it found himself in a room where an assembly of august personages were seated around a formidable table on which sprouted a brilliant green pasture. A white bull grazed among a herd of black and red cattle. The personages looked at him with contempt as he passed through to another door that gave access into a dark tunnel. Touching the walls on either side of him he journeyed through until he was confronted by the last door. He felt the lock and turned the handle.

The street lamps were burning in the grey light of morning. He stood for a while on the pavement and looked at the houses as though he had strayed into a foreign suburb. When he saw the Spider in the street he awoke to full consciousness. He scanned the street to see if there was anyone about who would recognize him. Then he hurried homewards.

10

Brooding over his broken life, the thought of killing Gool came to Mr Sufi again. As long as Gool existed he would be his quarry. He had failed to kill him in the way he had planned, but his failure had been due to his folly in trying to undertake the act himself. In fact, what he had done was to confirm Gool's power over him. Now, more urgently than before, the man had to be killed. But how? And by whom? After many days and nights the idea came to him like a sudden revelation. He was the patron of the supermen of the Spartan Gymnasium. The supermen were hunks of muscle without intelligence. All he had to do was to order them into action against Gool and the result would be predictable. Gool would either be killed or given such a fright that he would never trouble him again. The whole operation seemed so simple that he decided to telephone Riad immediately. He dialled four digits, then his finger froze as indecision gripped him. Riad's members were supermen, but they were men nevertheless. He had to convince them by rational argument that what he wanted them to do was morally and socially right. They would listen to him and since they would be sensible of how he could reward them, they would carry out his wish.

He spent many hours spinning the argument he would use to spur the supermen into action. When he felt satisfied, he telephoned Riad.

"Listen, Riad, can I meet you this evening together with the three men who took part in the contest at the Avalon? I have something to tell you."

"Of course, Mr Sufi. We will do anything for you."

He met them at the door of the restaurant. They were nattily dressed, their clothes fitting their powerful bodies perfectly. They shook Mr Sufi's hand and Brutus applied his usual vice-grip. Mr Sufi accepted it stoically.

A receptionist ushered them into a pine-wood cubicle with a beaded curtain and a trellis with intertwining leaves overhead. They sat down on chairs around a candle-lit table.

While sipping fruit drinks Mr Sufi asked Riad if the gymnasium was progressing.

"Your cheque did wonders. You should come and have a look."

"And exercise as well," Brutus said, lifting his hand above his head as though he were holding up a dumb-bell. He laughed in a gay baritone voice.

"Of course," Mr Sufi agreed. "A patron must not remain in the background."

The first course of the meal was served: cream-of-mushroom soup flavoured with mint and spice.

"How many hours do you all spend in the gymnasium every day?"

"Three to four," Riad replied. "It's hard training, but it has its rewards."

"Rewards?"

"Health, strength and beauty."

"Of course health and beauty are true rewards. But strength? Of what use is strength that isn't used, like armour in the museum?"

"We are not after strength," Julius said. "It sort of comes by the way."

"Perhaps you exercise to win contests?"

"Only I do," Brutus said, looking at his companions. Everyone laughed.

The second course was served: grilled peri-peri prawns and lobsters garnished with salad, olives and lemons.

"For how many months must one exercise before one can win a contest?"

"Months!" Brutus cried in a muted voice.

"I have been training for ten years," Julius answered.

"Ten years!"

"Yes, and I haven't won a trophy yet. Brutus always snatches it from me."

There was merriment.

"Perfection takes time," Riad said.

"It is perhaps a lot of wasted effort to win a trophy. You should be given countries to govern."

"We also exercise to win women," Brutus said, with an

arch glint in his eye.

Everyone laughed.

"You must have a harem," Mr Sufi said.

Riad smiled.

"I disagree about exercise bringing us women. Mr Sufi is a great Romeo and we don't stand a chance against him."

Mr Sufi enjoyed the compliment.

"Actually the gymnasium and women don't go together," Riad continued. "I advise my members to keep away from women."

They ate in silence for a while. Mr Sufi was quite content with the drift of the conversation. He had already presented in embryo the substance of his argument and would have no difficulty in going on to elaborate it and make the proposal he had in mind.

"I agree with you, Riad, about women," Mr Sufi said. "They weaken you so that you can't face up to life's problems."

"That's the advantage of being in a gymnasium. You forget the world and its problems," Anthony said.

"A little selfish, isn't it? I mean, trying to run away from life?"

"No, no," Brutus interjected. "We don't run away from life. We strengthen our bodies to face life."

"That's a sensible statement. Let's examine it a little. There is your strength which you gain by exercising your bodies for many years. But to what end? Can you give an example of how you will use it?"

"Strength can be useful when you are attacked," Julius answered.

"Excellent! In this world criminals are all around us and we have to protect ourselves."

The next course on the menu was served: spiced roast chicken, fillet steak, rice, herb-flavoured sauce and a variety of condiments.

Before they started eating, Mr Sufi took out an envelope from his pocket and handed it to Riad who looked a little puzzled.

"Open it. It is a donation."

Riad smiled, opened the envelope and found a cheque. He looked at the cheque with satisfaction and handed it to Brutus who blinked his eyes several times and smilingly gave it to Julius. Julius stared at the cheque in disbelief and handed it to Anthony who examined it, whistled, and returned it to Riad.

"Thank you, Mr Sufi," Riad said gratefully.

"To go back to our discussion about strength," Mr Sufi went on. "What good is your strength to you if you are not attacked? In fact, because of your strength you will not be attacked. This brings us back to the question of its use."

"Mr Sufi," said Riad, "you must not talk in this way. You will discourage my members and close the gymnasium down."

Everyone burst into laughter and Brutus slapped Mr Sufi's back. Fortunately, his arms were resting against the table and he was able to withstand the blow. The conversation now veered to films and Mr Sufi did not pursue his argument. He wanted them to enjoy the food and feel relaxed.

But when dessert arrived — fruit salad, pistachio ice-cream covered with a mantle of chocolate and crowned with cherries — he raised the question of strength again.

"I believe that if strength is not used positively, for instance against criminals, and is allowed to lie dead in you, it is a defect. Strength is not something like an ornament. What is your opinion, Brutus?"

The argument threatened the single-minded devotion of the Herculean quartet to physical perfection. They had spent so many years of their lives in the gymnasium that they felt they were useless men, like the antiquated armour Mr Sufi had spoken of.

"I agree," Brutus replied. "But can we take on what the police are supposed to do?"

"No, but there are some people who go on doing wrong without anyone stopping them."

Mr Sufi kept silent for a while to allow them to realize that he wished to enlist their aid.

The final item on the menu arrived: coffee and pastries.

"Friends," said Mr Sufi, "let me tell you what I have in mind. I am sure you will agree with me that while health and beauty are good in themselves, strength must be put to use. I don't say we should set out to destroy criminals, but we should put fear into them at least. For instance, we have the gangster Gool who goes about threatening people. Surely we can prevent him?"

For a moment the four men stopped drinking coffee and eating pastries as though they had suddenly discovered that Gool were eavesdropping. They sat like wax-work figures, eternally doomed to remain seated around a candle-lit table. Riad was the first to recover. As a tenant he knew that Mr Sufi had never shown a social conscience.

"We will have to think the matter over."

"I am prepared to go on supporting your gymnasium . . . pay all the expenses . . . give you each a cheque."

"We exercise for fun only . . . really."

Brutus, Julius and Anthony looked stupidly into their cups.

"The other thing," Riad continued in a conciliatory voice, "is that we are something like yogis, only we attend to our bodies rather than our souls. We don't care much about the world."

"You had some lovely women on the stage," Mr Sufi reminded him.

"They were only there to attract spectators."

"I see," Mr Sufi said, smiling ironically, desperately trying to conceal his disappointment. "Anyway, consider my offer. I am only trying to do something for society."

"We will think about it," Riad concluded, rising from his chair. "And now we must go."

Brutus offered Mr Sufi a limp hand.

11

One went up a flight of tiled stairs in a handsomely designed modern building in Mint Road to reach the office of the Editor of *Glitter*. In case one strayed there were six tablets gleaming with silver arrows and the inscription "Editor-in-Chief: *Glitter* " to guide the visitor to his office. One came to a door topped by a framed oblong glass on which the following words blazed in luminous orange: "*Glitter* — The paper by the Indians, for the Indians, and of the Indians. Be proud of it!" Inside the office, which was expensively furnished, carpeted and wall-papered, with Venetian blinds covering two large windows, was the Editor. Faizel Adil was busily tapping on his typewriter. He was a lean, curly-haired, doe-eyed man dressed in tight-fitting, gaudy clothing. He was below average height with the manner of a restless schoolboy. He tapped on his typewriter, referred to various notebooks scattered on the table, looked at some papers in a tray, asked his secretary — a prim, mini-skirted girl with an Afro wig sitting at the table near him — to sharpen a pencil; and then, as though some urgent matter had suddenly arisen, phoned several people. His secretary did hardly any work; she sat in her plush chair, did some knitting, read magazines, made tea, and displayed her ebony legs to the visitor.

"*Glitter* is the only paper exclusively for Indians and the kick-off has been great," the Editor said to the visitor from behind his glass-topped executive-type oak desk. "Sales are sky-rocketing. Fifty thousand copies have been sold within a few days and what would anybody expect after all the brainstorming I do. I work twenty hours out of the twenty-four. I am a human dynamo. If you know of anyone interested in journalism, send him to me. I require top-grade reporters, men with guts. You know what I mean."

He jumped out of his chair, went out of his office to the balcony, exercised with a couple of dumb-bells, took a few deep breaths, posed like a body-builder, and returned. "I have to keep fit in the newspaper game," he said, jumping into his revolving chair and spinning around.

The first issue of *Glitter* was priced at five cents. The entire first page was devoted to a policy statement by the Editor-in-Chief: "*Glitter* is going to be a great weekly chronicle, a pool in which the community will see itself, a community at play, at work, at social functions. But we are definitely not going to pull our punches when it comes to bashing the community when it needs bashing. We mean business, serious business. We are not interested in who gets hurt in the process. But if there is one thing we are not going to get ourselves messed up in it is politics. *Glitter* will not play the politicians' dirty game, whether White or Black . . ."

The first issue of *Glitter* antagonized all those interested in politics. And Dr Kamal, president of the Orient Front, issued a statement that *Glitter* was a "racist newspaper financed by Whites to undermine and divide the Blacks".

The first issue also antagonized all Hindus. An article by Aziz Khan on "Islam and Polygamous Marriages" included the following paragraph: "The lust of Hindus for the wives of others is amply demonstrated by the sculpture in the Ajanta caves in India. What could be more odious to the Muslim male glorying in the felicity offered by his several wives in the sanctuary of his home than the sight of the promiscuous contortions of the human animal in coition as represented in the caves? Surely the art of a civilization is a product of its morality. Islamic art is unrivalled for its purity."

The second issue of *Glitter* failed to appear on time. It appeared after a month due, the Editor-in-Chief declared, "to various difficulties best known to knowledgeable tycoons in the press game". The price of the paper was now twenty cents. The headlines proclaimed: "African Dolls Invade Fordsburg". A sub-heading stated: "Forty Indians lured away by black sirens every night". The article gave an account of "large-busted African call-girls from Soweto driving posh American limousines" invading Fordsburg every night "to carry away Indian males like helpless victims". In an interview a certain Ismail Yusuf gave a detailed account of his experiences with the Soweto sirens, concluding: "No normal man can satisfy their super-hot demands."

The second issue also contained two pages of letters from readers. One correspondent stated that the "dynamic Editor-in-Chief has hit the Indian world with a big load of TNT"; another from India said that "*Glitter* is unique in newspaper printing history as it caters exclusively for Indians outside India"; another that "the Editor-in-Chief has descended on the Asian scene like a fiery comet".

A number of male readers of the second issue, aspirant victims of the dolls, walked the suburban streets several nights in succession, but to no avail.

It seemed that the third issue of *Glitter* would never appear, though the presence of the Editor typing feverishly in his office and exercising on the balcony suggested that it would eventually be printed. It appeared after an interval of three months. There was no explanation for the delay this time. The price was now fifteen cents. The main story appeared under the headline: "School Scandal Rocks Community".

"Four Fordsburg schoolgirls have claimed that they have been forced to leave school by their headmaster because they were eight months pregnant. They refused to reveal the names of the males involved, but hinted that several teachers and senior pupils were responsible. An inquiry by *Glitter* and its newspaper sleuths soon made incriminating finds — contraceptives were found in several classrooms. *Glitter* is now able to reveal that our schools are hotbeds of corruption and vice, dens of drug-taking and marijuana-smoking where sexy schoolgirls sprint from desk to desk.

It is to the credit of *Glitter* and its staff that the vice going on in our educational institutions has now been made public." The story ended with a comment by "the renowned Islamic scholar Aziz Khan" who said that the Muslim community was "facing a moral storm and crisis".

Faizel Adil walked up the stairs to his office listlessly. He sat down in his chair and looked at the chair near him, his former secretary's. She had left because for the past three months he had not been able to pay her salary. On his left were stacks of unsold previous issues of *Glitter* which he had collected from various shops and cafés after the delivery of the third issue. In a tray on the table were bills from the printer, the furniture dealer, the motor-car dealer and others. There was also a reminder from the landlord of unpaid rent. He rolled up the bills into cylinders and put them back in the tray.

Why had his paper failed to sell? Had he erred, he reflected, by believing the public to be essentially naïve, foolish and gossip-hungry, requiring to be fed on a diet of melodramatic reports? He looked at the bills again and a pith of bitterness against the public hardened within him. He clenched his fists involuntarily.

He became aware of a buzzing sound. At first he thought it was from somewhere in the building, but as the sound increased in intensity he realized it was from the street. He went outside on the balcony and saw droves of school children assembling below him. They were carrying accusatory placards: "*Glitter* is Yellow"; "*Glitter* = Dirt"; "Down with the Editor-in-Chief". They began screaming and jeering at him.

He reacted by smiling and waving at the demonstrating

pupils. Then he quickly went to his office, returned with his camera, and began taking photographs. He shouted at the pupils to show "more guts" in their demonstration. It occurred to him that he was in an ideal position to deliver an oration.

"Silence! Silence!" he shouted.

The pupils, conditioned to taking orders, quietened.

"For the first time in history a newspaper appears for the exclusive benefit of the Indian community, and what does the community do? Bloody nothing! There are stacks of unsold papers in shops and cafés. Do you think that by not buying the paper you will make me close shop? My livelihood does not depend on your miserable cents. Do you understand? You duped fools!"

The pupils began howling. A fire was lit on the pavement with copies of *Glitter*. Faizel Adil shouted: "That's great!" He would not let them triumph; the final victory would be his. He ran into his office and returned with a bundle of copies of *Glitter* and threw it down into the blaze. He brought more bundles and threw them down.

"Burn them! Burn them!" he shouted and laughed hysterically.

12

Faizel Adil came to interview Mr Sufi. When he had telephoned him and said that he wished to speak to him in order to verify certain allegations made by his tenants, Mr Sufi had refused to see him; but when Adil explained that he would only have himself to blame if the public received a prejudiced report given by his tenants, he reluctantly consented.

Fawzia opened the gate to him.

"I am the editor of *Glitter*. I have an appointment with Mr Sufi."

She led him into the reception room next to her father's office. A variety of indoor plants — lovingly tended by Fawzia — gave an atmosphere of tranquillity to the room. She entered the office and announced the editor's arrival.

"Tell him to come in."

Mr Sufi was seated at his desk, examining some fresh bills that had been sent by shops having business dealings with Gool, among them one from Tabriz Gallery, a Persian carpet emporium.

"I am Faizel Adil, the editor of *Glitter*. "

He shook Mr Sufi's hand and sitting down on a chair took a notebook out of his bag, as well as past issues of *Glitter* which he handed to Mr Sufi.

"I have come to interview you, firstly, to authenticate — I am sure you understand the meaning of the word — a report that you are employing outlaws to threaten and beat up tenants. You had a tenant who complained about increased rent, and another who could not pay his rent because he was out of work, assaulted and terrorized by outlaws. What have you to say? Remember, as a journalist, I do not fear any man."

"That's good," Mr Sufi said, reflectively. "Tell me, Mr Adil, what is your age?"

"Twenty-eight and an editor."

"Twenty-eight and very clever."

"My profession demands a great deal of knowledge, Mr Sufi."

"If you don't mind, I should like to give you some advice. Why don't you write about things that interest the public, things like rape, suicide, love-affairs, elopements, and leave the property business to those who know about such things."

"My newspaper has a social concern . . ."

"There is nothing social about property. It is strictly a business. For instance, here on my desk are some bills sent to me by people I have no dealings with. I have to settle the matter myself. I don't have to go to a newspaper editor to complain that someone is trying to cheat me."

"If I were to listen to you no one would buy my paper. Now, to get back. Besides the allegations I have mentioned I have received another report. It refers to complaints by tenants about your properties. I intend publishing both reports if you don't have anything to say."

"Well, what are the complaints about my properties?"

"Your tenants speak of unpainted walls, blocked drains, toilets that don't flush properly, ceilings that are collapsing, dangerous balconies, corridors and stairs that are unlit . . ."

"Mr Adil!"

Mr Sufi rose from his seat, his face flushing as a turbid disorder swirled within him. Impulsively he picked up a letter-opening stiletto that lay on his desk.

"Leave my office now . . ."

Adil jumped up with his notebook and bag in hand, retreated to the door, closed it and left hurriedly.

He ran to the gate and found it locked. Fawzia, who was reading a magazine while reclining in a patio chair on the balcony, saw Adil looking flustered.

"What's the matter?" she asked, going up to him.

"No, nothing. Open the gate please."

She opened the gate and he passed through. He paused on the stair landing after the gate was safely locked, looked at Fawzia and said:

"You are beautiful!" Then he bounded down the stairs.

Mr Sufi sat down in his chair to calm himself. He began to realize that he had erred in losing self-control. If Adil published the information he had, he would damage whatever respect the public still had for him. He would give Adil enough time to return to his office, then telephone him to come back and complete the interview.

He looked at the copies of *Glitter* Adil had left on his table. He had seen the paper before but had never bought one. He turned the pages and read various paragraphs. A tremor of fear shot through him. If Adil did not come back, he must go to him and tell him his side of the story. Tenants were not entirely innocent and their grievances failed to reflect their own shortcomings, which were many. They were given to vandalism and wastage; they did not appreciate his own expenses in taxes and maintenance charges; their children were little better than hooligans; they were dirty in their personal habits; they failed to pay rent when due; and many were under the impression that his apartment buildings belonged to a charity organization. He would tell Adil the truth of what happened on the two occasions when the "outlaws" were involved; in fact he would confess to Adil how Gool was blackmailing him. Adil would pity him and perhaps even come to his rescue by exposing in his newspaper the activities of the "outlaws".

He feverishly looked up Adil's telephone number in a copy of *Glitter* and dialled.

"I am sorry, Mr Adil, for losing control of myself. Please

forgive me. Can you come over to complete the interview?"

"You are not my landlord!" Adil shouted, replacing the telephone on its cradle.

Mr Sufi held the telephone in his hand for a while, shaken by the tart rebuff. He telephoned him again and told Adil that if he published anything that was defamatory he would engage an army of lawyers to sue him.

"Did you say lawyers?" Adil asked, bursting into cynical laughter.

Riled, Mr Sufi telephoned Gool but stopped after dialling four numbers. The thought occurred to him that if Gool threatened or punished Adil he would have first-hand evidence of his complicity with the "outlaws". The threat of prosecution was sufficiently potent to deter him from publishing anything damaging.

The fourth issue of *Glitter* appeared so long after Adil had interviewed Mr Sufi that he had forgotten the existence of the man. He bought a copy at a street corner and recoiled at what he saw — it seemed as if a black gargoyle disgorged a torrent of fetid vomit on him: "Greedy Landlord Threatens Tenants With Outlaws". A smaller gargoyle croaked: "Building collapses on tenants".

The article began: "A well-known landlord is resorting to gangland tactics to terrorize tenants who complain . . ."

He angrily folded the paper, rushed home, then re-opened it and read the entire article. Though no mention was made of his name, it would be obvious to many people that he was the landlord involved. And the word "outlaws" gored him: it linked him with conspirators, anarchists and rebels. Adil had to be crushed, bullets pumped into his arrogant head.

He telephoned Gool who told him to come over to High

Road with the newspaper.

Gool read the report.

"What will you do to him, Gool?"

"He needs a visit. Come."

They found Adil exercising with dumb-bells on the balcony.

"In the newspaper game one must keep fit," he said as they came up to him. He held the dumb-bells above his head with difficulty.

"We are not here to watch you exercise," Gool said in a menacing tone. Gool took the dumb-bells from Adil's hands and placed them on the floor.

Adil, trying to look brave, led the visitors into his office and asked them to sit down.

"Now, gentlemen, do you wish to make a statement to the press?"

"Who wrote this report about the 'outlaws'?" Gool asked, throwing the paper on the table.

"One of my journalists. But it does not refer to you or to Mr Sufi . . . There are other landlords and other . . ."

"Other what?"

"It does not refer to you, Gool."

"Adil," Mr Sufi said, "didn't you come to see me over some complaints by tenants?"

"You are mistaken. I have never come to you."

"Liar!"

Mr Sufi, infuriated, rose from his chair, and shook both his fists at Adil. Gool stood up and placed a restraining hand on Mr Sufi's shoulder. He then addressed Adil.

"Listen, get this clear. I am not going to fire a bullet into you when I can blot you out more cheaply. Go immediately and remove all the copies of your paper from circulation."

"Yes . . . I will go now."

"Good."

As they were going out of the door Gool turned and said to Adil:

"Stick to politics and sport if you want to stay out of trouble."

In the street Mr Sufi told Gool of the day Faizel Adil came to interview him. At High Road, over liquor, Gool said:

"He could have destroyed you."

"Yes," Mr Sufi agreed, looking thankfully at his "protector".

"You know there is the small matter of the usual fees. I haven't had time to visit you."

Mr Sufi handed Gool his cheque book.

Gool wrote out a cheque, adding two extra zeros. Mr Sufi signed obligingly.

13

For Faizel Adil, the visit of Gool and Mr Sufi was not only financially disastrous (he had been forced to withdraw from circulation the entire fourth edition of *Glitter*); it had severely injured his vanity. He thought of revenge, and having enough time in his office to indulge in romantic fantasy, saw himself the hero in the following epic: trapped on a balcony was a princess, guarded by a dragon with stiletto-sharp claws. He was a princely warrior, and though lacking steed, armour and sword, had the pen and the word at his command. He would reach the captive princess and abduct her from her guardian monster.

He began a letter to Fawzia with the prologue: " 'You are beautiful!' These were my immortal words to you when I left you caged on the balcony, O Persian princess, as beautiful as a rose from the gardens of the Taj Mahal . . ."

When he had completed the letter and signed his name he went to Orient Mansions. He felt certain that Fawzia would appear at the gate. He would give her the letter and it would go to work for him.

He climbed the stairs and when he reached the top cautiously looked to see if the princess was standing on the balcony, lost in pensive reverie. There was no one. He pressed the bell-button. He saw Fawzia's form emerging from a doorway and withdrew a step.

When Fawzia reached the gate she saw no one.

"Fawzia, it's me," she heard him whisper.

She was slightly shocked, but when she saw Adil crouching to one side and pleadingly offering a letter to her, she recovered.

"Take this letter. Quick!"

He handed her the letter. She hesitated. No one had ever come in this furtive fashion to the gate. The letter fell at her feet.

Adil quickly disappeared down the stairs.

Curious, Fawzia picked up the letter. She returned into the house and her mother asked:

"Who was at the gate, Fawzia?"

"Only a hawker, mother. I sent him away."

Later, she read the letter several times. Slowly her body chemistry began to respond to the flattering references to her beauty and person and to the call of the male: "Break open the gate, descend the stairs and come into my arms, your dying-in-love prince . . ."

Fawzia had never received a love letter from anyone. Her ideas of love and marriage were conventional. One day her parents would receive a proposal of marriage from a relative, they would accept, and she would marry the man and love him. Her mother had already been preparing her for her eventual role as wife, and initiating her, with extreme delicacy, into the mysteries of bodily union and child-bearing. Now Adil's letter came to disturb her, with its appeal to her individuality and the power of her being over him. She found herself caught in the subtle joy of being desired and yearned to experience the romantic love he offered her at a secret meeting.

On the pretext that she wanted something from the shops, Fawzia hurried to meet her lover.

It was a brief meeting in a park. She returned home with her ears ringing with Adil's love rhetoric.

The next meeting led to a succession of others, and after two months Fawzia knew that she was pregnant. She confessed to Adil.

"I must marry you as soon as possible. Tell your father."

"My father!"

"Tell your mother to tell him if you are afraid. He will come to offer you to me."

Fawzia, dreading the consequences, confessed to her mother. Her mother was shocked and angry, but after several hours her protective feelings ruled and she began to accept the irreversibility of her daughter's condition. Fawzia must marry Adil as soon as possible. Although there would be gossip, it would come to an end when the couple settled down to domestic life. She would speak to her husband as soon as she found him in an untroubled mood. She had through the days and months sensed the stresses within him, stresses which she knew originated in his nexus with Gool. But her subject position had prevented her from reaching out to him.

She told her husband one night while serving him tea and cake in the dining-room. He had arrived from the cinema where he had seen a comedy.

"Fawzia is pregnant," she declared firmly.

She felt that a resolutely stated truth would be best as decisive action was needed if Fawzia — and the family — was to be saved from ignominy and disgrace.

"Pregnant?" he enquired vaguely while slicing a cream cake. His wife looked at him, bewildered. Had he failed to hear her? She repeated her words.

He ate some cake and drank some tea. Then he enquired, again vaguely:

"She's not married yet, is she?"

"No," she said. "But she must marry Faizel Adil soon."

She left hurriedly, went to her bedroom and wept.

The revelation had come to him like an instant inner explosion, a silent demolition which left his physical self intact and his neural reflexes functioning normally.

After he had had enough tea and cake, he sat for over an hour in a state of inertia. It was past midnight when his body, tenanted by some mobile being, led him to his bedroom.

Next morning Mr Sufi questioned his wife further and realized that there was nothing else to be done but visit Adil and arrange for his daughter's marriage.

He found Adil playing with a tennis ball on the balcony, flinging it against the wall and catching it skilfully as it rebounded. Mr Sufi stopped a short distance away, fearing to approach nearer as Adil seemed to be working himself into a frenzy, ball and man intertwined in some fierce battle. Suddenly the ball shot back from the wall at a tangent and struck Mr Sufi's head. "Ha!" Adil shouted, and with incredible acrobatic dexterity leapt at the ball as it rebounded. He caught it with a cry of "Good catch!" and flung it at Mr Sufi who thrust his hands at the missile. The ball struck his arm and was deflected over the balustrade to the street below. Adil jumped on the balustrade, and waving his arms, shouted at passers-by to retrieve the ball which had rolled under a motor-car. Mr Sufi, fearing that he would fall headlong, rushed towards him to save him.

"Come father," Adil said, jumping down. "I can see you have come to offer me something. Where is our friend today?"

They entered the office. Mr Sufi sat down on a chair and pretended not to have heard the question.

"Adil, you will have to marry Fawzia."

"Any minute, father. Bring the priest. She is beautiful and she is pregnant."

"Your parents . . ."

"I am an independent man, as you know, with my own newspaper. Nobody controls Faizel Adil's actions."

Mr Sufi was filled with intense loathing for the man. Man? He seemed to be the spawn of some foul brute and nasty sprite — a little while ago he had been perched on the balustrade, flapping his arms. If he had not come for his daughter's sake, he would have fled.

"You know, there are our customs."

"Of course. I have already told my parents. They will visit you in a day or two. They must hurry, otherwise there is going to be disgrace, for me, for you, Fawzia, the child, everyone."

"Yes," Mr Sufi said, a little pleased that Adil was perceptive of the consequences.

"And I shall also soon be in disgrace, father. And all because of your friend. Look at the papers in that tray before you."

He unrolled the paper cylinders and saw that they were letters of demand from the printer, stationer, furnisher, the landlord, the motor-car dealer and others.

"I may be in jail before the wedding takes place."

Mr Sufi examined the bills and felt a strange sense of pity for Adil pulse through him as though he too were the victim of an unscrupulous blackmailer. He took out his cheque book and began writing out cheques in payment of the accounts.

"I am grateful," Adil murmured as a cunning smile crossed his lips.

"You have an expensive car," Mr Sufi said, writing out the last cheque.

"It helps my image as Editor-in-Chief."

The words chilled Mr Sufi; they evoked reverberations of similar words he had heard before.

"Thank you," Adil said, taking all the cheques from Mr Sufi's hand. "I will rush my parents with the wedding arrangements."

"Let them come soon," Mr Sufi said, rising from his chair. He hoped that his gesture in paying Adil's debts would bind his future son-in-law to him. Though he disliked him intensely, there was the possibility that he might change.

"Your friend ruined me," Adil said, feigning misery. "Fawzia will have no wedding jewellery."

Mr Sufi looked at him for a moment, then wrote out another cheque.

After Mr Sufi left, Faizel Adil flung all the cheques in the air and gleefully watched them fall on the table. He chuckled, then laughed uproariously.

Adil's parents failed to arrive, and when after a week Mr Sufi telephoned him he received no answer. He went to Adil's office and found the door locked. He made inquiries from people in the building, but no one knew of Adil's whereabouts or of his family's. As day succeeded day, he realized that the man had fled. He told his wife of his suspicion and left it to her to tell Fawzia.

Fawzia was disconsolate for many days. She telephoned Adil's office many times and heard his telephone ring in continuous bursts of mocking metal laughter. She disbelieved her father's story of the cheques he had given Adil until he went to the bank and brought the paid cheques. Her sudden abandonment by her mercurial lover, her yearning for him, her ignominious pregnancy came as a traumatic experience.

Fawzia's agony and fate — who would marry her with an illegitimate child? Or even if the child were given away for adoption? — wrung the fibres of her father's being as nothing else had ever done, not even his involvement with Gool. Earlier the object of his preoccupation and worry had been himself. He now found the dimension of his suffering lifted to a new height. The sight of his daughter, doomed to an unhappy life by that mentally grotesque, sensual monster Faizel Adil (a monster who painfully revealed to him something of his own sensual image) filled him with profound love which he was unable to express, for he had never found the time to become part of the lives of his children. And he was seized by fear for the safety of his other daughters: they too were vulnerable. Love and compassion for them filled him.

To save Fawzia from having an illegitimate child and prevent the inevitable public stigma, he decided to send her to Cape Town to his wife's brother and ask him to arrange an illegal abortion. When he informed his wife of his plan she felt unhappy as she feared for Fawzia's subsequent health, but she bent to her husband's wish. He telephoned his brother-in-law and Fawzia was taken to the airport and sent off.

She returned after a month, looking pale and thin, physically and emotionally drained of life. She felt numb with bewilderment at the disastrous end to her love affair. Her mother consoled her as best she could — though in private she grieved at her daughter's fate — and undertook the task of restoring her to health again.

14

With the passage of days the idea that he was being persecuted by supernatural evil invoked by his tenants' curses germinated in Mr Sufi's mind. It was a fact that everywhere landlords were regarded with ill will by tenants who suffered from the chronic delusion that they were being swindled, and it was also a fact that their wealth and social standing aroused envy and hate. How else could his misfortune be explained? Gool, Abu-salaam, Mr Rahim, Faizel Adil, the thieves who stole the lamps, were all tied in a conspiracy against him. Of course they were not conscious that they were acting collectively against him. Even Fawzia's aborted love affair could be explained on the basis of a supernaturally inspired conspiracy. She had led a secluded life, never harmed anyone nor committed any evil. She was an innocent victim because she was his daughter. As for Faizel Adil, his very nature was inhuman; he was surely not himself when he set out on his knave's course. Gool himself, the man who had set evil in motion against him, was not to blame; he was merely the agent of some sort of unearthly Dracula. Therefore his attempt to marshall the help of the supermen of the Spartan Gymnasium had been doomed from the beginning. Even Mr Rahim, an otherwise charming man, had found himself filled with irrational hate for one who provided him with shelter. All the evidence suggested that he was the object of a visitation, and his only resource against it was to enlist the aid of men who were capable of pacifying the forces of evil. He would consult Molvi Haroon, the priest at the Newtown mosque. An amulet of various extracts from the Koran should successfully ward off all evil invoked by unbenign imprecations and perhaps the Molvi could also arrange some special prayer for him to perform. Convinced that these measures would bring an end to his misfortune, he resolved to seek the priest's aid.

The next day was Friday and he rose from bed earlier than usual. While having his bath, he considered whether he should consult Molvi Haroon at the mosque or at his home. If he spoke to the Molvi unceremoniously in the mosque gossip and suspicion could arise, and if he went to his home like a suppliant he would be demeaning himself. His best course was to invite the Molvi to lunch after prayers, and over lunch broach the matter. He emerged from the steaming bath and towelled himself briskly. He felt a certain glow and vigour returning to his body.

After leaving word with his wife that he would be bringing Molvi Haroon home for lunch, he went down to the basement, climbed into his Jaguar and drove towards the mosque.

It was no more than a few minutes from his house, and when he reached it he realized that noon prayers would not take place for an hour. He sauntered into the mosque yard and stood for a while gazing at the goldfish and the red water lilies. He sat down on a bench beside an oleander tree. The tranquil atmosphere filled him with serenity and he decided to enter the mosque and spend his time reading the Koran until the congregation arrived and prayers began.

When he entered the mosque he was surprised to see Molvi Haroon seated in a corner reading the Koran. The Molvi glanced at him and went on reading. He saw a Koran on the window-sill, took it and squatted on the carpet. As he had never bothered to read the Koran since his youth when he had attended a religious seminary, he now found the Arabic alphabet meaningless and he began to be afflicted by doubts about his coming to the mosque earlier than usual. However, when he had read repeatedly the first chapter, which he knew by heart as it was the prelude to every prayer, the Arabic alphabet unlocked its mystery.

When people began arriving they looked at him, head bowed over the Koran, in surprise. They had seen him at Friday prayers, but this was the first time they had seen him arrive before them and sit down to read the Koran.

He had stopped reading a little while ago, though he kept his eyes focused on a page. He was debating how to approach Molvi Haroon. Should he wait for him outside the mosque after prayers and then, as soon as he appeared, go up to him and invite him? Or should he stand close behind him during prayers and immediately afterwards take him by the arm proprietorially and lead him to his Jaguar? Both methods had this disadvantage: that they would draw the attention of the congregation and lead to speculation regarding his motives. Yet he could not delay in inviting him; there was the danger that someone else might do so first. There were always several people who wished to be hosts of the Molvi on a Friday.

More people entered the mosque, the muezzin went up the minaret to intone the call for prayers and the congregation was summoned. Mr Sufi stood behind Molvi Haroon and during prayers all his thoughts were concentrated on whether Molvi Haroon would accept the invitation which he intended making as soon as prayers were over.

When Molvi Haroon recited the final prayer, he braced himself to extend his hand in greeting. The prayer over, he rose from the carpet, but found himself prevented from moving forward by a heavy hand on his shoulder, the hand of the man who had prayed beside him — Gool! Gool took his hand and shook it and asked him how he was. Confused, in a state of panic, he did not know what to say, but was saved further bewilderment by Molvi Haroon who came up to them and greeted them.

"You must come home for lunch, Molvi Haroon," Gool said in Gujarati before Mr Sufi could gather himself and articulate his invitation. Nevertheless, unable to curb the words springing to his lips, he extended his invitation, but the Molvi declined saying that he was religiously bound to accept the first one. Gool asked Mr Sufi to join them but he said his family would be waiting for him. The trio left the mosque and when they parted Mr Sufi saw Molvi Haroon entering Gool's Spider with what seemed like a derisive look at him. He felt bitterly piqued at being slighted. Surely the holy man should have given precedence to an honourable man's invitation?

Though thwarted by Gool, he was determined to consult the Molvi that day, and after a solitary lunch — his wife and children never dined with him — and an hour of aimless driving in his car, he drove to the Molvi's residence in Lovers' Walk.

The Molvi was pleased to see him. He was dressed in a blue cotton smock and looked even more dwarfish than when dressed in his long coat, trousers and turban. That this physically stunted man — now looking so obsequious — had spurned his invitation rankled within him.

In the sitting-room Mr Sufi immediately confided, in Gujarati, his reason for the visit. Some misfortune had come his way and he wanted help.

"Yes," the Molvi said, "I will make up an amulet for you and also compile a schedule of prayers which you can recite at home without taking the trouble of coming to the mosque."

Mr Sufi thought his last few words to be barbed with an implied jeer at his religious indifference.

"Is there any fee, Molvi Haroon?"

"There is no fee, brother Sufi. But should you wish to offer a gift there is no restrictive law in Islamic jurisprudence."

"I should like to reward you," he said, as an idea unfolded in his mind. "When can I come to collect the amulet and the schedule of prayers?"

"Let me see . . . Monday morning should do."

Mr Sufi took leave, chuckling at the idea occupying his mind.

On Monday morning he told his wife to instruct one of the housemaids to take a box of lamps from the parlour and place it in his car.

He drove to the Molvi's residence. The Molvi gave him the amulet and the schedule of prayers, and also, as a special favour, recited a prayer for his welfare and happiness. When he had ended, Mr Sufi said:

"I went to a sale last week and bought some lamps. I want to give you some as a gift."

The Molvi thanked him gratefully, though he seemed somewhat surprised at the nature of the gift.

"Will you tell your housemaid to come with us to the car outside."

They went outside. The maid took the box of lamps and placing it on her head — much to the consternation of Mr Sufi, who thought it a risky way of conveying fragile (and stolen!) things — serenely carried it into the house.

He shook hands with the Molvi and left. He felt satisfied at his courage in giving away a box of the lamps. In future he would not allow people to impose on him; he would impose on them. His problems, he decided, were largely due to his lack of those qualities of firm resolution and positive action so vital in achieving success in this world, as the cinema screen so often testified.

When he reached home he tied the amulet, a black cloth sachet containing relevant extracts from the Koran, around his neck so that it hung like a pendant. Then he called the housemaids and boldly ordered them to remove the lamps from the parlour and store them in a vacant corner of the basement.

It was at this time that he made a surprising discovery. On each box appeared the inscription: Atlas Electrical Company. Contents: 100 Apollo lamps. He recalled that the figure 200 had entered his calculation during the night the lamps arrived. If only he had known the correct figure then! What a price he had paid for his error in terms of redoubled inner stress and mental attrition! The discovery reinforced his determination to respond positively to life.

One night while parking his car in the basement after returning from the cinema, it occurred to him that he could easily take several boxes of lamps in one of his cars into the country and there throw them over a precipice into a hollow. He quickly placed six boxes in the boot of his largest car, a Chrysler, and drove out. He was gripped by elation. He would spend the night transporting the lamps out of the city.

He drove along the highway. When he reached open country he turned onto a gravel road and drove on. The road went down a slope and past some gigantic boulders. When he neared a bend in the road he saw in the yellow shafts of the headlights a cluster of ruined huts beside some trees. He drove cautiously over a track towards the huts. The headlights showed broken walls, thatched roofs that had partly fallen, pieces of rusted zinc among some debris. He stopped near the huts, got out of the car, and opening the boot took a box of lamps and carried it into a hut. After he had placed all the boxes in the hut he drove back home. On his second journey he brought ten boxes; he placed some on the rear seat of the car.

He made several more journeys until he had brought all the boxes. He placed some in each of the huts, covered them with pieces of zinc and then carefully concealed them with wads of roof straw. Satisfied that the lamps would be safe for some time he returned home. Had he thrown them down some precipice he would have felt unhappy about their wasteful destruction. Now perhaps someone would find them, tell the owner of the farm, and he would return them to the manufacturers.

When he reached home it was past three in the morning. He went into the visitors' room and switched on the lights. He sat down in an armchair and was filled with a profound sense of relief. The incubus that had usurped his parlour had at last been dispelled.

In his bedroom he took a vow that he would undertake the obligatory pilgrimage to Mecca as soon as his affairs were settled. Now that the lamps were out of the way, he was in a position to stop Gool continuing to blackmail him. If necessary he would have him indicted in court; the cheques he had drawn would be sufficient evidence to have him imprisoned for a long time. Before going to bed, he read the "Prayer before sleeping" prescribed in the schedule. He slept peacefully and dreamt about Olga.

The next day was a happy one for Mr Sufi. He went to the cinema as usual and enjoyed himself. He felt that he was on the verge of regaining his former life with all its pleasures. In the evening he decided to go in search of Olga.

Since the incident in Nirvana Mansions he had thought of her several times. He had not fully appreciated her when he could possess her at will. Now her absence magnified her loveliness of character rather than her mellow body: her considerate nature, her soft speech, her courtesy. She had been the gentlest of his concubines. Even when he had told her of his intention to separate from her "for a while" she had not lost her pacific temper (as had some of the other women, who had turned upon him with fury). And before she had left her apartment she had written him a letter thanking him for keeping her and telling him that she would be staying with a sister in Fountain Road. Olga was the only woman he had ever thought of marrying as a second wife, but the fear that she too might bear him daughters had deterred him. He now longed to see her and to spend a few hours in her company.

He went to Fountain Road where a few homes seemed to be strangled by manufacturers' buildings and motor-car repair shops. He knocked at the door of a house and inquired. He was told that Olga lived across the road.

The house was a grey wooden structure on a concrete foundation. He entered a rusted gate and began to feel a little afraid. How would she receive him? He stood in front of the door, wondering whether he should not return home. Perhaps she was living with a man and he might find himself in an embarrassing situation. But his longing to meet her flowed strongly and reminding himself of his commitment to positive action he knocked at the door.

A young girl opened the door. He smiled in relief and said he wished to speak to Olga.

"Come in," she said.

He looked into a dingy passage and hesitated.

"Come in," she said again.

He entered. There was a curtained doorway on the left to which the girl pointed.

He parted the faded curtain and entered the room. He sat down on a chair, hearing a voice and the tramp of heavy feet on the wooden floor. A woman appeared through the curtain.

"Hullo," she said. "Olga will come in a minute. She is in the bathroom. What is your name?"

He told her and she left.

He waited, overjoyed that he had found her. He examined the room. There was a settee beside the chair he was sitting on; some of the cushion covers were torn and the plastic foam extruded. There was a display cabinet with a tarnished trophy of sorts and an antique photograph of an old woman. On the wall hung a faded bamboo scroll with a drawing of a Chinese rural scene.

He heard footsteps and Olga entered the doorway in a nightdress, with her hair turbaned in a towel to take the damp out.

"Olga!" he said, rising from the chair and taking her hand.

They sat down on the settee. Olga was glad to see him. He asked her about her health, what work she was doing, and whether she sometimes recalled old days. The poverty of the home in which she lived made him concerned about her welfare. She was no longer a physical body for his pleasure, but a complex being with a life of her own.

Before he left he asked her to meet him the next morning. He wished to take her out into the country for a drive.

She was waiting for him outside the house in Fountain Road. They drove out of the city southwards. When the highway came to an end they found themselves passing through valleys, skirting wooded ridges. He saw a gravel road branch away to his left and turned the car to follow it. The road ascended a brow of rising ground, then plunged towards a forest, passing through its shade. He turned off the road and drove slowly among the trees, avoiding fallen branches and stones. He stopped his car in a clearing.

Throughout the journey he had spoken little and Olga had sat quietly beside him admiring the passing landscape.

"Shall we take a walk?" she asked.

He agreed and they walked among the trees. He held her hand. The answering pressure of her fingers expressed her warm regard for him.

They passed through the trees into a glade. The sun was hidden by the clouds. A delicious coolness filled the air. There was birdsong on all sides. They sat down on the fallen trunk of a tree and spoke to each other. Olga told him that she had worked as a factory hand for a short period after they had separated and now depended on her sister. He told her of "certain financial and other problems" that had beset him, but were now, he was happy to say, in recession. She listened to him with sympathy and sensitive understanding and said that she looked to the day when he would be happy again. He realized Olga was a person now, a person whose worth transcended the pleasure she could give.

She had brought a picnic basket. She spread a cloth on the grass and they ate.

At noon they returned to the city.

In the afternoon Molvi Haroon telephoned to enquire how his affairs were getting on. Mr Sufi told him that they were improving and that he hoped the confidence he had placed in the Molvi would be kept a secret. The Molvi assured him of his honour in such matters, and then informed him that a deputation from the Crescent Charitable Trust would be happy to have an audience with such a distinguished

Muslim as he was. He readily agreed. Several years before a deputation from the same organization had approached him for a donation, but he had refused to give one on the grounds that he was assisting many other organizations in Durban and Cape Town. He had of course not mentioned that he did not consider charity to be a virtue as it generally confirmed in the lazy their bad habit of relying on others. Now he wished to offer them a donation. There was the possibility that his meanness had been a contributory factor in the genesis of the visitation which had afflicted his life. He was now presented with the opportunity of purging himself of a blemish and so clearing the way for the better working of beneficient influences. In fact the arrival of the opportunity to exercise generosity was in itself a manifestation of the working of such influences.

The deputation arrived in the evening. Accompanying Molvi Haroon were Mr Darsot, the spice merchant, Mr Khaled, an accountant, and Hajji Suleiman the draper, whose flowing henna-red beard was perfumed with attar. Mr Sufi, after shaking their hands cordially, invited them to enter the best parlour which was now open to visitors again. The deputation observed the warmth with which Mr Sufi received them in contrast with his coldness on the first occasion.

Molvi Haroon began with a recital from the Koran of various extracts and then went on to explain in Gujarati the Prophet's concept of wealth as a stewardship on which the poor had a rightful claim. He concluded by reciting other extracts that promised paradise to those who cared for orphans and widows.

When he ended Mr Sufi said:

"I am having some financial problems, but I will give a donation."

"In this world none of us are exempt from difficulties," Mr Darsot said. "We could come at a later date."

Molvi Haroon, sensing the danger in Mr Darsot's words, said quickly in Arabic and then translated into Gujarati:

"Allah blesses those most who give when they themselves are in need."

"Is there any specific sum you need?" Mr Sufi asked, taking out his cheque book from his coat pocket.

Hajji Suleiman looked at Mr Darsot (who was the chairman of the Trust) as if to say he should not let the opportunity slip and stipulate a sum. Mr Darsot, however, knowing Mr Sufi to be a man who kept a close grip on his wealth, feared to frighten him by mentioning a sum. The man had agreed to give them a donation; that was sufficient. They could always approach him later again.

"No specific sum, brother Sufi. We will be satisfied with whatever you give."

"Remember," Molvi Haroon said, "that our Prophet was an orphan and spoke on many occasions of the special blessings that would come to those who gave charity without caring about their personal welfare."

Mr Sufi wrote out a cheque for a very large sum of money, feeling that the multiplex force of the digits would help to fend off the visitation. He handed the cheque to Mr Darsot. Mr Darsot felt a sudden contraction within him for he himself had never given the Trust such a large sum of money. He handed the cheque to Molvi Haroon who smiled, showing his paan-reddened teeth. He passed on the cheque to Hajji Suleiman who, after hastily taking out his spectacles from his coat pocket, examined it with trembling hands. Mr Khaled, on receiving the cheque, looked at it with professional indifference.

Molvi Haroon then cupped his hands in thanksgiving prayer and exultantly read several extracts from the Koran. Everyone cupped their hands and looked reverent.

When Molvi Haroon ended Mr Sufi tinkled a bell and Fawzia and the kitchen maid arrived with tea and sweetmeats.

Before the deputation left Molvi Haroon offered a short prayer for Mr Sufi's prosperity and happiness.

For Mr Sufi the next two days came to approximate those scherzo times (the darkness of his recent life gave the past the dimension of a golden legend) when his life sparkled with women, motor-cars, cinemas, food, friends, and a matured bank account. Feeling confident that the combined force of the amulet, prayers, and his positive approach to life would soon bring back lost times, he visited friends and chose not to take seriously the alienation that had crept in since the ripening of his relationship with Gool. He spoke to his wife on several matters unconnected with their domestic life and gaily proposed a country excursion with the children on a bright Sunday. And to ensure that he was purged of all moral blemish he re-read all the letters (fortunately secreted in a drawer in his office) appealing to his charity: letters from individuals, schools, religious seminaries, orphanages, the Red Cross, sports clubs, political organizations (which he had always loathed and regarded as the creation of disaffected psychopathic individuals). He wrote out the cheques in a mood of almost hysterical benevolence. When he had signed the last cheque he thought of Olga. He wrote out a cheque for her and attached a note to it thanking her for her concern for him and for the happy day he had spent in her company. He went to the Central Road post office in the evening when the pavement was deserted and before posting the cheques read the prescriptive prayer from the schedule, entitled "Before doing anything important". When the last cheque went into the scarlet mouth of the pillar-box, he felt that he had finally suffocated the dragon which had plagued his life.

The next day being Friday, Mr Sufi went to mosque as usual. Molvi Haroon saw him after prayers, went up to him and said:

"How are your affairs getting on, Sufi Sahib?"

"Very well, Molvi Haroon. You have been very helpful. Already there is a change."

"Allah be praised."

He was about to take his leave, fearing that if Gool saw them he would come up to them, when Molvi Haroon detained him by placing his hand on his shoulder and saying:

"The lamps you gave me were very useful, Sufi Sahib. Some of the lamps in the chandelier of the mosque were burnt out, so I replaced them with those you gave me."

Mr Sufi looked up at the glittering crystal chandeliers hanging above him, and gazed at them as though he saw, at a great height in the heavens, the glowing fires of hell. If Molvi Haroon had looked at him then, he would have seen a bloodless face seized by terror and pain.

"I must go," he muttered feebly and hastily left the mosque. His sudden descent into spiritual damnation came like the blast of the anger of God. He was damned, eternally damned for having given a holy man stolen lamps which were now illuminating a sacred place. He had sinned against God Himself by desecrating His Sanctum. Of what use was the amulet and schedule for prayers now? He could never return to the mosque, for its very chandeliers would expose him — to God, to himself and everyone else — as a diabolical creature consigned to eternal perdition.

He went home, trembling in anguished confusion, his hope crushed.

15

Over the telephone Gool's words pierced like slivers into Mr Sufi's ears:

"There is trouble for you. Come over to High Road immediately."

"Trouble?"

"Yes. Serious. There is danger over the telephone."

He held the telephone in his hand for a while, disbelieving the doom-crack message. He went to his bedroom and sat down on the edge of the bed. Gool's words signalled the onset of final earthly calamity, a calamity he had secretly, fearfully known to be approaching — he had felt within him its destructive pulse — since the lamps began to burn in the Newtown mosque. He thought of suicide, of catapulting himself in his Jaguar over a cliff. But the thought was sterile. Gool's hold over him denied him even the freedom to destroy himself.

Later he roused himself, went down the stairs to his car, and drove to High Road.

Gool met him with his usual smile.

"Come into the office, Mr Sufi."

Gool sat down at his desk. Mr Sufi sat on a chair facing him.

"You are in serious trouble."

Mr Sufi looked down at his feet, his voice strangled. A coldness, bursting out from some Arctic frontier within, flooded his trembling body.

"There is trouble over the lamps. By the way, they must be very useful to you? You will have lights in your mansions for the rest of your life."

He felt like saying that the lamps had darkened his life, but could not articulate the words. The thought suffused him with gloom, a gloom that seemed to swell into a monstrous mushroom before his eyes.

"Your stairs are beautifully lit. No one need ever stumble in the dark again."

"Yes," he said timidly, almost in a whisper, as though affirming to himself the folly of having kept his stairs unlit. His gloom overwhelmed and smothered the tumult that usually swirled within him whenever any reference was made to unlit stairs. Gool appeared to him now like some hero of the cinema, taking revenge on behalf of tenants faced with the ordeal of ascending and descending the stairs at night.

"The lamps have a lovely name. Do you remember it?"

Mr Sufi tried to recall the name, but failed. The statue of Apollo, however, came to life in his mind's eye. The god frowned and gently flung a lamp at him for failing to recall his name. The lamp burst like a bubble as it reached him.

The vision dissolved and he heard Gool say, musingly:

"Apollo . . . a beautiful Greek god . . . beautiful."

In a state of abject depression, Mr Sufi found Gool's obsession with Apollo meaningless. The days of the pagan deities had long passed and he failed to see what they had to do with the reality of modern electrical lamps.

"To get to the trouble, the police have arrested them."

"Arrested?"

"Yes. They have confessed . . . those who delivered the lamps. There is a warrant of arrest against you."

Mr Sufi flung his head back and his arms upwards as though warding off the blows of an attacker, and shrieked as though several skewers were being plunged into various parts of his body.

Gool jumped up from his chair, filled a glass with liquor and poured it into his mouth.

Mr Sufi choked and coughed and gasped. He shouted, "No! No! No!" and rushed round the room, feeling weirdly legless, a torso whirling in a surrealist tempest. Broken, blinded, imprisoned in some torture chamber without hope of release, he pleaded miserably: "No . . . Don't let them . . . Gool . . . I beg . . . Don't let them." The room spun in feverish merry-go-round; desk and cupboard and cabinet and chairs seemed to be animated missiles charging at him, and Gool a many-faced spider pursuing him, constricting him, striking him.

When, after what seemed a timeless interval, he emerged from the hurly-burly of his convulsive experience, he found himself seated in a chair, exhausted and sweating, with Gool offering him more liquor. He sipped the liquor and felt calm returning. Gool assuaged him by saying:

"There is nothing to worry about. They will never arrest you while I am alive. Captain Green was here this morning and tore up the warrant before my eyes."

His fears dissolved and the euphoria bloomed within him. While he was under Gool's "protection" he was safe. He looked at Gool with admiration. Nothing would ever crack his imperturbable spirit.

"You know how to manage things."

"Yes, but I think the Captain expects a reward."

He produced his cheque book.

"We must remember he carries out orders," Gool said. "There are others, his superiors. Even the magistrate."

"How much do you think?"

"We cannot offer too much in the beginning. But eventually we must compromise. Give me a blank cheque and I will give them the minimum possible."

He signed a cheque, handed it to Gool and left the room.

In the street Mr Sufi entered his Jaguar. All the sap seemed to have run out of his body, leaving him like a bleached corpse rolling down a sand dune. He went home, crept into bed and slept through the day and night.

Towards dawn he dreamt of Apollo. The god stood beside him and said in Gool's voice:

"You are in serious trouble . . . You will have lights in your mansion for the rest of your life . . . Your stairs are beautifully lit . . . No one need ever stumble in the dark again."

He awoke in fear and drew the curtains beside his bed so that the pale morning light entered. The words lingered in his mind. Had Gool told him the truth? Could he be in "serious trouble" and also have lights in his mansions for the rest of his life? Had there been a warrant of arrest? Had Gool tricked him into giving him a blank cheque?

During the next few days Mr Sufi reviewed his desperate

situation. Since the time when his involvement with Gool had gone beyond the threshold of the early "protection" period, he had been driven into the labyrinth of schizophrenic distraction. Socially, his status and respectability were irrevocably lost. Many people avoided him, and when meetings were unavoidable they showed no eagerness to speak to him. His friends had stiffened. He was an untouchable. There had been a time, he recalled, when days were serene and nights imbued with the charm of love. He was now a recluse within his agony, a prisoner in the void of inner exile, unable even to find comfort in those nearest him, his wife and children. To Fawzia, caught in the vortex of his affairs, he had brought mildew, damaging her young life. Morally, he was contaminated: he had drunk liquor, which was forbidden; he had joined in a debauch and led two of his former concubines to sinful fornication; and he had been a party to the violence committed in Nirvana Mansions. Spiritually, he was damned by the sacrilegious burning of the lamps in the chandeliers of the Newtown mosque from which he had excommunicated himself for ever. Criminally, he was implicated in a theft, perpetually exposed to the threat of arrest. And, finally, threatening doom, his financial empire was reeling: the digits in his bank account that buttressed it were tumbling, and the revenue from his apartment buildings was diminishing — for many of his tenants, either unable or unwilling to pay the inflated rents imposed by him, or fearing his association with a dangerous man, were beginning to leave.

16

Several months later, while Mr Sufi was having breakfast, the telephone rang. Gool informed him that he had an "exciting proposal" to make to him that would convert him into a millionaire in a short time. He should come to High Road where he would give him the details.

He left his breakfast unfinished, went to his bedroom and sat down on the edge of the bed. The "proposal" aroused no excitement in him. For a week now he had made his bedroom his hermitage; it was here, on the pretext that he suffered from migraine, that he spent long hours, garrotted by defeat, loneliness and self-pity.

Yet, as he lay in bed, all his wants solicitously anticipated by his wife and daughter, listening to their voices as they went about their domestic duties, he came to realize that only in relation to them did his life take on meaning. His wife's love for him had been expressed not by words, but by her silent devotion to his well-being. On a more profound level, he gradually became conscious of the beauty of his wife and children — not only of their physical beauty but also of the primary beauty of their beings to which he was emotionally, spiritually and organically united. A yearning to have them near him seized him: he wanted them to sit beside him and talk to him, even about the most trivial matters. Several times he attempted to draw them into conversation, but their respect for him made them listeners rather than participants. He rued his decision to banish his wife from his bed, for now he was overcome by that natural yet most profound of human longings: to hold another being's hands. And what intensified his agony was that, while all he need to say to his wife was that she should return and she would do so unhesitatingly, he could not do so: his will had snapped. Especially the voices of his daughters, ringing with innocence and happiness as they played on the balcony, affected him deeply; he craved to hold them in his arms and kiss them. At such moments came the crushing realization of their mortality: they would grow up, eventually grow old and one day perish. This thought wrung his being with such inordinate, bitter anguish that he was filled with overwhelming, compassionate love for them.

Later he went to see Gool.

"You have heard of Elysia," Gool said to him as soon as they were seated, each with a glass of brandy in his hand. "I have spoken to a lawyer about you and his opinion is that the best way of multiplying your wealth is to invest in land in Elysia."

Mr Sufi sipped the liquor and felt a raw sensation in his gullet.

"If you think I am trying to make you invest in something worthless, then let us go and consult a lawyer. You can decide afterwards."

He had read in the newspapers of Elysia and the government's plans to make it an exclusive area for Asians. Under the plan all properties in Fordsburg would be expropriated and sold to whites. Controversy had raged in the press regarding the motive behind the Group Areas Act, and the Orient Front and the People's Movement had condemned Elysia as a racial ghetto. He had attended a meeting of property owners to decide on a course of action. It had been a rowdy meeting, for some tenants also turned up with placards proclaiming in scarlet: "It is your turn to be evicted now!"; "The end of tyranny by landlords!"; "Our own homes in Elysia!". Some of his former tenants shouted his name jeeringly and made obscene gestures at him. The eccentric landlord Joosub appeared at the meeting in Arab garb. He was accompanied by two of his servants dressed as Cape coons, whom he declared to be his "lawyers". He insisted on praying on the stage in the hall and there was silence while he performed the usual genuflections. When he had finished he announced that he had received a divine message that if all landlords stopped accepting rent from tenants, Allah would send his archangel Gibrail to settle matters. He was wildly applauded by the tenants. Then he lapsed into silence and sat on the stage flanked by his two "lawyers". The meeting ended with a resolution to petition the rulers to grant an extension of five years before they began to expropriate. Though Mr Sufi had consented to the resolution he had remained silent. Even without the government's threat he would have been compelled to sell some of his properties to keep himself financially buoyant, and the sale would have given rise to questioning, gossip and humiliation. Now he was presented with a reason for selling them, and even though he risked accusations of betrayal by fellow landlords, he would be able to stand up to them. Ultimately the government's bulldozers would triumph.

Shortly after Mr Sufi had returned home from the meeting, four young men came to see him. As soon as they were seated in the guests' parlour Ebrahim, the leader of the group, said:

"We are members of the People's Movement."

He looked at them critically. They were a racial motley;

they were dressed gaudily; their hair was long, giving them the appearance of nubile girls; they carried themselves like arrogant braggarts.

"Is there anything I can do for you?"

"Nothing for us, but for yourself."

He was mystified. Had these hermaphrodites been sent by some secret People's Court to fetch him? Or were they merely a gang of freaks and perverts out to rag him?

"We are here to help you," Ebrahim said. "You know about Elysia. We intend to launch protest rallies."

His imagination lit up a multitude of people, anarchists, nihilists, communists, snaking through the streets, holding aloft banners, and shouting slogans.

"To help me?"

"Yes, of course. Your properties are in danger. We intend to stand by you."

"I am afraid I don't take part in politics."

His answer elicited a rapid fire of questions from the quartet.

"You are not interested in what happens to you?"

"You want to be evicted?"

"You wish to be destroyed?"

"You refuse to accept our aid?"

He cringed.

"Gentlemen, I inherited . . ."

"Inherited or not, they are yours," Ebrahim interrupted. "We intend protecting you from the Herrenvolk landlords."

"The bloodsuckers!"

"The Caesars!"

"The fascists!"

A moment of silence followed. Then Ebrahim went on, in a conciliatory tone:

"Mr Sufi, please understand that we represent the oppressed people and have to carry out our responsibilities. We are your friends, though you may not think so. We are prepared to sacrifice our lives for you."

"I understand," he whispered, touched.

"Now you are reacting as a true son of Liberty. You will appreciate that resistance goes hand in glove with the instruments of resistance. What I mean is that we need funds to help us in the struggle to help you. You know how we operate. We need money for paper, duplicating machines, premises; we have to hold conferences, transport delegates and supporters; then there are lawyers' fees, and bail and other expenses that run into thousands."

He felt awed at the vast protest machinery that was to be set in motion for his sake. He wrote out a cheque quickly and handed it to Ebrahim.

"You will understand that the sacrifices we are making cannot be counted in terms of money," Ebrahim said, taking the cheque, glancing at its value and tearing it into confetti. "We spend our lives trying to protect innocent people like you. It is certain you will be eaten up by the Herrenvolk shark if you don't help us to help you."

Mr Sufi saw himself in a sea of blood. He took his pen and wrote out another cheque.

Gool was about to lead the way out of his office when he said, turning:

"Come see what I bought yesterday."

He went towards a shelf, opened a cardboard box and carefully removed a statuette of Apollo.

"I was passing an art shop yesterday when I saw it in the window."

He placed the statuette on a small, semi-circular table.

"I would give anything in the world to look like him," Gool said in admiration.

Mr Sufi looked at Gool. The man was obviously obsessed by an image. But it occurred to him that perhaps Gool's good fortune in life was a result of his adoration of an idol. With a feeling of personal inadequacy he examined the statuette.

"That's Apollo," he whispered.

The beauty of the god, of the ideal human form thrust itself upon his awareness.

"Whenever I look at Apollo I think of lamps," Gool said.

Mr Sufi was brought trenchantly back to himself, and to the tumour within.

The lawyer's office was in Fox Street. When they entered the reception room they were met by a slender lady with blonde curls and blue eyes. She greeted them and led the two men through a carpeted passage to a glass door.

The lawyer was seated behind a large table. He had a round face, fleshy cheeks, curly hair and a small beard. He reminded Mr Sufi of a goblin who had run away from the woods and usurped a modern office of filing cabinets, an oak table laden with the usual pens, papers and files, and shelves fitted with formidable phalanxes of books.

"Sit down, gentlemen. I am at your service."

"Mr Mohamed, this is Mr Sufi," Gool said.

"I am very happy to meet you, Mr Sufi. As you know I am an adviser to many property owners. By my advice many a man has become wealthy. Though unluckily for me my fate is that of all advisers. We are soon forgotten. Sometimes we are killed."

He laughed in a series of sharp muted barks.

"When I was at school," Mr Mohamed continued, "I acted the part of Polonius and was killed by Hamlet."

"You will be killed again," Gool said facetiously, "if you don't tell Mr Sufi of the advantages of buying land in Elysia."

He laughed again.

"My advice to you, Mr Sufi, is to buy land now. The petition by property owners is not going to succeed. Mr Mia and Mr Darsot have realized this and submitted their applications. Several properties in Fordsburg are already up for sale to whites. Look at these."

There was a file on his table. He opened it and showed Mr Sufi some newspaper advertisements.

"I speak as an authority on the Group Areas Act. Within two years land prices in Elysia will rocket and you could be a millionaire. Land is power, that is a legal saying. Have you visited Elysia?

"Let us go there now," Gool said.

"Excellent! My other clients can wait."

He lifted the telephone.

"Tell John to bring the car."

The lawyer rose from his chair and his clients followed him. In the reception room he introduced them to Helena, the lady who had met them on arrival. She was dressed in a grey silk blouse and a short blue skirt. Around her neck were two strings of multi-coloured beads.

"Helena is a descendant of Helen of Troy," Mr Mohamed said jocosely.

She answered with a smile, her scarlet lips revealing rows of even teeth.

Mr Sufi recalled the classical Helen. A year ago he had

seen the film — Gool had seen it too, at the Lyric — entitled *The Face That Launched a Thousand Ships*.

"Mr Sufi is an important figure in the community, Helena," the lawyer said. "You are going to see a great deal of him."

"That will be lovely." And she smiled at Mr Sufi, who stood near her.

"By the way, how many sisters have you?" the lawyer asked.

"Two."

"Three Helens!" Gool exclaimed. "When can we meet the other two?"

"Any time."

"Mr Sufi, our luck is in," Gool said smilingly.

"To Elysia now, on business," the lawyer said, moving towards the door. "Later, maybe this weekend, we shall abduct the three virgins."

Helena made an arch enquiry and there was merriment. Mr Sufi managed a smile.

"Helena, lock the door and come with us," the lawyer said as they stepped out onto the pavement.

In the street a car was waiting for them, the doors open.

Mr Mohamed sat next to the chauffeur. Helena sat between Gool and Mr Sufi. On the way to Elysia Mr Mohamed spoke of the bright future that awaited Mr Sufi.

"Our politicians can go on protesting, but you are among the fortunate few . . ."

As the car passed through the city and reached open country Mr Sufi began to feel like a condemned prisoner taking his last ride. The bronze rocks along the roadside, the sentinel-like trees in rain-blessed sunlit fields, and perfumed Helena beside him (with her hands, languid and heavy with rings, in her lap, her left thigh nestling against his) reminded him of tranquil evenings in the apartments of his concubines, of mornings when the bathroom tap gurgled and the aroma of breakfast filled the kitchen, of days that held undiluted promise.

They reached Elysia after an hour and got out of the car. In the distance was a low mountain range; below its slopes were clusters of homes that formed part of the government's resettlement housing scheme. On their right was a wood of acacias.

"Beautiful virgin land," Mr Mohamed said.

"What is the price of land here?" Mr Sufi asked.

"It is not expensive when compared to other areas. Can you see our city on the horizon? It is marching south."

"I haven't sufficient capital," Mr Sufi said regretfully.

"That's no problem. I can sell your properties immediately to whites and raise the money. Let me handle your affairs for you, Mr Sufi. I shall do my best since you are a friend of Mr Gool."

A paradise widow bird flew past, trailing its long black tail. They looked at it.

"Leave everything in Mr Mohamed's hands," Gool advised Mr Sufi. "You cannot leave it in my hands. I might be killed at any moment by my enemies."

Gool's words, though spoken in a matter-of-fact tone, reverberated painfully within Mr Sufi.

Mr Mohamed now went on to speak of the link between wealth and land and concluded with these words: "History offers us this lesson: when men are without land they are lost."

"Then they have to look for a bonfire to throw themselves in," Gool said laughing.

"Or find comfort in a woman's arms," Helena said, smiling at Mr Sufi.

Mr Sufi walked several paces away from the group. He looked at the fields before him and at the serene expanse of the sky and experienced for a moment (though he was urban in his soul) a feeling of communion with natural beauty.

Several yellow birds flashed past on whirring wings and Mr Sufi rejoined the group.

"Mr Mohamed, I think you can put my properties up for sale."

"I congratulate you on your decision," the lawyer said, placing his arm over Mr Sufi's shoulder. "Let us now return to the city and business."

And Mr Sufi got into the car.

The noise of the city overtook them suddenly. They were in the midst of shining motor-cars, roaring excavators, screeching drills, blaring hooters, coloured neon signs, scurrying pedestrians. The car swung around a corner and came to a stop.

In the lawyer's office all the relevant documents were prepared after Mr Sufi had gone home and brought a briefcase full of papers. The details were checked with municipal records by telephone. They adjourned to a nearby restaurant for lunch and returned to complete their business. Mr Sufi signed the documents with Helena and Gool as witnesses. By the time they had finished an hour remained before dusk.

"Gool," Mr Mohamed said, "I think we need some diversion after the day's work."

"Let's go to High Road and have supper," said Gool.

"Helena," Mr Mohamed said, "you go with John and bring

your two sisters to Gool's place. We'll meet you there."

The three men went to High Road. They sat in the lounge and drank wine, waiting for the arrival of Helena and her companions. The lawyer spoke of the bright future that awaited Mr Sufi, and went on to say:

"Of course the sale of your properties will realize more money than will be needed to buy land. The surplus can be used in a number of ways. For instance, we could invest in shares yielding high percentage returns. We could also . . ."

By the time Helena and her companions arrived Mr Sufi was feeling convivial. Cheryl was a tall, rather gawky brunette with a bronzed skin and Josephine a small, buxom woman, much made up.

Supper was served on a candle-lit table. After supper they returned to the lounge for coffee, liqueurs and cigars or cigarettes. Mr Sufi showed keen interest in the ladies and when Mr Mohamed proposed that they should all go picnicking on a Sunday, Mr Sufi reminded him:

"You know what you said today before we went to Elysia? 'We shall abduct three virgins.' " Everyone laughed.

Later that night the three women were taken home. They lived in an apartment on the tenth floor of a building in Hillbrow. The men were invited up for a drink. The building was modern and the apartment carpeted, centrally heated and well furnished. While having drinks Mr Sufi thought of his own buildings and felt happy that he had decided to sell them. They were disgracefully ugly and not worth possessing. He had spent his entire life guarding them as though they were strongholds of treasure. He felt grateful to Gool and the lawyer for convincing him that it was time to sell them. In Elysia he would own an apartment building like the one he was in; in fact he would have several such buildings erected.

"Friends," he said, "one day we shall all live in a beautiful building in Elysia."

"Excellent!" Gool exclaimed, and applauded. They all applauded.

"I promise," Mr Sufi continued, moved, "that I shall share my wealth with you. You are all my friends."

They applauded again and Gool rose to go.

"Ladies, good-night. We shall meet again."

"No, you cannot go yet," Helena said to Mr Sufi, hanging on to him.

The others encircled them as she pressed her lips to his.

Mr Mohamed was taken home first, then Gool. Finally Mr Sufi returned to Orient Mansions.

It had been a long, eventful day for him, beginning with the visit to the lawyer and ending in the company of the three women. A variety of emotional states and inner movements, ranging from the penumbral misery in his bedroom to the sudden gust of sensual energy from Helena's lips, had pulsed through him. In one day he seemed to have passed through an age of living.

He stood for a while in the foyer of the building where he had spent so many years. It would soon be sold and later crushed to rubble by the sledgehammers of demolishers. It had been the nave of his life's pattern. He felt that in some way he had betrayed the building, that its eventual destruction was the result, not of a government order, but of a personal inability to protect it. The sense of betrayal worked on him as he walked up the illuminated stairs. He knew now the urban doom that awaited him, and the end of his days as an affluent landlord.

In his bedroom a surge of pessimism overwhelmed him. When it receded he felt that only as a derelict, freed of responsibility, of being, would he be able to evade determination by worldly things, preoccupation with his own fate, regret at times past, yearning for the nebula of the future, the power of Gool, the cunning of Mr Mohamed. Like flotsam driven by currents out at sea, he would go wherever life took him.

During the night sleep came to him fitfully, and dreams in morbidly garish colours reeled in his febrile brain . . . He was in a crowded arcade surrounded by howling, gyrating maenads . . . He was in Elysian fields where gay, one-legged nymphs romped beside pools echoing with weird laughter . . . He was in a wilderness where Apollo, standing on a granite crag, held aloft a flaming brand; where harpies shrieked obscenities in Helena's voice; where Mr Mohamed, his head impaled on the bonnet of his car, rushed vengefully towards him; where a smiling spider that was Gool looked on. Then the earth opened and he fell, down a screaming stair.

His wife found him lying helplessly on the floor, his face contorted. She flung herself down beside him and held him.

"What's the matter?" she cried. "What's the matter?"

He clung to her, breathing convulsively, sweating profusely, seeking solace, compassion and love.

His cry awakened the children and they came into the room, frightened.

"Your father is ill," their mother said. She caressed her husband's forehead tenderly for a while and then held his hands. He sat up, called his daughters to sit near him and touched them fondly.

"My children," he said, looking at their beautiful faces.

Uanhenga Xitu

THE WORLD OF 'MESTRE' TAMODA
£4.95/US$8.95 paperback   £9.95/US$16.95 hardback

The archetypal bush lawyer, mock rhetorician and speechifier Tamoda was conceived in an Angolan colonial prison, but his continuing adventures go beyond the absurdities of white rule to encompass the split between rural and urban life, the rapidly deteriorating African landscape, and the fleeting vision of a possible non-racial society, freed from southern Africa's burden of racial division and violence.

"There is something of him in all of us...like those mimic-men who had no underpants but made sure they wore good-quality trousers." Antônio Jacinto, 1986 NOMA prizewinner.

"Xitu's insights into village life, and the world of pre-independent urban Angola, are both acute and valuable." Caryl Phillips in *The Guardian*

Henri Lopes

THE LAUGHING CRY
£4.95/US$8.95 paperback   £8.95/US$16.95 hardback

An irresistible cock and bull story with the ring of truth. To the sound of military marches over the State Radio, into the Presidential Palace steps Marshal Hannibal-Ideloy Bwakamabé Na Sakkadé, familiarly known as "Daddy," Chief of State, President of the Patriotic Council of National Resurrection, and Recreative Father of his country. Noted Congolese writer Henri Lopes has created the supreme African dictator — a brilliant, ferocious burlesque. The adventures of "Daddy" in the bush, the bar and the bed are a devastating, comic portrait of African power politics today.

"Lopes has captured the truth about Africa." *International Herald Tribune*

"Lopes' book is satirical, tender, bawdy, savage, and filled with love and hope." *Washington Post*

"An Africa that vies with Céline...a beautiful book that will be talked about for a long time." *Nouvel Observateur* (Paris)

African Titles from Readers International

Njabulo Ndebele

FOOLS AND OTHER STORIES
£4.95/US$8.95 paperback   £8.95/US$14.95 hardback

In these powerful yet delicate narratives, winner of the NOMA African literature prize, Njabulo Ndebele evokes township life with humour and subtlety. Ndebele rejects the image of black South Africans as a "passive people whose only reason for existing is to receive the sympathy of the world... The mechanisms of survival and resistance we have devised are many and far from simple." Instead, he focuses on the complexity and fierce energy that complicates their lives. The title story *Fools* explores the confrontation between two township men of different generations and the women who bind their lives. Zamani, a disgraced, middle-aged school teacher meets Zani, an angry young activist, and an intense relationship of conflict and growing understanding develops between them.

"For formal elegance and originality, *Fools and Other Stories* surpasses anything else I've encountered in South African fiction, such excellent works as *Burger's Daughter* and *Life and Times of Michael K* included." *Village Voice*

"Everything in this book demonstrates splendidly that as a writer Mr Ndebele has chosen to make his own version of what Nadine Gordimer called 'the essential gesture'...and he convinces us of the genuineness of his vision in everything he writes." *New York Times Book Review*

"These begin where the post-Soweto writing gets stuck; they move on from *apartheid.*" *The Nation*

READ THE WORLD—Books from Readers International

Nicaragua	**To Bury Our Fathers**	Sergio Ramírez	£5.95/US$8.95
Nicaragua	**Stories**	Sergio Ramírez	£3.95/US$7.95
Chile	**I Dreamt the Snow Was Burning**	Antonio Skármeta	£4.95/US$7.95
Brazil	**The Land**	Antônio Torres	£3.95/US$7.95
Argentina	**Mothers and Shadows**	Marta Traba	£3.95/US$7.95
Argentina	**A Funny Dirty Little War**	Osvaldo Soriano	£3.95/US$6.95
Uruguay	**El Infierno**	C. Martínez Moreno	£4.95/US$8.95
Haiti	**Cathedral of the August Heat**	Pierre Clitandre	£4.95/US$8.95
Congo	**The Laughing Cry**	Henri Lopes	£4.95/US$8.95
Angola	**The World of 'Mestre' Tamoda**	Uanhenga Xitu	£4.95/US$8.95
S. Africa	**Fools and Other Stories**	Njabulo Ndebele	USA only $8.95
S. Africa	**Renewal Time**	Es'kia Mphahlele	£4.95/US$8.95
S. Africa	**Hajji Musa and the Hindu Fire-Walker**	Ahmed Essop	£4.95/US$8.95
Iran	**The Ayatollah and I**	Hadi Khorsandi	£3.95/US$7.95
Philippines	**Awaiting Trespass**	Linda Ty-Casper	£3.95/US$7.95
Philippines	**Wings of Stone**	Linda Ty-Casper	£4.95/US$8.95
Japan	**Fire from the Ashes**	ed. Kenzaburō Ōe	£3.50 UK only
China	**The Gourmet**	Lu Wenfu	£4.95/US$8.95
India	**The World Elsewhere**	Nirmal Verma	hbk only £9.95/US$16.95
Poland	**Poland Under Black Light**	Janusz Anderman	£3.95/US$6.95
Poland	**The Edge of the World**	Janusz Anderman	£3.95/US$7.95
Czech.	**My Merry Mornings**	Ivan Klíma	£4.95/US$7.95
Czech.	**A Cup of Coffee with My Interrogator**	Ludvík Vaculík	£3.95/US$7.95
E. Germany	**Flight of Ashes**	Monika Maron	£4.95/US$8.95
E. Germany	**The Defector**	Monika Maron	£4.95/US$8.95
USSR	**The Queue**	Vladimir Sorokin	£4.95/US$8.95

Order through your local bookshop, or direct from the publisher. Most titles also available in hardcover. *How to order:* Send your name, address, order and payment to

RI, 8 Strathray Gardens, London NW3 4NY, UK
or **RI**, P.O. Box 959, Columbia, LA 71418, USA

Please enclose payment to the value of the cover price plus 10% of the total amount for postage and packing. (Canadians add 20% to US prices.)